Tigerheart

Tigerheart

PETER DAVID

DEL
REY

Ballantine Books · New York

Published in the United States by Del Rey Books, an imprint of The Random House Publishing Group, a division of Random House, Inc., New York.

Del Rey is a registered trademark and the Del Rey colophon is a trademark of Random House, Inc.

Library of Congress Cataloging-in-Publication Data
David, Peter (Peter Allen)
Tigerheart / Peter David.
p.   cm.
ISBN 978-0-345-50159-2 (acid-free paper)
I. Title.
PS3554.A92144T54 2008
813'.54—dc22   2008000454

Printed in the United States of America on acid-free paper

www.delreybooks.com

2 4 6 8 9 7 5 3 1

First Edition

Book design by Lauren Dong

To Ariel David,
for the title;
and
to Sir James Barrie,
for the inspiration

Tigerheart

The Bird Who Told Him So

Young Paul Dear stared at his reflection one evening for a very long time. When his reflection began talking back to him, Paul began to think that perhaps he himself was actually The Boy of Legend.

In order to understand how that came to pass, it is important to learn of the events directly preceding the moment Paul's reflection stuck its tongue out at him and threw several cocky and very saucy challenges his way.

Paul knew about pixies. He knew about elves and leprechauns. He knew about mermaids who dwelt beneath the chopping whitecaps from the times when his father and mother, Patrick and Colleen Dear, took him to Brighton on holiday. They would watch the surf and his father would tell him stories of such fancies as he knew. Sometimes Paul's father would lean in and say softly, "Don't look at your mum when I say this. But she is, in fact, part leprechaun, what with having the Irish in her blood. Hush! Are you not listening? If you look at her sidelong with a suspicious eye, she will disappear just out of the habit of her kind."

"So I am part leprechaun as well?" Paul said eagerly. His father simply smiled in that puzzling way he had. It is, as we all know, the way that parents always smile when they want you to think they know the answers, and perhaps even want to convince themselves as well.

Paul did not press his father on the answers, knowing that he had learned all he was going to. However, if he had known that his father was going to go away, he might well have been more insistent in trying to determine the truths of the world in general and himself in particular. Paul did not know that his time with his father and mother was limited, for to all children time is an inexhaustible commodity and childhood an endless haze of day after day.

Paul was a fair-skinned boy, with short black hair cropped in neat, even bangs and the redness of cheeks that comes from adoring relatives pinching his face and saying, "Look at that lovely little face! Why, we could just EAT HIM UP, yes we could!" For a time, Paul lived in fear of being fattened up and devoured, and thus did everything he could to prevent himself from becoming a potentially tasty treat. This was a period which you and I would think of as Paul's desperate and ongoing attempt to thwart some cannibals, but Paul's parents simply referred to it as "That time when Paul was such a finicky eater, we have Absolutely No Idea how he managed not to starve himself to death, the poor lad—whatever is it that gets into children's minds?"

Paul's father, as we noted, was full of magic and mischief, while his mother was full of the ability to tolerate magic and mischief. As such they made a superb pair, with Paul's mother smiling and shaking her head at her husband's shenanigans.

Paul was a bit unclear as to exactly what his father's profession was. Patrick simply said that he was a paid, professional liar. Paul would ask various of his friends what a paid, professional liar was, and he would receive answers ranging from barrister to politician to writer to clergyman, depending upon the friend's age and level of cynicism. His mother, all curls and patient amusement, mainly seemed to exist to say "Oh come now, my dear, really!" in an ongoing endeavor to bring Paul's father up short. It never worked for long.

Paul's sense of time, however, changed utterly, as did his world, with the arrival and startlingly quick departure of Bonnie.

Bonnie first made herself known to Paul when he was lying on the couch in the family drawing room, gazing at the blazing fire in the fireplace one chilly autumn London night. His head was resting on his mother's lap, and she was gently stroking him about the shoulders and cooing soft words about what a kind and loving and excellent boy he was. It was at that moment that his mother's stomach kicked him in the back of the head. This was an unusual occurrence in and of itself, augmented by his mother's abruptly calling out for Paul's father and announcing, "She kicked!" Paul was puzzled by his mother's suddenly referring to her stomach as "she," and his bewilderment only grew as his parents sat him down and explained to him that a baby was growing in his mother's stomach. A baby girl, his mother insisted, although his father said that they didn't know yet, but his mother said they did—or at least she did—and that was quite enough for her.

Paul gazed in wonderment at the passenger within his mother's stomach. He was quite distressed to discover that she (for he had taken to calling her "she" since his mother seemed so confident) was bereft of clothing and toys, and at one point he came to his mother with some outgrown baby clothes of his and a rattle that he'd found during a walk in Kensington Gardens. He proffered the treasures to his mother and urged her to swallow them so the baby could clothe herself properly and have something to play with besides. This caused great laughter in his mother and his father, and for all those cannibalistic relatives whenever the story was told and retold. Paul never understood quite why it was funny, but since he liked bringing smiles to people's faces, he never let it bother him too much.

He watched with continued fascination as his mother's belly expanded in a manner that he never would have thought possible. As it did so, Colleen would spend inordinate amounts of time reading both to Paul and to his soon-to-be-sibling. It was not as if she had been stingy with her reading time before a baby had been placed into her stomach through mysterious means. But now she read far more often and even told Paul to join in. She said that it was wise to familiarize his little (probable) sister with the sound of his voice so she would not be completely bewildered as to who was who when she finally was removed from her place of residence by the doctor (through other equally mysterious means).

Colleen would read the tales of fancy that Paul's father foisted upon them, although always with one eyebrow raised in grudging patience over such frivolousness. The aforementioned elves and leprechauns and mermaids—and jolly rousing adventures of piracy and wild Indians and such—paraded through the lad's active imagination. And every day he would go out in the backyard and pass the tales on to whatever animals happened to be lounging about.

Still in all, Patrick's practice of speaking tales pulled wholly from his memory rather than refracted through the prism of another storyteller were the ones that Paul truly adored, because they were more personal. And of all those, the tales of which he was the most fond were the ones involving the individual who had achieved fame far and wide as "The Boy." The most splendid boy in the world, as he would not have hesitated to tell you given the slightest opportunity.

There was some confusion as to The Boy's whereabouts, according to Paul's father. He said that some claimed The Boy was an infant who rode on a goat in Kensington Gardens after lock-out, playing his pipes and cavorting with the woodland sprites that supposedly populated the area. Other times, The Boy was reputed to reside in a land called the Anyplace, which could be reached by flying to the third star on the left and continuing until morning. When Paul asked eagerly if his father had ever encountered The Boy personally, his father became very quiet and then seemed wistful, as if he was either remembering something he had accidentally forgotten or trying to forget something he had no desire to remember. Finally, instead of responding with a simple yes or no, he asked Paul if he thought he might have run into him in the course of his dreams.

Paul considered it for a time, and then said he had some vague memory, as a number of youngsters did, that had something to do with The Boy during one cloudless night. His mother had come into his room and woken him, and told him that he had been creating a frightful ruckus by clapping his hands together in his sleep and shouting, "I believe! I believe in pixies!" Paul had no recollection of doing so, and could not fathom why he might have; but his mother just sighed in some odd, knowing way and said, "It probably had something to do with the Anyplace," and then settled him back down to sleep.

"Well, if the Anyplace was involved, there's every likelihood that The Boy was as well. Maybe the pixie involved was his."

"The Boy had a pixie!"

"Oh yes," Patrick said. "And redskins who combated him

and an enemy named Hack, a pirate with a hatchet instead of a right hand, who was so vile that even Long John Silver feared him. And others, but their names blur," he said with a frown. "The memories one takes from the Anyplace are fluid at best, vapor at worst."

The Boy sounded like a perfectly marvelous fellow to Paul. It was hard to dislike someone who flew and dispatched pirates and cavorted with redskins and pixies and such. Still, in some ways Paul disapproved of him; for, by all accounts, The Boy was a showy fellow, and uncaring, and really not all that heroic unless it suited his vanity. Paul was of the opinion that if one was going to be a hero, it should be from selflessness, not selfishness. His stated beliefs had prompted Colleen to say, "You are quite wise beyond your years, Paul. Well done and keep at it, and you shall be a grown-up in no time!"

When she said that, Paul felt a chill wind blow across his spine. He had no idea why that should be so.

That evening, lying in his bed in his nursery, he thought he heard something. A voice, perhaps, calling to him. It wasn't speaking his name, though. Instead it was making sounds . . . animal sounds. A lion growling and then a clucking like a bird, followed by a crowing as if from a rooster. None of them sounded remotely like "Paul" and yet, in an odd way, they all did.

He slid out of his bed and crawled around upon the floor, looking under the bed to see if the sounds were originating from there. When he couldn't find them, he stood and glanced around in the darkness, modified by only the illumination that came from the night-light his mother insisted be in his room.

Then he saw a movement in the mirror. His reflection, he would have thought, except he swayed back and forth experimentally and the reflection stayed right where it was, a smug grin on its face and an impish twinkle in its eyes.

Paul might have been dreaming or might not; he was in one of those places where the borders between the two became indistinguishably thin, but he did not know that. Slowly he crept toward the mirror, staring fixedly at it. His reflection continued to gaze back at him, chin pointed upward in a defiant manner.

"Hullo," said Paul cautiously. "Are you . . . *him?*"

"Are you?" said the reflection. Then it stuck its tongue out at Paul, at which Paul was slightly taken aback. Paul was generally well behaved and well schooled, so it was odd to see himself acting in such a manner.

"I don't think so," Paul said.

"Then how am I supposed to know?"

Paul was mildly irritated at the vagueness of the exchange. "Look here," he said firmly, "I asked you a question. You don't have to play games."

The reflection laughed. "If you think I don't have to play games, then no wonder you don't know if I'm him or you're him. You don't know anything important!"

"I do so," Paul said defensively. "I know——"

"Stop," said the lad in the mirror, holding up his hand in a preemptive manner. "Are you about to rattle off all sorts of things from school?"

"Well . . . yes."

The reflection turned away, making a dismissive, snorting noise. Then Paul suddenly said, "Oh! And I know about gnomes and pixies and—and The Boy . . . which is who I think you are."

The lad in the mirror snapped back and grinned, and then vaulted straight up, leaving a bewildered Paul craning his neck and trying to see where he'd gone. Then The Boy dropped back into view and bowed deeply. "So you *are* him," Paul said.

"Am I truly marvelous?"

"Yes."

"Then who else would I be?" said The Boy, flashing his pearly baby teeth. He leaned forward, motioning for Paul to do the same. For a moment, Paul thought The Boy was going to pull him right through the mirror. Instead The Boy looked him up and down and stroked his chin thoughtfully. Paul mimicked the gesture as if he were the reflection and The Boy the reality, which for all he knew might be the case.

"There is some me in you," The Boy said at last, "although not much. A passing resemblance at most."

"You think so?"

"Maybe. Or maybe I'm lying. I am, after all, half brother to Coyote, the trickster god." The Boy always made boasts along those lines whenever his veracity was questioned. In this case, it was indeed a lie, because being Paul's reflection, he was in fact identical. Then, his voice soft and edged with the echoes of a thousand crafty plans, he said, "Would you like to learn some things?"

"Yes, please."

So The Boy taught him.

This happened repeatedly over a series of nights, although since Paul spent them in that delicate dividing line between sleep and dream, he lost track of how many and how often. His parents did not notice for the most part, although his father did look rather surprised when—while telling Paul about various adventures The Boy had had—Paul offered polite but firm corrections or clarifications. Plus there were other talents that Paul acquired, although it wasn't so much acquiring them as discovering that he had always had them at his command and didn't know until now, as if waking from a long sleep.

I can more or less guess what is going through your mind. For one thing, you wish to know what Paul did learn. Not flying—I can tell you that. The specifics, I regret, we must withhold for the present time, as more pressing matters are commanding our attention. A child's birth has a way of doing that.

One day when Paul came home from school, he discovered a neighbor there and his mother and father both gone. This caused him some brief consternation until the neighbor explained that his mother was off at the hospital having the baby removed from within her stomach. This was of tremendous relief to Paul, since he had become convinced that his mother was going to become so large that either she was going to float to the ceiling, or even out the window, or else she was going to explode like an overinflated balloon. Neither turned out to be the case, and his mother came home several days later with his little sister, Bonnie, cradled in her arms.

Bonnie did not look at Paul, no matter how much he tried to convince her to do so. Instead her eyes wandered about almost independently of each other, and she would occasionally make small chirping noises.

"She still thinks she's a bird," Paul said. This was one of those things that Paul had learned. "All babies are birds before they become babies. Sometimes they forget and fly away. That's why it's best to keep the windows closed."

"That's a very good reason," said Patrick. "You never know when children may fly away."

"Oh, stuff and nonsense," said Colleen. "Why do you say such things to him, Patrick?"

"I don't know. They just come to me," Patrick said guardedly, and left it there.

Colleen turned back to Paul. "It's best to keep the windows closed, dear," Paul's mother said with infinite patience, "so that she does not get influenza."

Paul had no idea who Enza was, or why she flew in, but his mother seemed quite certain that she was not welcome, and Paul was not about to disagree.

Many was the time during Bonnie's short stay that Paul would gaze high into the night sky, trying to determine which star on the left was the third one, since there seemed to be ever so many. On occasion he became convinced that he saw not only the star but The Boy himself, small and glowing and cir- cling the glittering balls of light in the sky. Invariably, however, he would call his father's or mother's attention to it, and they would know for sure that it was an airplane merely passing, and not a magic boy reluctant to age. It was probably for the best, though, because if Paul indeed was The Boy, then naturally he couldn't be in two places at once.

At least he didn't think he could. Then again, confronted with the prospect of something he couldn't do, The Boy tended to dismiss the notion as absurd. He was a wonderful boy, and if he could imagine it, then it could be done. So Paul didn't know what to think. He asked The Boy about it during one of their late night mirror sessions, but The Boy simply chuckled and said, "What a silly question. If you *are* me, you're in two places *now*, aren't you?" He stuck out his lower lip, pulled it, and let it snap back into place.

"I suppose," said Paul.

The Boy shook his head. "You'll never be me if you just sup- pose." Then he flew away from the mirror, leaving Paul with no reflection for several days, making brushing his hair quite a challenge.

Bonnie left on a night when the skies were starless. She had been there just over a week. Paul had barely had the time to be- come adjusted to her, and then she was gone, like a relative who had just poked her head in because she'd forgotten to take her hat with her and swung around to pick it up before abruptly de- parting once more.

He did not understand why she had left or where she had

gone. All he knew was that there was a great deal of tumult late one evening, and the next morning, her bassinet was empty. His mother spent a full week sitting in a rocking chair in the nursery, staring at the empty bed, saying not a word, while his father stood somberly by and occasionally rested a hand upon her shoulder.

They did not speak to Paul much about the matter except to say that Bonnie would not be with them anymore. Paul, being a wise young fellow, considered the matter and asked if Bonnie had fallen out of her pram and been taken away to the Anyplace by The Boy, making a rare exception and adding a girl to the ranks of the Vagabonds.

Paul's father said gently, "Something like that," and his eyes were a bit wet.

But Paul's mother's eyes were not wet at all. They were hard as steel, hard as the metal of a blade, and her voice as cutting, and she said, "You are not to fill his head with such nonsense anymore. He must learn to accept the world for what it is, with all its unfairness and cruelty. You have treated him like a child and left him ill prepared to deal with reality, and I insist you stop at once."

Paul had never heard his mother speak in such a way. It was as if she had been transformed overnight. Paul knew and understood about changes. Knew that at some point, child turns nearly overnight into adult through some mysterious event, the nature of which no one could quite explain to him. He had never, though, considered the possibility of adults likewise undergoing a change and transforming into something as different from adult as adult was from child. That, however, was what happened to Paul's mother; and whatever it was that she had become, it left her like the mother he'd known in name and visage only. It was as if someone else had set up housekeeping within her. His mother was a mere shade of herself.

Paul, she simply treated indifferently. She would speak words of love on rare occasion, but they were distant and halfhearted. Paul's father appeared even more bewildered by the metamorphosis, and she seemed angry with him day and night. Paul could not conceive what his father might have done, and Bonnie herself was hardly in a position to shed any light on the subject, what with being restricted to sitting out on a branch and not entering Paul's room.

His parents knew nothing about Bonnie's return or her new place of residence, for she cautioned Paul repeatedly that it would be best if he said nothing at all. Nevertheless, it finally slipped out one night when he heard his parents speaking very, very loudly, in such harsh tones that they were almost unrecognizable as themselves. He heard his father say something about it not being his fault, and his mother said she knew it wasn't; and he claimed that he was being treated as if it was, and she claimed he was wrong and being unfair to her and being insensitive; and for that matter she had been concerned that the baby looked off somehow and she had wanted to call the doctor but he had said no, she was imagining it, and if only he had listened; and then he replied that, see, there she was blaming it on him, and on and on until Paul could stand it no longer.

He thudded on their bedroom door, standing there in his newly laundered pajamas with the feet on the bottom because he was always losing his slippers and the bare wood floors could be quite cold these winter days. Patrick Dear threw open the door, his eyes red as if he were about to cry, the very notion of which terrified Paul because he was of the opinion that mothers cried rarely and fathers never. "Satisfied? You woke him!" said his mother, and she looked angrier than Paul had ever seen her; but he knew that the next words out of his mouth would surely make everything all better.

"Bonnie is happy," said Paul. "I just thought you would want to know that. I speak to her every day and she's perfectly content; and if it's her absence that's making you upset, you can stop now. Because you always say that you just want me to be happy, and I figure it's much the same for her, isn't it?"

His parents looked at him in puzzlement, and his mother scowled fiercely at him then and told him not to joke about such matters.

Paul explained very patiently that he was not joking at all. That his initial questions about whether Bonnie had flown off to the Anyplace had been answered by Bonnie herself, who was perched out on the tree branch that came near Paul's bedroom window.

"There's naught but birds there," his father said in bemusement.

To which Paul said, "Yes. Exactly. Remember that all babies are birds before they come to live with their families? Well, some babies, when they forget and desire to fly but cannot because the windows are closed, change back to being birds and slip out up the chimney or when the front door is open. And this is not such a terrible thing; because babies like that weren't truly ready to give up being birds in the first place, and would have been terribly miserable children and adults if they'd been forced into it."

"Really," said Colleen Dear in a voice that sounded as if it was supposed to be a question, but wasn't actually.

"Yes. Bonnie told me so. She's a house swallow now. She perches outside my window every day, and we talk and laugh and she tells me about what being a bird is like and I tell her what being a person is like. Honestly," Paul added a bit sadly, "she doesn't seem all that interested in the life of being a person. I told her I couldn't imagine spending my life eating worms, but she told me she couldn't imagine spending her life not flying. And I can understand that. I'd eat worms if I could fly. Wouldn't you?"

"I might at that," said Paul's father. "To fly like a bird . . . or The Boy . . ."

"Right. That's it. Close the door," said Paul's mother in a voice that sounded not angry or cutting but as vacant as an empty cookie jar—once the home of something delectable but now devoid of any hint of sweetness.

Paul went back to his room and climbed into bed, hoping that what he had told his parents had helped matters. Instead, later that night, his father stole into his room, kissed him gently upon the forehead, and said, "Your mother and I think it would be best if I left for a time."

"All right," said Paul, unfazed, for he was accustomed to his mother and father doing what they thought best, and did not expect them to change their behavior at this late date. "When will you come back?"

"I wish I knew," said his father.

Paul stared at his father for a long moment, the slightest glimmer of what was being said beginning to illuminate his brain. "I thought grown-ups knew everything," he said.

"I wish we did." He ruffled Paul's hair, which was something Paul had never been too fond of, but he offered no protest now. "Take care of your mother."

"I think she's supposed to take care of me."

"Yes," said his father, "but for the time being—perhaps a very long time to come—you are to be the grown-up man of the house."

"But I do not wish to grow up."

"All children, except one, grow up."

"Am I that child?" Paul watched his father's face carefully for a reaction. "Am I The Boy?"

Patrick did not answer him. Instead he hugged him once more, then stole out of the room, noiseless as a shadow.

Paul sat there in the darkness for a long, long moment, and then there was a tapping at the windowpane. He slid out of bed, padded across the floor, and opened the window wide. A small, brown swallow fluttered in and nestled on his outstretched finger. It cocked its head slightly and said, "You told them, didn't you?"

"Yes," Paul said with a sigh.

It fluffed its feathers and said, "I warned you not to. I knew this would happen. I told you so. Why didn't you listen to me?"

"I did," he insisted. "Listening and doing don't always have to be the same thing."

"Fair enough," said the swallow.

"Can you stay with me always?" Paul said.

"No, because I'm already forgetting about my time as a baby. I'm thinking more and more about nests and winter habitat and such. Soon I will simply be another bird, and no matter how much you remind me, I won't recall."

"I will always remember you," Paul assured his sister.

"We'll see," said the swallow, and then turned on his finger, hopped off, and flew away into the night sky.

Chapter 2

The Irishman with the Curious Profession

Things don't happen all at once.

Even those things that do seem to happen all at once, such as automobile accidents, don't really. They are the last act in a lengthy series of actions that have led, slowly but inevitably, to the supposedly "sudden outcome." You may be standing on a street corner and your head snaps around and, two drivers—one in a blue car, one in a white car—are sitting there, looking quite stunned, having collided with each other, because this was not remotely what they had planned for the day. Be aware that the first step along the long and treacherous path resulting in this "sudden" happenstance occurred twenty-three years earlier when the driver of the blue car was told by his mother, "Today is the day! You're getting your first haircut!" Off they went to the barber, who had a rather superb tonsorial facility; and there he had a haircut that was most revelatory because suddenly this mass of stuff hanging from the top of his head was no longer obscuring his vision.

So splendid an experience was it that he resolved, right then and there, to come to this very barber once a month, on that same Monday, so the hair would not hang in front of his face again.

Had the haircut been any less superb, had the day been anything other than Monday, he would never have been in the wrong place at the wrong time and run afoul of a speeding motorist who had his entire own story with which we will not bore you. The point is that he brought himself to this pass, and it may have seemed accidental; but looking back at the course of his life, it was unavoidable. This is what is referred to as foresight aftersight. You may as well perfect it, because there are some walks of life where it is an absolute necessity. In any job, for instance, where one of your responsibilities is determining how to blame other people for various mishaps.

So for Paul, although it may have seemed very sudden that he was sitting in front of a doctor explaining recent events of his life and being told how he was going to be taking some medicine so that he wouldn't be sick anymore—the fact was that it was not sudden at all. Rather, it was the culmination of a series of events that had led, inevitably, to discovering that he was apparently quite ill. Which was odd because he had never felt quite so healthy.

The beginnings of his abrupt meeting with Those Who Would Help Him stemmed from his ongoing endeavors to be the man of the house, as per the instructions of his father. His first attempt to meet this vital need was to strut around and say, in what he fancied was a most grown-up voice, "Looks like it's going to be one of those, eh!" or "I should say!" or "Tut-tut" or "Will we be attending that thing this evening?" But his mother kept looking at him oddly and finally told him to stop talking that way because he was ridiculous. He wanted to be grown-up, not ridiculous, and he did not realize you could be both at the same time, and oftentimes are.

So he decided to seek out advice from others on the best way to proceed. Normally he would have gone to his father for advice, but if his father had been around, he would not have been in this predicament in the first place. Instead he decided to seek guidance from the denizens of Kensington Gardens.

He sought out the pixie folk, but couldn't manage to hold their attention long enough to ask his questions. This is a common problem when it comes to pixies. If you flip a coin in the air while calling "Heads or tails?" a pixie will as likely cry out, "Coin!" or "Beer!" or "Balloooooon!" The pixies did, however, tend to give him very queer looks, as if they thought they should know him but were not quite sure.

So he consulted whatever animals he could find. He spoke to the birds nesting in the trees, the mice hiding among the high weeds, and the cats who were seeking out the mice but were generous enough to take a few moments to chat with Paul. He asked all of them what he could do to assume his mandated position as Man of the House.

Being animals, all their advice centered upon bringing home the fruits of a good hunt to feed the family. The notion intrigued him, especially since all the animals seemed rather set that it was the wisest course. He was embarrassed to admit, however, that he had never hunted anything in his life.

He had *pretend* hunted, and this may seem like something of a digression, but it is actually terribly relevant. So kindly do not jump ahead but instead pay strict attention.

Paul had pretend hunted during a number of his excursions into the Anyplace. The circumstance of the hunt had been real enough, but the locale assured it of being merely pretend. Thus

Paul had not felt any guilt over, say, taking the life of a helpless creature.

His partner in the endeavor—more than his partner; his mentor and spiritual guide—had been the merely magnificent snow tiger.

He could not remember the first time he had encountered the snow tiger on the shores of the Anyplace. He had always simply *been* there, and he had belonged to Paul and only Paul— if animals could be said to belong to anyone other than themselves. The snow tiger, as his name suggests, had fur as pure white as untouched snow; and when he moved, his muscles could be seen stretching and snapping taut beneath his hide. It may well have been the snow tiger who, at Paul's birth, bequeathed him the ability to converse with animals that The Boy had eventually helped him master.

Many was the time that Paul would run through the jungle or along the shores with the snow tiger at his side in adventures so vivid that—when Paul awoke—he needed to pick brambles from his bedclothes or sand from between his toes. Sometimes he would even sit astride the great beast, and the ground would blur beneath them as the snow tiger sprinted in pursuit of his prey.

Occasionally the snow tiger would express interest in hunting other humans, but Paul would sternly scold him about the practice, and the snow tiger would back down. Paul always suspected in the back of his mind that the snow tiger might well be off hunting humans when Paul wasn't around. When asked about this, the snow tiger would hem and haw and then point out how absolutely perfect the weather was, and shouldn't they be off stalking small game, for the gnawing in his stomach was becoming impossible for him to ignore. And Paul would fix him with an annoyed look that he inevitably could not maintain for long, and then they would be off on their adventures again. Adventures that Paul typically could not remember but wished he could.

Paul loved the snow tiger more than he loved himself. And since humans put their own interests above anything else (even the most unselfish of them—and you know who you are, so do not offer protests, because you will not impress me), that was and is a remarkable achievement.

Anyway . . . that is Paul's snow tiger.

Back to Paul's present situation, which presented a quandary to the animals upon learning that most humans did not hunt for their food but instead depended upon others such as grocers to provide it for them. Several of them loudly expressed their astonishment that such creatures as humans, lacking even the most fundamental self-reliance, had not simply starved to death long ago. Finally, one noble mouse took pity on Paul and volunteered his services. Instructing Paul to take the mouse's tail ever so gently between his teeth, the mouse then dangled from Paul's mouth in an ever so convincing act of playing dead. Paul had told the accommodating rodent that his mother would most likely have no interest in eating the mouse since she was, in fact, a vegetarian, but certainly she would appreciate the gesture and realize that Paul was at least endeavoring to step up to the responsibilities that had been thrust upon him.

The actuality of how matters subsequently unfolded did not meet with Paul's imagined scenario. In fact, the moment Colleen Dear turned around in the kitchen and saw her son with a seemingly dead mouse hanging from between his lips was so calamitous for all concerned that we would be best served if we glossed over it. Suffice to say there was much screaming and scampering and then leave it there. We will instead mercifully draw a curtain over the entire sorry affair and move on, rather than dwell upon the most tragically misunderstood gift since that day long gone when the denizens of Troy peeked out from behind their walls and said, "Look at the smashingly thoughtful wooden horse the departed Greeks have left us to apologize for ten years of harassment! Let's bring it inside, make merry sport, and drink ourselves into a stupor, for what harm could possibly befall since our enemies are nowhere near?"

Of far more import to our narrative are the events that transpired after Paul's majestic shot at adulthood woefully misfired.

Paul's mother brought him straightaway to a doctor. But it was not the doctor that Paul normally went to. His office didn't have that odd smell to it, and, cheerily, his mother assured him that no needles would be involved.

Furthermore, the thing Paul found most exciting about the experience was that he got to be in the office with the doctor, just the two of them. Since every other trip to a doctor had involved his mother being there the whole time and doing all the talking, Paul had to believe that this was a step closer to the coveted grown-up status.

The doctor, whose full name was Doctor Something Very Long That Ended with "witz," had a round face and a smile in his eyes. He said gently, "All right now, Paul. Tell me why you came home with a mouse hanging from your mouth."

So Paul did just that. He told the doctor all about the mouse and birds and pixies and cats, and how all of them spoke to him. He spoke of how it seemed the most natural thing in the world, and he had always been able to do it except he had not known it until recently when his mirror image began speaking to him. And the mirror image, by the by, turned out to be that of The Boy, which made Paul think that perhaps he himself was The Boy and had simply forgotten it somehow. But he was not sure, and needed to reflect upon it further.

He spoke of all these things, and also felt obliged to inform the doctor that the doctor's shadow had been making all manner of mocking gestures on the wall behind him. Shadows always do that when no one is watching. The doctor obligingly turned and looked and, of course, the shadow snapped back to its normal quizzical "why are you looking at me?" manner.

The doctor then held up a mirror to Paul and asked to speak to The Boy. There was The Boy in the mirror, as he usually was these days, save when he was being petulant; but in the spirited gamesmanship so typical of him, The Boy chose that moment to imitate—down to the slightest gesture—everything that Paul did, making him indistinguishable from a normal reflection.

Finally the doctor gave some medicine to Paul's mother, and explained to Paul that although he actually wasn't feeling sick, that was okay, it wasn't a sickness like a cold but rather a kind of sickness that came from sadness. Paul was to take this medicine, and then he would feel much happier and better and calmer, and never ever walk around with mice in his mouth (which didn't upset Paul) and never ever talk to animals or pixies or whatever again (which did upset Paul). He was not at all anxious to stop talking to his friends, but his mother said to him sternly, "Paul, you must be grown-up about this." Well! That was all that was required, for Paul knew the importance of such a goal, and so he downed the medicine without complaint.

The next day, his reflection was merely glowering at him, and when he would call The Boy by name, The Boy simply turned away.

By the day after that, The Boy wasn't acting like The Boy, but instead like Paul.

By the day after that, Paul was beginning to wonder why in the world he'd ever thought he was The Boy.

Now—let us talk about the Irishman.

It should be noted that the Irishman was a witness to all that transpired in Kensington Gardens. We made no mention of him at the time because it was really Paul's business that was under discussion. The man would have intruded into the tale in a very noisy fashion; and he was disinclined to do so, because ultimately he is a rather polite sort, even if he does claim piratical leanings. So we respected his wishes and kept him out of the proceedings for as long as we reasonably could. But now we must clear our throat; tap on his virtual, if not literal, dressing room door; and bring him to center stage in order to proceed.

The Irishman had a grizzled beard and tufts of white hair, and tended to squint through spectacles that were perpetually perched upon the end of his nose. He was shabbily dressed, sported a battered felt hat, and wore a small placard tied around his neck. At the moment the placard was backward so that whatever words might have been printed upon the front were unviewable. When he was not working, if his work could be called working, he would hang about in Kensington Gardens to see if there were any children worth killing. He did notice one or two on occasion, but could never quite muster the energy.

When he watched Paul going about his business, however, he instantly knew Paul as the type of boy who could, should, and must be killed. Every day he would sit upon his favorite bench, watch Paul yammer and chatter in an easy fraternal manner with the subtler residents of the Park, and come up with all the best ways to bring terminal mischief upon the lad.

Paul stopped coming by Kensington Gardens during the week or so it took the medicine to work its magic, which the Irishman did not know. We could have told him, of course; but we find it's preferable to let the characters in the drama find these things out for themselves, lest they discover too much too fast and wind up stampeding toward the end of the book having learned none of what they were supposed to in their journey. The Irishman had almost given up hope of having the opportunity to kill the lad, but was both delighted and dismayed to spot him one day ambling through the Gardens in much his normal routine, briefly thought abandoned.

He watched Paul walk away down the Broad Walk, without—as always—a mother in tow. This was fine insofar as the Irishman was concerned; for in his experience, mothers were nothing but a blamed nuisance. Paul got ahead of him and seemed to disappear and reappear almost at will, leading the Irishman to conclude that one of Paul's parents was probably Irish, explaining possible leprechaun leanings that the Irishman could usually spot at twenty feet away.

The Irishman stalked Paul while trying to remain casual, and finally caught up with him at two small tombstones. One read "W. St. M." and the other "13a P. P. 1841." Paul was staring at them, his hands behind his back. The Irishman came up slowly, prepared to both stab and shoot Paul just to make certain. He was prevented from doing this by two things: Paul's suddenly turning and looking him right in the eyes, and the fact that he was unarmed.

"I used to wonder if The Boy was buried beneath that one," said Paul.

He was pointing at the tombstone with "P.P." upon it. The notion took the Irishman aback, and he looked leeways and sideways and thriceways at Paul, and then said, "I don't think so. The year's wrong."

"Maybe not," Paul reasoned. "Maybe The Boy is just a boy who died and doesn't know it, and won't admit it, so he's stuck in between, too lively to be dead, too dead to be alive."

"He was wounded. By Hack. Wounded and nearly died

from it. How could one nearly die from a wound if one is not truly alive?"

Paul nodded but then said, "He liked to pretend. Perhaps he pretended he was wounded."

"That could be," allowed the Irishman. "That would be like him. To have the last laugh on Hack by being unkillable, since he's already killed."

"So you know the stories of him, then?"

"Stories? Who said we were talking about stories?"

The true significance of the words filtered slowly through Paul's mind, and then he turned and looked up at the Irishman as if truly seeing him, and understanding him, for the first time.

"I was making things up just now," Paul said. "Talking about The Boy as if he really was, when he's just the stuff of dreams."

"Why should he be any different from the rest of us?"

Paul tried to determine whether that was wise or just obscure, and didn't bother to decide. Cautiously he asked the question he'd been afraid to voice, because it seemed to get him into trouble when he did. "Am I The Boy?" he said.

"No," said the Irishman, and then looked at him closer. "You look a bit like him though. Around the eyes. Enough around the eyes to stir up some bad memories."

"Were you about to kill me, then?" Paul said.

"No. No, no, no. Yes, but no. Yes, in that I intended to do it, but no, in that I intended to lie about it."

"Have you killed many boys?"

"Not hereabouts. Not for a while. If ever. My memory on that score is a bit patchy, I'm sorry to say."

"Oh. Well, I wish you wouldn't do it now."

The Irishman considered this, then shrugged. "All right, then. I'll do the next best thing to killing you. I'll help you."

"You can't kill someone by helping him."

"Course you can," said the Irishman. "Best way, in fact. Whole races of people, poor devils didn't know how unhappy they were, and the only way to help them was to kill off every last one of them. So what do you need helping with, then?"

"Well," said Paul, "I told a doctor about how I talk to animals and pixies and such, and he gave me medicine for it so I'd stop talking to them."

"Ahhh," said the Irishman, and he began to walk. "Does it make you happy, taking it?"

"No. I was hoping it would make my mum happy, but it's not. But she's unhappy about so many other things."

"What else is she unhappy about?"

So Paul told the Irishman about all that had transpired. At random times the Irishman interjected such thoughtful comments as "Tut-tut!" and "I should say!" and "Looks like it's going to be one of those, eh?" which was how Paul would have known he was speaking to a genuine grown-up, had the whiskers not been a dead giveaway.

"Well," the Irishman said at last, once Paul had finished his recitation, "it's fairly clear what needs to be done, eh?"

"Is it?" said Paul, politely bewildered.

"Isn't it to you? If your mother is so upset about the loss of a baby daughter, then what's the obvious answer?"

Paul gave it a good deal of consideration. "To find her another?"

"Exactly!" said the Irishman, who actually had figured that putting poison in the mother's tea, or perhaps blowing her up, was the most elegant means with which to deal with the woman's sorrow. But Paul's suggestion seemed workable as well, plus it had the merit of not attracting the local constabulary.

"Perhaps the Anyplace can help me!" Paul said with growing excitement. "It is the place where dreams are given substance.

So if I can go there and dream of making my mother happy, perhaps I can return from there with the means to do so."

"What," said the Irishman with genuine interest, "does your Anyplace look like? They vary, you know."

"Lately, my Anyplace looks much like my nursery, with my mother simply glowering at me or staring at an empty infant bed, and I've been unable to tread upon the more distant shores. I used to have a white tiger—fur white as snow—that stalked the Anyplace. He was mine and I his, and we moved through the jungle together while all others faded away from us in fear; but I haven't seen him or the jungle for a very long time."

"There is a shop," the Irishman said abruptly. He told Paul where it was, and I will not repeat it to you here, for it would be precipitous and possibly send far more people to the shop than its proprietor would care to handle. If you give it a great deal of consideration just before you go to sleep, perhaps you will find the location whispered to your nearly dreaming mind. Whether you can keep it with you upon waking is entirely your own problem, and best of luck to you.

"If you have the stuff of it," the Irishman said, "you will find what you need there."

"And what is it that I need?"

"You will know it when you see it," the Irishman said. "And if you do not see it, then you will never know it, and that's the truth of it. Now, if you'll excuse me, I have to go to work."

"What work is that?"

The Irishman turned the card around, and Paul read the words: THE ONLY MAN CAPT. HACK FEARED. Below that, in smaller but equally meticulous print, it said, HANDSHAKES, ONE QUID. PHOTOS, TWO QUID.

"The proprietor's name is Starkly," said the Irishman. "Tell him the Irish pirate sent you. And tell him that the Irish pirate told him not to kill you." He lowered his voice and added, a bit abashed, "Our killing days are long past us, truth to tell. Plus, there's a depressing lack of boys trying to kill us, and without them having at us, it seems bullying to have at them. Being a pirate is one thing, but we don't have to be bullies about it now, do we?"

With that confession off his chest and feeling far better for it, the Irishman swaggered off, moving as if he were still striding the deck of a pirate ship.

Late that afternoon, Paul pretended to take his medicine, but he did not do so. He crawled into bed at the appointed time. Long minutes turned into hours, and hours into days and years and centuries, for that was how long it seemed to Paul that he lay there. Finally, unable to stand it any longer, he flung off the bedclothes and stomped to the mirror.

His reflection stood there, defiant, indistinguishable from himself. But he wasn't fooled. He knew it was The Boy. He was taunting him. Confusing him. Leaving Paul unable to determine whether he himself was The Boy, or if The Boy just existed in the mirror to torment him; or perhaps it was another scenario entirely that he couldn't begin to comprehend.

"Boy!" he said in his most commanding tone. "Come here, Boy!"

The Boy in the mirror mimicked him, mocking him with the perfection of his imitation. A pantomime. "I need to go to the Anyplace!" Paul said. "I need to know how, or learn how, or remember how! I need you to teach me or remind me! I need to find happiness for my mother. And you've got to help me!"

Nothing. Nothing to indicate that he was anything except a simple mirror image, except... there. There in the eyes, the slightest flash of the mocking contempt in which The Boy obviously held him.

"Why are you doing this?" said Paul. "Why are you being this way? Why? Why?"

And The Boy, from the protection of the mirror, said, "Because I thought you were different. I thought you were like me. But you are not. You want to be like them, and go places I do not, and, deep down you wish I wanted to grow up as you do. You even wanted to make me go away so that you could keep your mother happy. Mothers betray you. Always. Always," he said sharply, angrily. "And you want to leave me behind so you can make her happy, then wonder why I'll have nothing more to do with you?"

"I need you," Paul said. "I need you to bring me to the Anyplace. I need your help."

"No," The Boy said carelessly. "I've other things to do and other games to play. I'm done playing with you."

"But I'm not done with you," Paul said hotly. "I'll—I'll find another way to get there, then! I'll make you help me! I will!"

The Boy, gay and heartless as always, threw wide his arms and laughed.

And Paul grabbed at the mirror, yanked it as hard as he could, and sent it crashing to the floor. The mirror shattered, sending glass everywhere. The impact brought his mother running in, and she surveyed the damage with wide eyes, shaking her head. Then she looked at Paul and said intensely, "Did you take your medicine today?"

Paul, who had kept the pill tucked in his cheek until he found a private moment to spit it out, lied to his mother for the first time in his life. "Yes," he said.

She grunted, not looking entirely convinced, and told him to step back away from the glass until she could return with a broom and dustpan to clean it up. When she walked away, he carefully picked up a shard of glass. He saw smirking lips within.

"I'm coming for you," he whispered.

"Catch me if you can," said the mouth of The Boy.

Chapter 3

"Did You Not Hear That?"

Even with the address in hand, the next day Paul had a good deal of trouble locating the shop to which the Irishman had referred him. It was in a bustling market area, the exact type of place where a young lad could very easily feel overwhelmed. Paul did not feel overwhelmed, nor underwhelmed, but simply whelmed. It was a task, to be sure, but merely the first task on what would doubtless be a lengthier undertaking; and so he set his mind to achieving it as efficiently as possible.

He was loath to ask any of the passing adults for the curio shop run by the fellow named Starkly, because he had long ago noticed—as I'm sure we all have—that adults in these types of situations are far more interested in asking their own questions than providing answers. Watch: Just to show you, Paul will ask the first adult crossing his path where to find Starkly's curio shop.

"And what is a young fellow like yourself doing out and about on his own, eh?"

You see? Simple question, nonanswer. So we shall allow the adult to go on his way by calling to him in a loud voice so as to distract him, permitting Paul to slip sideways and disappear into the crowd of noontime buyers. After all, do we really wish to drag truant agents and such into a nice day as this? Certainly they have better things to do, as do we all.

Paul made his way past the array of bookstores, fruit stands, clothing shops of endless variety. He was certain he was in the correct general area, but was still having trouble finding specifically the place he was looking for. Then he hit upon a notion. He recalled all the times that his mother had said that something was always in the last place one looks for it. So Paul resolved, in order to save time, to skip all the other places and head straight to the last one. Naturally he found the shop immediately.

There was the door right in front of him, with a sign that said CURIOS etched in fading gilt letters. There was no mention of the name "Starkly," but that did not deter Paul. He was quite certain that he was in the right place, and the reason was that he heard the bell calling him.

Paul didn't head straight into the shop. Instead, he stared at the dust-smeared front window, trying to make out anything there that might have some sort of value. And as he stood there, the front door to the place kept opening and closing, not because a flow of customers was steadily entering and leaving the shop, but because the (presumable) proprietor kept poking his head out, looking around, and then closing the door again, not unlike a rabbit peeking out of its hutch to make sure there were no predators about.

Each time he did so, a small bell that hung upon the door chimed musically. But it did not ring in the same manner as other bells that Paul had heard in his life. Instead, it almost seemed to be calling to Paul, with a sense of urgency.

Paul glanced right and left, not because he thought he was being observed but because that was simply what one was supposed to do when embarking on an adventure. Then he scampered across the busy street, walked up to the door, and thrust it open.

He was powerfully struck by the thick, musty smell. It was almost as if he were entering another world altogether, for the one in which he lived seemed always to be focusing on what was happening next, whereas this place smelled of a past that would always be and a future that would never come.

He sensed rather than saw a movement in the darkness, and then a man was standing over him. It was the very proprietor who had been poking his head out. He had a round club that Paul instantly recognized as a belaying pin, and he was holding it high over his head with the obvious intention of bringing it crashing down upon Paul's skull.

He froze as Paul stared at him. Nothing was said for a long moment, and then Paul said, "Are you planning to try and kill me with that?"

"This? No," the man immediately said. He had a gentle, soft-spoken manner, something more common to a schoolteacher perhaps. "I was simply holding it up to the light to see it better. Would you mind turning away, please? I can examine it better if you're not watching."

"Is your name Starkly?"

Starkly said nothing at first but merely pondered all the ways in which he could answer the question . . . none of which, as it happened, had the slightest relation to the truth. Paul, meantime, wisely decided not to wait for the answer to be forthcoming. "The Irish pirate told me to come here. He told me to tell you not to kill me."

"Oh. Did he?" Starkly lowered his arm and actually looked

a bit relieved. "Probably all for the best. I'm out of practice killing young boys."

"So is the Irish pirate."

"Yes, but he was never particularly skilled at it, even in his best pirate days. Poor sod never knew what he was on about." Starkly leaned in toward Paul and squinted at him. "Do I know you, young sir?"

"You might. I'm not sure." Paul tilted his head, trying to look cocky. "I think I may be The Boy. Do you think I am? Do I look anything like him?"

"No," said Starkly dismissively, but then he took a second look. "Well . . . maybe a little. Around the nose, I think. Yes, the nose is a bit evocative of The Boy. So what do you want?"

"I want to go to the Anyplace."

"Oh, do you." Starkly made a face of nearly unveiled disgust. "And why do you want to do that? To fly like The Boy? To harass and kill perfectly noble pirates? To cavort like a heathen and never grow up and have no care in the world?"

"No. To find a lost girl, if there be any, and bring her home so my mother can have a little daughter and not be so angry all the time since my previous little sister vanished from her crib, never to return."

Starkly took all this in, and something in his look and demeanor changed. It was far too subtle for Paul to note, but since we are standing just outside and slightly to the left of the situation, we can perceive what Paul cannot.

"Well, I certainly don't know what to tell you. Why in the world did the Irishman send you here?" When Paul merely shrugged in response, Starkly shook his head with the air of one greatly put upon. "Well, feel free to look about. If you find anything you think can be of help to you, we'll discuss price."

"I don't have any money," said Paul.

"Best not to tell me that," Starkly said, "because now I have to throw you out. On second thought, I won't do it myself. I'll have to find someone else to do it. Hang on." Starkly promptly walked into the curtained-off back area, leaving Paul alone in the shop.

Nervous, his heart pounding, Paul began sifting through the many shelves, looking for he didn't know what. A book, perhaps, or a map or a magic wand or secret words scribbled down upon a piece of paper, written in an ancient tongue that would grant Paul special powers when read aloud. Something, anything, that would be of use to him. All he could find, however, was miscellaneous bric-a-brac, none of which appeared to serve any useful function and all of which seemed to be there solely for the purpose of making him have to look at it all.

His eye almost went right past something as he scanned the bottom shelf in the farthest corner of the room. But then his gaze was drawn back to it, as if something had tossed out a fishing line, snared his eyelid, and drawn him irresistibly back to the place he had initially overlooked. On his hands and knees, he leaned forward, craning his neck around so that he could make out whatever it was more clearly. Limited in his ability to do so, he reached back and pulled the dust-enshrouded object from its hiding place.

It was a detailed wood carving, a statue about the size of the palm of his hand. At least he thought it was a wood statue. The material felt odd and looked even stranger. More "mummified" than carved, really. Yes, that had to be it. It was a representation of an Egyptian mummy, produced through some marvelously clever means. It was a female, definitely, because her curves were in the right places. She was upright, her hands crisscrossed upon her breast in the near universal depiction of one at her final rest. Her eyes were closed in solemn slumber. In-triguingly, she had a pair of wings upon her back. It was difficult to tell what they would have been like in life, for they were as solid and unmoving as the rest of her. She was clad in a skeleton leaf, or at least the remains of one, and she was a bit rounder in the hips than most women preferred—which was not some-thing that Paul noticed, being a boy and not understanding women.

But take heart! If he is fortunate enough to survive all that is. going to happen to him before we take our leave of him—and we must tell you that his survival is not remotely guaranteed—then his reward, such as it is, will be to become an adult man and still not understand women.

"What have you there?" said Starkly, having reappeared so abruptly that Paul jumped, startled. Instantly he thrust the mummified female into his pocket and stood up with his hands wide open and presented for inspection. Starkly did not seem impressed. "Did you take something with the intention of steal-ing it?"

"No. Nooo, no, no, no. No."

"I think I don't believe you," Starkly said. "Aren't you aware that thieves will be killed, just as it says on the sign?"

"What sign?" said Paul innocently. He looked where Starkly was pointing, but saw nothing.

Now Starkly looked where he was pointing and made an ir-ritated noise with his lips. "Someone must have stolen it," he said. "Well, it seems you'll be getting off lucky this day. Best be off with you, then, before the sign turns up and something un-fortunate happens to you."

Paul started to reach into his pocket to remove the mummi-fied woman and replace her, but Starkly did not give him the opportunity. Instead, waving the belaying pin in a very authoritative manner, he said, "Off with you! Immediately! Don't even think of putting your hands into your pockets in order to take something out of them, or I assure you it will go badly for you."

"But—"

"No butting. Butting is for goats. Are you a goat?"

"No."

"Off with you, then," he said firmly.

Paul went to the door, opened it, and immediately was struck by the total absence of the sound of the bell. "Did you hear that?" he said.

"Hear what?" said Starkly with a tilt of his head.

"Did you not hear that?" Paul said. He looked up at the bell that was hanging on the edge of the door. "The bell kept ringing, and now it's not."

"That bell has not rung since the day I took over this store," Starkly said. He reached up and tapped it with his finger. It produced no noise, not even the slightest tinkling. "See? Nothing."

"But I thought—"

"Boys don't think," Starkly said. "Boys do. Boys believe. Go do something you believe." And with that, he closed the door firmly, leaving Paul out in the street and the bell thumping soundlessly against the door.

Chapter 4

The Crooked Old Lady with the Hooked Nose

If any of you are sitting snug in your homes and wondering where The Boy might be at this point in the narrative—whether he's actually Paul, now living a normal life as a youngster struggling to find his way back; or perhaps residing in some world existing only in the shadow realm of mirrors, not unlike that blond-haired girl in another tale; or perhaps he was just strutting around the Anyplace and far too taken with whatever had lately caught his fancy to concern himself about anything else—take heart that several of his most devoted followers were wondering much the exact same thing. And since their particular situation was far more dire than yours, you can be cheered that a small bit of impatient frustration is a pale thing compared to worrying that you are going to die with The Boy not there to aid you.

The foremost of his followers was a young lady who served a peculiar function in The Boy's life. She was a petite British girl named Gwenny, an occasional visitor to the Anyplace rather than a permanent resident. There are some very curious aspects to Gwenny, beyond some of the more head-scratching aspects—such as that sometimes The Boy saw her as his mother and other times as his wife, arbitrarily addressing her sometimes as "Mother" and other times as "tut-tut, my dear" (which is what he thought husbands called wives). But this part is about Gwenny, not The Boy's peculiarities.

So: the curious aspects of Gwenny. Once upon a time, Gwenny and her brothers would sleep peacefully in their nursery and dream of the Anyplace, playing upon its colorful shores and hobnobbing with its varied and sundry residents. They would see lions and wolves, savages and gnomes and a strange old lady with a hooked nose, and princes with six brothers, and just about everything that they could imagine and you could imagine. The Anyplace was about all these marvels and more besides. And every night their mother would sort through their minds, as mothers always do, so as to make them all nice and orderly for the morning's activities, and she would find bits and pieces of the Anyplace strewn about. It was in this manner that she first learned about The Boy, setting into motion an entire sequence of events that no one could have foreseen.

Gwenny and her brothers made their initial flight to the Anyplace when they were of a certain youthful age. There they had many great adventures, including notable and epic confrontations with Captain Hack, who eventually went to his end in the jaws of a beastly serpent. They then returned home, Vagabonds in tow ("Vagabonds" being the group name for The Boy's followers—parentless young boys gathered by The Boy to return to the Anyplace and accompany him in an endless reverie of unending childhood). The Vagabonds were adopted by Gwenny's parents and put on the path to the inevitable destruction that is called maturity.

A year later, The Boy returned and brought Gwenny and her brothers back to the Anyplace for spring cleaning, just as he had promised...although it should be emphasized that time moves very differently in the Anyplace than it does in our own world, and The Boy easily crammed a lifetime's worth of adventures into the same period that Gwenny was cramming fractions, history, and astronomy.

The positive aspect of this was that The Boy's existence was one of constant challenge. The negative aspect was that, since Gwenny and her brothers were far less ambitious in their experiences, they were able to retain the knowledge of the things they learned; whereas events unfolded so quickly upon The Boy, and in such number, that they pushed one another out of his head. Gwenny was dumbfounded to learn, for instance— upon her eventual return to the Anyplace—that The Boy had no recollection of Captain Hack. The Boy didn't consider this remotely unusual, explaining that he tended to forget people after he killed them.

Even more shocking was that he had no recollection of Fiddlefix, the glowing pixie sprite who had been his constant companion. When Gwenny did all she could to stir his memory on the subject, he opined that she was probably dead, since pixies tended not to live for all that long.

It was odd that this should have left Gwenny unhappy. Fiddle (as she was called) had done nothing to hide her disdain and dislike for Gwenny, and had even tried to engineer her demise on more than one occasion. To Gwenny, though, pixies were amazing creatures, and Fiddlefix was no less amazing than others of her sort. It had been almost touching how much she had wanted Fiddle to like her; and the fact that she would never be able to accomplish that aim weighed sadly upon her.

That first spring cleaning visit was gloriously active otherwise; and, although The Boy's forgetting about Hack and Fiddlefix distressed Gwenny, the Anyplace is such that sad memories tend not to linger. So Gwenny and her brothers were able to enjoy their share of experiences without too much concern about those missing from said experiences, both friend and foe.

After that occasion and their return home, The Boy did not come back for her for several years, and when he did, he was unaware that he had missed all that intervening time. Gwenny's brothers were absent, off on a school holiday, when The Boy came for Gwenny; but that did not daunt him, since he didn't recall her brothers either. Indeed, it was miraculous and a measure of the depth of feeling he had for Gwenny that he remembered her. So he can be forgiven for overlooking that Gwenny was wearing a new frock, one that hid—as best as possible—the fact that she was on the cusp of becoming a young woman.

The danger signs were there for anyone who chose to see them. Since The Boy chose not to, however, naturally he was oblivious to them. He did not know that the ravages of time were not about to let up upon Gwenny and her brothers any more than they passed over any other children...except, of course, for him.

But that was a tragedy for another time. Currently we are dwelling upon the tragedy unfolding before us now.

When Gwenny had first voyaged to the Anyplace, the Vagabonds and The Boy had resided underground. She had not been enamored of that living situation, asserting that young boys needed to be surrounded by fresh air and sunshine rather than dirt. So The Boy and the Vagabonds had obediently constructed a house secured high in a tree. They had all moved in there and, even after Gwenny and the original Vagabonds had departed (the former to return to her parents, the latter to be adopted and destroyed), The Boy had continued to reside there as he went about his business gathering new Vagabonds. Upon her return, Gwenny found herself once again the mother of children who needed one more desperately than any other children in existence.

The circumstances were markedly different, though, due to the total absence of The Boy and more than half the Vagabonds.

Gwenny, having arrived in the Anyplace after a dizzying and dazzling flight that fairly took her breath away, met a half dozen new Vagabonds that The Boy had acquired from various points around the world. They were a scruffy lot, and there was something in the eyes of many of them that Gwenny found a bit disturbing. This was due partly to the fact that Gwenny was no longer the young, wide-eyed girl that she had been when she had first come to the Anyplace at The Boy's behest. The adult eye that resided deep within her head was opening wider and wider, and causing her to look down upon the youngsters that she had formerly looked at directly. Where once they had been lacking merely a mother—a role that Gwenny was more than happy to fill—now she saw they were lacking other things. Compassion. Joy. The sheer thrill of childhood. This new crop of Vagabonds was . . .

. . . sinister.

Not all of them. Two of them evoked memories of the gentle, credulous enthusiasm that she had seen in all the Vagabonds of days past. One was a young, skinny, slightly twitchy fellow who took great pride in knowing his name, since it had been on a tag on the shirt he'd been found in: "Irregular."

The other was very different from Irregular in that he was broad shouldered, even stocky, with an open and eager expression that made him appear so eager to be liked, it was impossible not to like him. He was French, and he was called Porthos. He tended to dress like an oversized dog, with a headdress of floppy fur ears; and he was remarkably strong but was one of those who was easy to bully because he didn't know his own strength.

Within a day of Gwenny's arriving, The Boy was gone, and he had taken most of their "sons" with him, leaving behind only Porthos and Irregular.

This action, in and of itself, did not alarm Gwenny. The Anyplace was a place of vast and endless adventure. Many had been the times when The Boy had hustled off on some exploit or another, sometimes gone a day, even two. He would invariably return and strut about, pumping his arms and crowing over his varied and courageous deeds. Gwenny and the family would ooh and aah; and if they did not do so with sufficient enthusiasm, Gwenny would say firmly, "Now, show proper respect to your father, children." Whereupon they would sustain their oohs and aahs for far longer, allowing The Boy more time to puff and strut.

That was when The Boy was being the father and Gwenny the mother. There were other times when The Boy wanted to be treated as a child as well, although Gwenny confusingly remained in her role as mother in those instances. In his inability to decide whether he wanted the most significant female in his life to be his mother or his life mate—and perpetually alternating between the two—The Boy was closer to the attitude of adult men than in any other aspect of his nature.

When The Boy departed with the balance of the Vagabonds that first day which would mark a major tragedy in their lives, Gwenny went about the usual routine of spring cleaning. Naturally she had no true idea how much time or how many springs might have passed in her absence, but she dealt with the considerable mess with her usual aplomb. The day slid easily into night, and Gwenny told her two young charges stories and settled them in bed, while assuring them that their father would be back by the morning.

The morning came and went and brought no sign of The Boy. The evening followed as had the previous, and by the time of the third morning, Gwenny's assurances that all was well rang hollow in her own ears.

Time passed, and passed some more. In The Boy's prolonged absence, the Vagabonds were responsible for food gathering, and they did an adequate if not spectacular job. They would come home with armloads of plants mostly, but tell great stories of how the vegetation had put up a mighty fight. Gwenny would ooh and aah, but her efforts to do so were halfhearted as her concern grew.

Gwenny lost track of how long The Boy was gone. That wasn't all that difficult to do, for the Anyplace was adept at draining one's awareness of times past or present, encouraging its residents to live only in the now. But every so often her mind, or the thoughts of the Vagabonds, would return to their missing father and siblings, and the concern would grow once more. Eventually it took such deep root that no amount of the Anyplace's influence could distract them from their anxiety over their father's prolonged absence.

"What if he's dead?" Irregular whispered to Gwenny, thinking that he was the only one who was doing so when in fact so was Porthos.

"He's not dead," Gwenny said firmly. "He is far too wonderful to die, and he would be the first to tell you, if given the opportunity."

"Then I hope he has that opportunity soon."

Then one day, Gwenny woke up with the distinct feeling that this day was going to be significantly different from those that had gone before. She didn't know why she thought it, but it was an ill-at-ease that she could not escape. She continued to try to put up a brave front for the others, but they picked up on her worry, and it permeated the entirety of their day.

Day once more rolled into night, and Gwenny let out a deep sigh of relief that her premonition appeared groundless. But the sigh caught in her throat when Porthos suddenly tugged at her arm, pointed, and said, "Who is that?"

Gwenny didn't initially see at what he was pointing, but then she did. From her vantage point in the tree house, she spotted an elderly lady, crooked and bent, standing some distance away.

"Are you going to invite her up?" Irregular said, never praying more that the answer was going to be no.

Gwenny obliged him. "Stay here," she said, and vaulted off the edge of the house.

With The Boy having been gone for so long, and no ready supply of pixie dust to supplement them, flight was problematic. In some measure, it was The Boy's own belief in their ability to fly that enabled them to do so, and with The Boy gone, flying—like every other Anyplace activity—became far more difficult. But Gwenny was still able to float a bit when needed, and she did so now, drifting like a feather to the ground. She was extremely worried and nervous, for she had no idea who this lady might be or if she presented any sort of danger. Gwenny told herself that she could handle anything, especially if it involved a threat to her children, whom she would defend like a tigress.

She landed gently on the ground, making sure to keep her hands upon her thighs so that her frock didn't billow up and around her. Gwenny was all too aware of the eyes of the lads upon her from above, watching and listening to every move. She tilted her head slightly and said as properly as she could, "May I help you?"

The crooked lady with the hooked nose took a step forward, moving from the shadow of the tree to a sliver of moonlight that fell upon the ground before her. Gwenny was taken aback. The lady had a smile fixed upon her face that came nowhere near her eyes. Eyes that burned with a hatred that was cold and hot all at the same time and seemed to illuminate what features of her face Gwenny could make out. Her black cloak and gray garments hung loosely around her, making her body look like a formless mass. Her most prominent feature, her nose, was long and distended. It not only hooked in general, but the tip of it extended a bit longer and farther down, curving back and pointing ever so slightly at her mouth. A few wisps of hair, gray streaked with black, stuck out from beneath her hood.

"Are you the Gwenny?" said the old lady.

"I am, yes. And who are you?"

"My name is unimportant," said the lady. "I am here merely to send you word from The Boy."

"The Boy!" Gwenny said, and she heard the collective breaths of her boys being drawn above her. She took two steps forward and then, her caution gainsaying her, took one step back. "Is he all right? Where is he?"

"He will not be coming back."

Gwenny didn't take in the words at first. "I beg your pardon?"

"He has left you." The lady cackled, then cleared her throat. "He has decided that he no longer desires to be father to your brood or play your husband. It is a game that no longer suits him."

"But ... he can't!"

"You are young," the crone said, "and not knowing of many things. But one thing even you should know is that there is nothing The Boy cannot do if he puts his mind to it."

"He has responsibilities!" Gwenny said. "To me! To our children! He cannot forsake them and us. What are our children supposed to do without their father?"

"Well," the old lady counseled her, "my suggestion would be that they grow up as quickly as possible."

"But no child should have growing up thrust upon him, simply because one of his parents has wandered off."

"I wouldn't dispute that, actually," said the old lady. "But no one asked me. I am merely conveying the message."

The boys, upon hearing this, let out a distressed moan and cries of "We don't want to have to grow up! It's not fair!"

"I would agree," the crone commiserated. "Your father has many fine qualities, but unselfishness is not among them. What's fair is what's fair for him, and the rest must simply live with what is." She turned to Gwenny and said, "That, child, is the way of things."

The old lady, however, was not dealing with the child Gwenny. This was Gwenny on the cusp of adulthood, and she was not easily cowed or condescended to. "You have not answered my question," she said sharply. "Who are you? What are you to The Boy? What influence do you have over him?"

"I have told you. I am merely a messenger—"

"That is what you are but not who. You," said Gwenny, pointing an accusing finger, "are a villain. Admit it, and give up your villainy immediately."

Gwenny advanced upon her, and something suddenly cut through the air. Gwenny stumbled back, looking down at her arm in surprise at the thin ribbon of blood that was now upon it. Her sleeve had been neatly sliced open, and Gwenny clutched at it in shock. The wound was not wide nor deep, but it stung and certainly got her attention. She looked up at the crone in astonishment.

The crone had her left arm raised, and her sleeve had fallen away to reveal her left wrist. At first glance, Gwenny thought the crone was holding a sword. She was not. Instead the sword was actually affixed directly to a metal cuff upon her wrist. Despite her age, she nevertheless whipped the glistening blade back and forth warningly with a vigor that belied her advanced years.

"You dare!" screeched the crone, her voice becoming higher and higher. She was trembling with indignation, and her face was turning purple. "You dare speak so to me! The gall! The sheer presumption! In all my years, *I have never known anyone to—to—to—*!"

Then she stopped, just... stopped. She closed her eyes and drew in several deep breaths. Gwenny could not be sure, but she thought that just for a moment there was a hint of fear in the old lady's face, as if the notion of completely losing her temper in the way that she almost had could have extremely unfortunate consequences. Perhaps, Gwenny reasoned, she had a weak heart or some such and needed to moderate her attitude. Eventually the crone calmed herself, restoring her breathing to its natural rhythm. When she opened her eyes and spoke again, she sounded almost maternal.

"There are no heroes or villains in these matters, child," said the old lady, "just victims." She brought the flat of the sword up and touched it lightly to her forehead in a mocking salute, and then stepped back into the forest, allowing the shadows to swallow her as if they'd just become reacquainted with an old friend.

Chapter 5

How the Pot Became Repaired

Any number of times in the past, Paul's mother had asked "Where have you been?" when he came in the door. In the days when he had entered at his father's side, it was a musical, inviting question, asking him to share with her whatever adventures he had undertaken that particular afternoon. On those occasions when he had been out playing on his own and come back a little later than he really should have, the question was fraught with cautious concern.

Nowadays, however, it was an inquiry delivered with the same sort of weary frustration that she might have used upon, say, errant keys that had caused her to be delayed on her rounds.

Paul stood in the doorway, his hand still resting on the knob. "To the marketplace."

"The marketplace?" Her eyes narrowed and Paul could sense her picking through bits of his mind, trying to determine what he had been up to with the sort of deep suspicion that she approached everything having to do with him these days. "Why did you go there?"

"No reason," said Paul, which was probably the best thing. Understand that we do not believe in lying to one's mother. It is, in fact, a most unfortunate pastime and beneath even the very lowest of the low. Yet children do so whether we approve or not. And they will do it for the most self-serving of motivation: to hide some great misdeed in vain hope of not being caught out. Yet when the truth comes out, as it always does, the children are forgiven sooner or later, usually sooner. Paul's motivation, on the other hand, was purely to make his mother's life better. There was no selfishness in him. So if miscreants can receive absolution, certainly we would be rotters to withhold similar dispensation from Paul.

So it is that he earns no loss of esteem in our eyes when he lies to his mother about having no reason for his trip to the market and for his withholding from her his encounters with unemployed pirates, and the small dried-out figure he had in his pocket. Likewise we extend forgiveness to him when he goes on to reassure his mother that his days of conversing with animals, pixies, and such were continuing to be long gone.

She eyed him thoughtfully, but said no more of it as she went off to prepare dinner for them. Paul, meantime, hied himself upstairs, where he removed the precious cargo and set it upon his small desk. Then he rested his chin upon his hands and stared at it levelly, waiting for it to blink, to move, to *something*. "I do believe in pixies," he said. "I do. I talk to them all the time. I do believe." But no response came. He tried clapping a few times, and then even more emphatically, and he kept saying over and over, "I do believe. I do believe in pixies. I do, I do believe," and clapped harder and harder.

Suddenly a shadow cast itself upon his wall, and he turned,

crying out "The Boy?" but it was not. It was as far from The Boy as it could be. It was instead his mother, standing there in the doorway, stirring the contents of a pot. She could have ceased her stirring when she'd heard the commotion that Paul was making upstairs and gone to check, but it was one of those recipes where to stop stirring, even for an instant, would bring disaster upon that meal and possibly all future meals for several generations.

"What are you doing!" thundered his mother, and she tried to reach out for the diminutive figure on Paul's desk. But in so doing she ran out of hands and the pot fell from her grasp. It clattered to the floor, spilling its contents all over, and incurring a sizable dent and bent handle besides. "Now look what you did!" said his mother, who had done it herself. "You lied to me! You promised me! Enough of this foolishness, and give that here!"

Paul scooped up the tiny figure and held it close to his breast. "It's mine," he said sullenly.

"It is perfectly hideous! You will give it here this instant, Paul, and we will return to the doctor and get you even stronger medicine, and we will drive these fantasies from your mind once and for all!"

And Paul grew up.

Not for long. Only for an instant. Just enough to summon the anger and energy that he would possess as an adult and blend it with the innocent outrage that only a child can command. For if his mother felt betrayed, it was as nothing compared to what Paul was feeling, and he bellowed, "No! It is mine! It is more mine than you are mine, for you are not my mother, or not what my mother was! You are all darkness and stormy seas and a crooked shadow of what you were, and the only thing that makes you happy is making me unhappy, and you're punishing me because I stayed while Bonnie left, and I believe in pixies because I don't believe in you anymore! You are a villain and I hate you!"

Paul's mother remained exactly and precisely where she was, frozen and as unmoving as the figure Paul clutched close to him. There were many things tumbling through her mind at the moment, and we could examine them here for you. But we have explored this poor lady's pain so thoroughly that it is probably far more decent to leave her to her private thoughts and focus instead on her actions.

With nary a word, she walked down the hallway out of sight. Paul, never easing his grasp on the tiny figure, held his breath as he heard water running at the far end in the loo. Some moments later she returned with the pot now clean and empty. She placed it down carefully on the floor. It looked rather pathetic, dented and bent as it was. Were Paul of an older and more literary mind, he might have seen some resemblance between that battered pot and himself, but he wasn't and therefore didn't. Instead he remained silent, huddled in the far corner, watching, as his mother used several towels to sop up the spilled mixture. As she did so she was shaking her head slightly the entire time. Having finally cleaned up to her satisfaction, she rolled the towels one into the other so that the sopping sides would be inward.

There were so many things Paul desperately needed her to say at that moment. Unfortunately not a single one of them was what she did say.

"Good night."

She reached up, extinguished the light. Darkness settled into the room, and once she closed the door, the darkness was complete.

Paul did not realize until that very moment how terribly

angry and lonely he had been since his mother's strange trans-
formation. There, in the darkness, it all came crashing home to
him. He held the figure tighter than ever, held it so hard against
his chest that his heart was practically thudding around it. His
face became unaccountably wet.

There, in the strange, dark, forbidding territory that his
room had become, where he could not believe in his father, for
he was gone, and his mother, because she had been swallowed in
gloom, he reiterated with new fervency the one thing in which
he did believe as his tears flowed freely upon the mummified
figure in his hands. "I do believe in pixies, I do, I do believe in
them—"

He lost track of how many times he repeated it. Perhaps it
was some number with potent magic meaning, such as three or
seven or thirteen or eighteen or eleventy-twelve or forty-nine
and a half. Perhaps it was part of some grand design that everything happened just so in a unique set of happenings; or perhaps it was just a purely random happenstance in a purely
random universe, where things occurred—good or ill—for no
reason at all, no matter what other people might have you believe.

All he knew was that suddenly he was able to see better than
he'd been able to moments earlier, and the reason for it was that
light was seeping through his fingers. He lowered his hands and
gazed in wonderment at the figure he'd been clutching. The
moisture from his burning-hot tears, which had practically
seared his face on the way down, were infusing the figure
with—what? life? energy? the endless potency of unbridled
want? We cannot say—not because we do not know, but because we're afraid that, as with most gloriously wonderful
things, if you speak of them out loud, you will inadvertently at-
tract the attention of the sort of people who would be overjoyed

to take them away from you at the first opportunity. And since we have no desire—nor do you, we'd wager—to deprive Paul of this small miracle, we will not question it or comment on it beyond to say that, lo, it transpired thus:

Paul fell back, his hands dropping away from the glowing light that was hovering directly in front of his face. He had seen pixies and such in Kensington Gardens, but this was very much something else. Pixies who resided in the city were quite civilized things, posh and polished. They were not pixies of the wild, and bore as much resemblance to the creature confronting Paul as a finely trimmed poodle did to a timber wolf, even though they nominally had the same ancestors.

This pixie was the dehydrated figure brought to throbbing, pulsing life, stretching her arms and yawning as if awakening from a long slumber. She was low to the ground, for her wings were not moving very quickly at first, but then they began to speed up as she stretched them, sending her higher and higher until she thudded her tiny head against the ceiling. This prompted a stream of surprisingly raw invective from her. It struck Paul as tremendously funny to hear such common language spewing from the mouth of something so ethereal; and he laughed in response.

The laughter seemed to reinvigorate her in some manner, and she darted down toward Paul so quickly that he thought she was about to slam into his face. He flinched as she halted her dive mere inches from his nose. She checked her reflection in his eyes, primping slightly so that she was just so. When she spoke again, it sounded like the chiming of a series of small bells, very different from the pixies in the Gardens. Yet Paul, whose great gift continued to be his ability to converse with just about everything under the sun or moon that mere mortals should, by all rights, not have been able to comprehend, cut through the rapid-fire language with no problem and found, at its core, pure emotion. The pixie spoke the language of the heart in all its varied and conflicting tonalities.

"Boy?" she said. "Is it really you, Boy?"

"I've been wondering that myself," said Paul. "Perhaps you can answer at last. Am I him? Am I The Boy?"

She stared at him long and hard, examining him this way and that. He forgot to breathe, so intent was he upon hearing her response.

"I thought you were," she said at last, "but there's no resemblance."

"Others have said around the eyes, there is. Well, one said. Another said the nose."

"Not at all. Well," she said, "perhaps around the mouth a bit. Yes, very much around the mouth. That same confident pucker, that cocky smirk. No other place in you looks like him, but most definitely the mouth. What is your name?"

"Paul."

"Where is he, Paul?" There was the slightest edge of danger to the pixie's voice, but Paul didn't quite discern it. That was unfortunate, because if he had, he would have told her what she wanted to hear, even if it was a bald-faced lie. Instead he had a serious mental lapse and told the truth.

"I don't know."

That was clearly not the answer she wanted or expected, and it only angered her. She reached up and grabbed him by the front lock of his hair and pulled sharply, again demanding, "Where is he? Where are you keeping him?"

Yelping in pain, Paul brought his hand around and swatted the pixie in the way one would swing at an irritating mosquito. "Stop that!" he said, sending the pixie tumbling end over end, skidding across the floor in a little ball of rolling illumination.

Instantly he felt contrite, for one was not supposed to hit girls, even teeny, tiny ones yanking one's hair.

But the pixie was not a girl, not even a teeny, tiny one. She was a pixie, a very different creature. Which is not to say that Paul should have struck her but merely that she felt no pain from it. She was, however, disinclined to let the incident pass without comment or response. Her response, as we're sure you can foresee, was to rebound at Paul even as he began to say "I'm sorry" and thump him soundly in the forehead. Paul flumped backward, stunned, as the pixie landed on his chest and wagged a scolding finger at him.

"Stop hiding him!" she said. "You must know where he is, you silly ass! For that matter"—she glanced around—"where am I?"

"This is my room," he said, rubbing his forehead gingerly. "In the city. And I don't know where The Boy is, but I wish I did, because I could use his help."

"His help!" The pixie laughed sourly at that. Her glowing aura revealed the pot lying on the floor, and immediately she bounded from Paul's chest over to the pot with one graceful leap. She began thumping on the place where the pot was dented, and then twisting the handle, venting her frustration while simultaneously repairing the damaged cookware. "He's an even sillier ass than you! Cares about no one except himself and his games! After everything I did for him!"

"You're *his* pixie!" Paul said with sudden realization.

"I am not his pixie! I'm no one's pixie. Pixies belong to none save themselves," she said archly. "Only animals can belong to people." Then her nostrils flared slightly. "An animal belongs to you, and you to him," she said after a moment's assessment. "I can smell him on you. A tiger. A powerful one, of the Any-place."

Paul marveled at her olfactory skills, but he didn't want to give her the satisfaction of looking impressed because his head was still smarting from where she'd thumped him. "You're Fiddle!"

"Fiddlefix, if you please."

"I know you! It was you!" His voice was growing more and more excited. "When I clapped in my dreams, it was for you!"

This brought Fiddlefix to a halt. Slowly she set the pot aside and stared fixedly at Paul, brushing a stray lock of hair from her face. "You clapped for me?" she said slowly.

"Yes. The Boy urged me to. Urged all children. And I tried to remember it clearly since that night, and I could, but not entirely clearly. Then I look at you, and your light illuminates it all for me. What a superb pixie you are. The greatest, most wonderful pixie in all the world."

Well, if there's one thing that pixies are, it's vain. And not only was Fiddlefix not the exception to prove the rule, she was, rather, the rule incarnate. She lifted her chin proudly, adjusted the leaf that was her garment, and then chimed at him, "Clap for me now."

Paul was quite happy to do as he was bidden, banging his hands together enthusiastically. And Fiddlefix brought one arm across her middle, swept her other arm back graciously, and took a deep bow. Then she curtsied in a vague attempt to suggest the sort of manners she didn't truly possess before bowing once more.

"Well done!" Paul said. "A splendid bow! You are truly the most marvelous creature I've ever seen."

"You are no doubt right," Fiddlefix said approvingly, but then she flopped down upon the floor in a manner so lifeless that Paul thought, for one horrible moment, that he'd gone and lost her. But her glow did not diminish. Instead, she was simply paralyzed by sadness. "The Boy did not think so. He killed me, you know."

Paul was aghast. "No! I'm sure you meant so much to him! I don't believe—"

Fiddle immediately sat up, her eyes wide in horror, which puzzled Paul until he realized that the absolute worst thing you can say in the presence of a pixie is any sentence beginning with "I don't believe," for if two fatal words follow those, it will not go well for the pixie. So Paul hastened to finish the sentence as he'd always intended, which was, "he would do such a thing on purpose."

Fiddlefix glowered, the light around her actually darkening to reflect her black mood. "He is heartless," Fiddle said. "He was never the same after the wretched Gwenny came and went. Oh, he played at being the same, because, you know, that's what he does. But he wasn't. I could tell. And he despised me because I could tell."

"The Gwenny?" said Paul. "Who is the Gwenny?"

So Fiddlefix proceeded to tell him the entire tragic (as she saw it) history involving the intrusion of the Gwenny, along with her brothers, into the Anyplace. Some of it sounded passingly familiar to Paul, for the history of it had seeped from the reality of the Anyplace into the dreaming Anyplace, and from there into the deepest minds of children everywhere. That happens on occasion. Dreams usually go one way, toward the Anyplace; but from time to time something of enough significance happens to reverse that trend, and it becomes one of those things that children just "know." Most of the songs and taunts common to childhood, for example, originated in the Anyplace. The waterspout upon which the eensy, weensy spider crawls drips water in the Anyplace; and the liar whose pants are perpetually on fire resides there; and the rhymes for choosing up

sides, such as "My mother and your mother were hanging up
clothes," were first chanted there; and yes, believe it or not,
there exists in the Anyplace a solitary chicken whose sole mission in life is to get to the other side of the road.

So now you know.

"And The Boy was going to bring her back for spring cleaning," Fiddlefix concluded, her chiming voice rising as her ire
rose. "And I told him she would be nothing but trouble, mark
my words. And he said—"

She stopped. It was clearly hard for her to continue, and
Paul was loath to urge her to do so. But then she took a deep
breath and forced out the words. "He said he didn't believe. In
me. In pixies. The Boy, of all people, said it."

"But he could not have meant it. He knew it not to be true,"
Paul said. "He may have said he did not believe, but he didn't
believe in not believing."

"The Boy believes what he wants to believe, when he wants
to believe it. And right then he said it because," she said tragically, "he wanted to see me die."

Paul gasped. For all that he had thought The Boy at least
somewhat heroic, this cold and capricious act was simply staggering to him. "That . . . bounder!"

"Yes."

"The heartless cad!"

"He is rather," Fiddlefix said carelessly, as if the matter were
of little consequence to her rather than the greatest thing in the
world. "And this is the person you seek?"

Paul explained to her as quickly as he could what his intentions were. Fiddlefix listened, nodding thoughtfully. "It's possible," she said at last. "I haven't been in the Anyplace for a while.
I've no idea of the lay of the land. But perhaps there are young
lost girls now who would serve your purpose. For that matter,

perhaps there's a mother Indian who would not miss her papoose if it disappeared."

"I would think she would," Paul said uncertainly.

"Hard to say. Mothers are difficult to predict."

Paul pictured the lady his mother had been and the one she'd become. "That's true," he had to agree.

"The Boy had a very low opinion of mothers," Fiddle said, "except when he was busy trying to pretend the Gwenny was his mother. He wasn't happy unless he was either pretending or making himself miserable, and he never knew what he wanted. Except me. He didn't want me," she added in that same tragic tone that simply ripped at Paul's heartstrings.

"What's to be done, then?" Paul said. "How am I to seek the help of someone who can treat another so badly?"

If Paul had been older or wiser or a bit cannier in the ways of pixies in general and Fiddlefix in particular, he might have perceived the scheming in her voice. For Fiddlefix was nothing if not a conniver. She didn't do it maliciously. It was just the way she was. "You can go to the Anyplace and avenge me against The Boy," she said with growing excitement.

Paul gasped at the very notion, and even glanced around to make sure that no one was listening. "Me?" he said. "Go up against The Boy? But... I couldn't!"

"If you haven't, then how do you know you couldn't?" Fiddle said reasonably.

"And—The Boy? He killed Captain Hack!"

"He did no such thing," Fiddlefix said. "Hack threw himself to the serpent that had pursued him all those long years, after The Boy fed him Hack's right arm. Perhaps The Boy might have defeated him, perhaps not. I can help you, though."

"But I have no experience in adventures. Not real adventures. Adventures when I'm sleeping, yes, but this..."

"I will aid you," said Fiddlefix. "We will have the element of surprise. Why, I'd wager my wings that The Boy doesn't even remember me anymore."

"I would never forget you," he said with full passion.

"A bargain, then," said Fiddlefix, twinkling with glee. "Come with me to the Anyplace. Aid me against The Boy. And I shall find you a new sister to set things right and restore your mother to you—presuming, after spending time in the Anyplace, you have any interest in having her back."

Paul felt no end of trepidation over the notion, but Fiddlefix was looking at him expectantly, and he felt caught up in forces that were beyond his ability to control. Which is, when one thinks about it, not unlike the first true steps to adulthood. But Paul didn't see it that way. All he knew was that pleasing the females in his life had suddenly become the most important thing of all. One of those females was a mother who had been there all his life but had emotionally abandoned him, and the other was a female who had been in his life for less than half an hour and made him feel like the most important boy in the world.

"I am yours," he said to her.

Fiddlefix chimed with joy, so loudly, so purely, that Colleen Dear, sitting downstairs in the study—the cobbled-together leftovers now serving as her dinner growing cold on the table—heard it. She had no idea what it was, but despite appearances, she knew one thing it was not: a bell. She responded to it in a primal manner that she would not have thought herself still capable of possessing. She ran up the stairs, her mind racing, trying to determine what the source of the noise could have been, how she was going to deal with it—all that and more.

For the first time in a long while, fear for Paul created a crack in her veneer. She began calling out his name in a manner that, had he heard it, would have given the first true lift to his heart that it had felt in quite some time.

As it was, he did not hear it, for he had received a lift of a very different sort. And so when Colleen Dear burst through the door into the room, all she found was her pot, deftly repaired, shutters banging open in the wind, and no sign of her son at all.

Chapter 6

Dark and Sinister Boy

See him there? Pull him up in your mind's eye now, and he should be clear to you.

The Boy, walking about the deck of the *Skull n' Bones*, a rakish-looking craft, foul to the hull. See the swagger in him as he develops his sea legs, swaying back and forth. Occasionally he will lash himself to the wheel in anticipation of a storm possibly blasting him off the deck, even though the sun is shining down upon him. Realizing then that it has missed its cue, the sun will scuttle behind clouds to accommodate him and a storm will come rolling in, pounding harshly upon him while he grips the wheel, turns it sharply, and bellows, "Stay the course, ye scabrous dogs, or every man jack of you will feel the lash of the cat before we're done!"

It is a sight that brings a smile to our lips, or at least to mine, and very likely to yours as well. A boy at play, pretending that he is a pirate with the same enthusiasm that any other child might . . . except any other child is conjuring his sailing vessel out of pillows or sofa cushions or large cardboard boxes.

The smile fades slightly, however, when one notices a few things. Gone is the forest raiment that The Boy was sporting when he returned to London to fly Gwenny away for spring cleaning. He has instead donned the suit that Gwenny once made for him, right after Hack had abandoned himself to the jaws of the serpent. It is an evil suit, made from the wickedest garments in Hack's wardrobe. Moreover, The Boy has developed the curious habit of straightening his right arm and chopping it, as if it bore a hatchet the way that Hack's had, waving it around every so often and threatening those of his crew who make the mistake of drawing near during one of his foul moods.

That, however, believe it or not, is among the lesser of our concerns. Our greatest concern stems from this: that one judges a man, or a boy, by the company he keeps. The company that The Boy is keeping is of the most disturbing variety, so much so that we almost hesitate to tell you lest they take root in your dreams and make it impossible for you to sleep well. You might wake up one awful night screaming, for instance, "The Terrible Turk is coming for me!" If that should happen, I must confess that the chances are the Terrible Turk is, in fact, *not* coming for you. But my advice to you is that it'd be best if you stayed awake until sunrise on the off chance you might be right; and I would hate for you to believe otherwise, leaving me feeling responsible for your sudden and violent demise.

Let us survey the deck of the *Skull n' Bones* as the crew goes about its business, all under The Boy's watchful eye. Let us discuss, in more detail than before, the remaining Vagabonds who accompanied The Boy when he heartlessly abandoned Gwenny for his newfound activities.

First among them is Big Penny, The Boy's second in command: bold and brassy and tanned almost to a copper hue and hard as the coin for which he's named. When The Boy swaggers, Big Penny swaggers as well.

Big Penny is busy bossing the other Vagabonds . . . except we should backtrack and make clear that they, in fact, no longer go by that name. Big Penny, you see, presented the notion to The Boy that it was a misnomer, considering they were not aimless wanderers, as vagabonds most certainly were. Instead they had a home, aim, and purpose. Pondering Big Penny's words, The Boy finally agreed it was a valid point, and promptly changed their name to the Bully Boys. It suited their nature, and they very much took to their new moniker, as we shall soon see.

The other Bully Boys, then. Over there is Yorkers, small and shifty and master of unfair play. Nearby him is Roomer, with fiery hair and repulsive disposition, never happy except when he is speaking ill of someone else behind his back. And Caveat, the most intelligent of the Bully Boys, prone to throwing elegant-sounding foreign words in his speech, and the most insidious in thinking of ways to hurt others with minimal risk to himself.

Those then are the Bully Boys but, scarily enough, they are not the largest cause for concern.

Once upon a time, you see, The Boy and the Vagabonds fought and killed pirates. Indeed, they commandeered the *Skull n' Bones* over the dead bodies of Hack and his entire crew, save two whom you've already met, and who have served their purpose in our narrative. Yet now The Boy captains Bully Boys, not Vagabonds, and they all work side by side with—brace yourselves and cover your ears lest the news be too terrible for you—pirates.

The villainous-looking lot that served under Hack was more fearsome than any who had hung in a row on Execution Dock, and yet they pale in comparison to those who stalk the deck now. They are Barbary pirates through and through, with not so much as a single gentleman in the bunch. There are fifteen of them, most of them walking about shirtless, since The Boy—unlike the Eton-schooled Captain Hack—has failed to institute a strict dress code. Their muscles are thick and glistening; and many of them were slaves who revolted, took over their masters' ships, and continued plundering, making them doubly desperate and doubly dangerous.

Some of them are Moriscos, fearsome and scowling, such as the formidable Suleyman, with his shining shaved pate and gold tooth. Near him is the aforementioned Terrible Turk, all bristling beard and gleaming scimitar. Perched in the crow's nest, looking for possible plunder on the seas, is Simon the Dancer, so deft on his feet that when you think you are about to cleave him with your sword, you discover he's suddenly behind you and you are doomed. Scowling off in the forecastle is the mulatto, Agha Bey, his naked chest covered with tattoos that say unspeakable things in foreign tongues. And those are just the ones whose names we dare speak. Most of the others don't even have names, which, as you know, makes them all the more formidable. To know someone's name is to have some degree of power over him, even a little. These others are pure wild cards, and we know not what they will do or to whom or when.

And, overseeing all of them, walking among them and smiling and nodding, is the crooked old lady with the hooked nose.

We will tell you more of her later, since you must suspect by now there is a great deal about her to be learned (not the least of which is why such a scurvy and repulsive lot as this would tolerate the existence of a woman on board). For the time being, all you really need to know of her is this: She never strays all that far from The Boy. She coos in his ear, whispering sweet nothings of adoration, telling him what a wonderful job he is doing and how he is the greatest captain who had ever sailed the seven seas. She dotes on The Boy, and The Boy in turn dotes on her words of praise. Mother to son? Older sister to younger brother? A bit of both, but the result is that The Boy never sways from his course, secure that he never misspeaks; never makes mistakes; and never does anything that isn't justified, no matter how unjustified. Thus are the dangers of living in an insular world surrounded by those who tell you only what you want to hear rather than what you need to.

Do you still hold out hope that this is mere playacting on The Boy's part? That he still maintains a solid grasp on the difference between right and wrong, hero and villain? One has to admit that he always had a tenuous hold on the differences at best, but now we will see that matters have deteriorated.

What is the best way to show it?

Let us choose an ally of The Boy's and see how he responds.

The Boy has many allies throughout the Anyplace, people and races who have come to know him and respect his sense of adventure, his flashing sword, his heroism when it suits his fancy. We have done a quick drawing of lots and made our decision as to who shall be brought forward and given the honor of being victimized by The Boy, all to prove the point. Our apologies to the six princes; the bishop of the Gnomes; the Swan Princess; and, most tragically, the troupe of Hungarian acrobats. We will instead select for the purposes of demonstration the Indians of the Picca tribe.

In the past, The Boy and the Piccas had formed a bond of trust and friendship as a result of The Boy's rescuing their beloved first daughter, Princess Picca, at Rotter's Rock. In the past, as a result of that bond, they fought a great fight and lost many braves to the cutlasses of Captain Hack and company, all to protect The Boy and the Vagabonds.

So let us see now what transpired when Simon the Dancer, up in the crow's nest, called out to The Boy, "Savages, Captain! In canoes! Off the port bow!"

The Boy, who had been standing at the wheel, staring at his hand, immediately looked up with interest. Sure enough, coming in from the left were two canoes manned by small Picca fishing parties.

"They mean to attack us, Captain!" Roomer said, slithering within range of The Boy's ear. "You can see it in the fierceness of their bearing!"

The Boy pulled thoughtfully at his imaginary beard. He looked quite striking in his splendid garments: a black frock coat with gold trim, white shirt, gray cuffed pants with black buccaneer boots, a plumed tricorn hat, and his sword tucked boldly through a red sash around his waist. He strode to the port bow and studied the braves, the old lady behind him, petting him affectionately on the arm.

The braves had no weapons on them. Instead, three to a boat, they were sitting there with fishing cable dangling in the water. They had paddled their boats to get into position but now were bobbing in the water, having just the paddles so as not to scare the fish. Upon seeing The Boy staring at them, they waved in leisurely fashion and then went back to the lazy craft of catching fish.

"They obviously mean business!" The Boy said. "And what sort of lords of the seven seas would we be if we didn't answer in kind!"

"Well spoken, my pet, well spoken," the crooked lady said. She straightened his collar slightly so that he would look his best, taking care not to step upon his shadow as she did so.

"*Roll out the guns!*" said The Boy.

"Roll out the guns!" Big Penny repeated, and the order was chorused one to another to another, until the formidable Suleyman—the best shot of all of them—had the cannon up to the port side and angled directly at the peaceful Indians.

One of the braves noted the cannon aimed right at them, and began shouting in alarm to his fellows. At first they didn't believe him, but then they saw, and they very much believed. They grabbed their paddles and quickly started trying to get to shore.

Too late! Too late!

The cannon unleashed its deadly burden, and the braves leaped clear just as the cannonball smashed into their canoe, ripping it asunder. The pirate crew laughed merrily at the sport as Suleyman reloaded the cannon. He needn't have bothered, for the rest of the Indians had already vacated their canoe, swimming as fast as they could toward the shore. This didn't deter Suleyman, who aimed and fired with terrible accuracy, blasting apart the second canoe.

Just to drive home the point, The Boy leaped into the air, drew his sword, and flew off the ship. While his crew pointed and chortled and egged him on, The Boy swept down toward the Indians. Then he paused and said, "Oh! It's you! This is all a vast mistake, my friends! Truly!"

"Truly?"

"No, not truly, for I am first cousin to Puck and say what I like to mere mortals." Swinging his sword at the Indians while hovering just above them, he was out of reach of their hands but they were well within reach of his sword. The Indians kept being forced to dive far under the water to evade The Boy's sword thrusts, but every time they came up for air, there he was, dive-bombing them while crowing continuously.

It was a truly tragic day for the Indians. They finally managed to get back to shore with only a few cuts and nicks, and one brave had lost his magnificent braid of hair, since The Boy had swept down and slashed it off with one deft flick of his sword. Once they splashed up onto shore, however, they heard a low growling and saw burning yellow eyes from deep within the undergrowth. The Indians backed up, moving along the shoreline; but they were too slow, for a fearsome tiger came bounding into view.

He was a great and terrible beast, with the largest head that any of them had ever seen and fangs as long as the arm of any one of them. Had the Indians been armed, they still would have been hard-pressed to defend themselves. Unarmed, they had no chance. The tiger took down two of them beneath its claws and gnashing teeth while the others managed to effect their desperate escapes.

As for The Boy, he returned to his ship, where he danced merrily upon the deck, playing his pipes and singing praises of himself while the others joined in. There had been no plunder in the harassment of the Piccas, but at least it had provided some sport.

So it went, day after day and night after night. Sometimes they made life miserable for the various residents of the Anyplace, and other times they sailed away from the immediate area in order to plunder and steal from other realms. We will not go into detail here, although we will mention that The Boy's confrontation with the *Flying Dutchman* was particularly memorable and deserves a book unto itself.

Still, there were times when The Boy was unsettled and disturbed, which was neither a familiar nor a pleasant sensation for him. At those times he would take up residence in his cabin and stare at the wall. We will now be a fly upon that wall on one occasion when the crooked old lady—the only one who could approach him at such times—spoke to him. Stroking his hair lovingly, as moonlight filtered through the cabin windows, she asked him what ailed him.

"This morning," The Boy said, "the Turk and Agha Bey were complimenting me on the previous night's assault on the merchant vessel *Drake*. They said I was particularly fierce, my sword work formidable and terrible to behold. They said I had rarely seemed so evil and piratical."

"What of it?"

He looked up at her, concern crossing his face. "I don't remember it," he said.

"And so?" The old lady laughed. "Why should that disturb you? You forget things all the time."

"Yes, but not that quickly," The Boy said. "From one night to the next morning? And there have been other nights, or even days, other occasions, when the men talk to me about some special bit of nastiness that I embarked upon, but it's gone from my mind. Also..."

"Also what?"

"When I forget things, it's because I didn't think of them as being important enough to remember. I remember what's important."

"Of course you do. After all, you never forget your own name, nor your own magnificence, nor how to fight or fly—"

"Yes, yes," The Boy said. "I know that. The thing is... I feel like I'm forgetting things that I should be remembering. And here is the most curious thing: It's not like I'm just forgetting these things. It is as if... I never did them at all."

"But, pet," said the old lady, "of course you did them. They say you did them. They saw you do them."

"Yes, but—"

"No 'yes, but,' " the old lady said firmly. "I tell you, there's naught to worry yourself about. Have I ever lied to you?"

"I do not know," The Boy said honestly. "I do not remember how we met, or where you came from, or how you came to be here. Maybe you have lied to me."

"I would tell you if I had," said the old lady.

The Boy accepted the assurances, because, despite her outwardly fearsome appearance, she spoke with an amazingly soothing and mellifluous voice, honey dripping from every syllable.

Yet, even though he accepted them, there were things that still niggled at him, like insects buzzing about your face in such a way that you can't quite swat at them. Furthermore, there were times The Boy would drift to sleep and have strange dreams about himself. This made a certain degree of sense, for The Boy's own Anyplace was simply a reflection of what already existed, folded in and back upon itself like an envelope turned inside out. And if we tend to forget our dreams upon our own awakening, then naturally The Boy would forget his even faster. The sense of them remained within him, however; and that sense of them was that somehow, in some way, he was endeavoring to summon aid, even though he did not think he was in trouble and did not believe that—even if he were in trouble—he needed any succor beyond that which his good right arm, keen blade, and dazzling flight could provide.

So was the uneasy balance upon the *Skull n' Bones*, and now we come to the flash point of events.

It so happened that the pirates were getting restless from recent inactivity, and the Terrible Turk had suggested to the crooked lady that the time had come to wipe out the Indians once and for all. This notion intrigued the crooked lady, and she in turn took it to The Boy, who considered it. At first it seemed a rather pointless exercise in cruelty, but then he felt a distant scratching along the bottoms of his feet, and somehow after that it all made more sense.

"Best of all," said Caveat in his superior manner, "the mission can be accomplished with minimal muss and fuss, at absolutely no risk to us. In one stroke, we will be able to administer the koop dee grace."

"The what?" said Yorkers.

"It's Italian," Caveat said airily. "It means 'the final blow.' "

"What's that have to do with Grace? Who's she, anyway?" Yorkers said, looking to Roomer for clarification. Roomer simply shrugged.

"If you want to say 'final blow,' then just say it," Big Penny snapped at Caveat, fed up as he always was with Caveat's dazzling command of so many complicated languages.

The Terrible Turk glowered at the Bully Boys. He and the other Barbarys made little secret of the fact that they felt infinitely superior to them and had no patience for the boys' discussions or boasts. He strode across the deck, snagged Caveat by the front of his shirt, and lifted him off his feet. Caveat let out a squeal of alarm. The Boy, testing his balance by standing atop the steering wheel while not moving it, paid them no mind, far more interested in his exercise in equilibrium.

When the Turk spoke, it was always in a frighteningly soft voice, the sort that made you stop doing whatever you were up to and work hard to hear everything he was about to say. "How would we go about this?" he said. The other Barbary buccaneers scowled fiercely behind him.

"Their camp," said Caveat nervously. "It's around on the back of the island, up on a cliffside. We simply fire into the side of the cliff, blast it apart, and send the entire cliffside crashing to the ground along with the Indians."

"And if they have valuables," Suleyman said, "we can pick them out of the rubble."

"Makes sense," Yorkers piped up, and received a glare from Agha Bey for his contribution.

The crooked lady turned to The Boy and said, "What say you, Captain?"

"Aye!" said The Boy, who had not heard a word of the discussion and had to be filled in later as to the specifics of the plan he had just endorsed.

The *Skull n' Bones* set out. The wind puffed against her sails; and with The Boy's firm hand on the tiller, the ship cruised briskly around the coast of the Anyplace. The Boy watched the shoreline move past him, and was vaguely aware that he had once cavorted and frolicked upon those shores. But those days were long past, as if belonging to another person who shared his name but had gone on to other, greater things.

Soon they drew within range of the cliffside to which Caveat had alluded. The Bully Boy had been completely correct. There, high at the top of the cliff, was the peaceful Picca camp. Pulling out his telescope, The Boy gazed upward and was even able to see Princess Picca in the midst of her people, engaged in a ritual dance that he recognized as asking for a successful harvest. Well, what a crop he had to share with them, eh? A crop of cannonballs, sure as shooting.

"Roll out the carronades! All of them!" The Boy said, and the Bully Boys and pirates worked together swiftly as a team, dedicated to the single goal of wreaking a glorious day's havoc. As per The Boy's orders, four fearsome eighteen-pound guns were positioned, poised to be armed, readied, and to perform dazzling feats of destruction. The Barbarys braced them in position.

Everything was ready. The Boy sailed through the air, landing on the mainmast, grinning in a most fiendish manner that didn't seem anything remotely like play. "Ready!" he said. "Aim!"

"Captain!" said Simon the Dancer, the most eagle-eyed among them. "Floating toward us from the direction of the cliff-side, coming 'round the island from the far side ... it's a raft!"

"A raft?" said The Boy. Instantly the Indians, if not forgotten, were at least a distant second in his priority as this new curiosity presented itself. "Heading *toward* us? Not *away* from us?"

"Madness," growled the Terrible Turk. "Have they no idea who they're dealing with?"

The crooked lady looked in the direction of the small vessel that was indeed moving on a straight intercept course with the fearsome pirate vessel. "The nerve of them! We'll have their guts for garters, we will."

"We?" The Boy said, looking with a faint aspect of danger at the old lady.

She turned to him, smiled, and said silkily, "You will, my dearest. Only you."

The Boy could, of course, have flown out to the raft to see what was what or to harry the people upon it as he had the Indians. This time, however, it struck his fancy to remain on his ship and play the part of pirate captain to the hilt. He bounded to the foredeck, calling for a megaphone. Roomer tossed one to him. The Boy caught it deftly, brought it to his mouth, and said, "Ahoy the raft! Who goes there?"

A voice floated back to him, apparently without aid of a megaphone; but it was firm and strident and The Boy was stunned to hear it.

"Boy!" came the voice of Gwenny. "Is that you?"

The Boy blinked in surprise, than rallied himself and said, "No! I am Captain Boy, the deadliest pirate ever to menace the Spanish Main! I am he who the Sea Cook feared! I am—"

"Boy, this is nonsense!" Gwenny said. "The Anyplace is abuzz with your actions! We made this raft to come fetch you home and away from this—this terrible environment you've put yourself in."

"Ignore her," said the crooked old lady. "She is simply angry that you have found a more entertaining game to play than being husband to her and father to a brood of brats."

"Away with you," The Boy said to Gwenny, "before I give you a taste of the round shot! Avast, *arrrh!*" he growled to add piratical authenticity.

As the raft drifted closer, he could see that Gwenny was not alone. Irregular and Porthos were with her. He was pleased to see, even from this distance, that there was terror etched on their faces. Why shouldn't there be? They knew who was the true power in the Anyplace, and it was most definitely not the bold girl perched in the middle of the raft.

Yet Gwenny was not acting in the manner of someone who knew the truth of things. Instead, her attitude was defiant, as if she were holding vast amounts of power instead of none.

"Boy," she said firmly, "you have responsibilities to me and to these brave lads. I will not see you gallivanting about, deep in the midst of your games, ignoring those who count on you. You must accept those responsibilities, Boy, and come back to us. It's not right to do this to your family. To just—just pretend that we don't matter."

"It's not right," Big Penny said mockingly; and now the other Bully Boys joined in, pitching their voices in a feminine manner and throwing Gwenny's words back at her. The Barbary pirates picked up on it, and they mimicked her as well. In short order, the entire *Skull n' Bones* was echoing with contemptuous imitations of Gwenny.

If they were endeavoring to make her lose her temper, they

were not succeeding. In fact, if we are to be embarrassed for anyone, it is for the crew of the *Skull n' Bones,* jumping about like foolish apes. Gwenny never lost a shred of her dignity; and the pirates kept at it for some time before they realized that she was not breaking into tears or pleading with them to stop holding her up to ridicule. Like the infinitely tolerant mother that she was—or would be or played at being when in the Anyplace—Gwenny simply took the jibes in the endlessly patient manner of one who knew that boys will be boys no matter how old or how cruel they were, and that this, too, shall pass.

In time it did pass, as the crew felt increasingly foolish in failing to garner the response they wanted. Their catcalls and howls tapered off; and Gwenny said sternly, "Boy . . . it's time to come in now."

For one of the few times in his life—perhaps the only time—The Boy hesitated. He had not budged from the foredeck, but he was teetering slightly, as if his sea legs were losing some of their security.

"Kill her," whispered the crooked old lady, little drips of poison flecking from her lips to his ear. "Kill them all. End it now. End it clean. You know it's the only way."

"Let us blow them out of the water, Captain!" said the Terrible Turk, beard bristling as fiercely as ever. Suleyman was ready to light the nearest gun, waiting eagerly for his captain's order.

"Kill them," repeated the crone; and the urging was taken up by the others until it was a chant, over and over. The Boy felt a pounding in his head, and he desperately wanted to lash out but could not decide at whom.

A cold chill gripped his spine and straightened it, and he turned. "Back away from the carronade," he snapped to Suleyman. "You are not to fire on them."

"But, Captain!" said Suleyman.

The Boy strode from the foredeck, shoved Suleyman away, and snatched the match from his hand. A grim smile spread across his face. "I'm going to do it myself." He turned, readied the cannon as the raft floated helplessly within range, and said, "Gwenny! Consider our marriage at an end!"

"But what of the children!" Gwenny cried.

"I'm giving custody of them to Davy Jones's locker," The Boy said, and brought the sparking flame down toward the fuse.

Chapter 7

Straight On Until Morning

Flying came far more easily to Paul than he would have thought possible. Part of that may have stemmed, however, from his conviction that he would be able to fly. That's all it takes, really. Pixie dust facilitates it, to be sure; for science can be a harsh and pesky mistress, and it has a love affair with gravity that cannot be ignored. A little magic, however, will counter even the most stubborn science any day; and so the magic that comes from sprinkling pixie dust is a handy ingredient in making something as difficult to swallow as self-aviation go down far more easily. Think of pixie dust as flight's answer to a spoonful of sugar aiding the swallowing of medicine, and you will understand more fully.

Paul did not need to understand. Paul believed, and that was all that was required.

It was but the work of minutes to leave the spires of London behind and fly in the direction of the third star. Soon he and Fiddlefix were out over the ocean, the waves chopping beneath, licking up as if hoping that they would be able to bring the fliers down. Paul considered it most strange. In some ways, it seemed as if he were truly awake for the first time in his life. In that awakening, he discovered that the world was far more "real" than he had once thought. Shadows seemed to watch him with excessive interest; the branches of trees leaned toward him as if to try and pick up passing comments he might make. Now, over the vast waters that lay between England and the Any-place, it seemed as if the very ocean had come to life and was displaying untoward curiosity about him. He had never consid-ered the notion that the earth around him might be alive and thinking. Paul had to admit it did make a strange kind of sense. It nicely explained earthquakes, storms—all manner of disas-ters. It was simply that sometimes the world was in a good mood and sometimes far less so. The people who resided upon it sim-ply had to tolerate it, the same way that fleas were required to put up with whatever was going through a dog's head on any given day.

Still and all, Paul was not thrilled with the way the ocean was looking at him, and he made certain to stay sufficiently high above it.

This was not always easy, because the flight was a long one and every so often Paul would start to fall asleep and drift toward the water. Fortunately the divine Miss Fix was alert and attentive to her subject. When she heard him beginning to snore or noticed a decaying trajectory, she would buzz over to his ear and chime at him loudly enough to startle him awake. At one point Fiddle had gotten too far ahead of him and barely managed to get back in time as a shark lunged from the water, snapped viciously, and narrowly missed taking off Paul's leg be-fore Paul was rousted from his light slumber in time to angle away from it. The shark splashed back down into the water and watched him fly away with its dark, soulless eyes.

As Paul drew alongside Fiddlefix once more, he started talking with her to make certain that he didn't fall asleep again. "You said The Boy had a low opinion of mothers. Why?"

"Don't you know?" Fiddle asked.

"No," Paul said, sounding reasonable about it. "If I knew, I wouldn't have asked."

"Well . . . The Boy made the mistake of trusting his mother long ago."

"Trusting mothers is a mistake?" Paul said. He was rather uncomfortable with that notion. Despite the difficulties he'd had with his own mother recently, he still at core wanted to believe that mothers could be counted on in general.

"It was in The Boy's case, at least," said Fiddlefix. "You see, when he fled to Kensington Gardens, he always thought that he could return at his leisure and that the window to his nursery would always be open. When he finally did return, however . . ." She sighed heavily, causing a mourning bell-like peal that sounded almost funereal rather than her usually far lighter tone.

"However what?" said Paul urgently.

"He found that the window had been locked to keep him out. Not only that but his mother was sitting there, cradling a new child. He had been replaced."

"Replaced?"

"Yes." With great sarcasm she said, "A new horse had been fitted with a bridle to take up the reins of receiving a mother's love." Then she lowered her voice and continued soulfully, "I think that's why he was so interested in that annoying Gwenny. He believes he's entitled to his share of a mother's love, and isn't all that particular about the mother it comes from. I mean, obviously he's not particular, if he was willing to receive it from the Gwenny."

"So he doesn't like mothers in general . . . but wants the love of one just the same. That seems mixed up."

"He doesn't know what he wants. He doesn't know what's good for him."

"How do you know that?"

"Well," she said as if it should be painfully obvious, "he didn't want me, did he?"

"Want you to be his mother, you mean?"

Fiddlefix flipped over so that she was on her back, flying and looking at him with a combination of amusement and annoyance. "You silly ass," she said after a time, and flew on ahead of him. It was all that Paul could do to keep up with her after that, and she seemed uninterested in talking about The Boy any further.

More time passed, and more, and Paul felt fear creeping into him. He had come this far on faith; but the water stretched on and on in all directions without letup, the night seemed endless, and his home was ever so far away. Who was to say that Fiddlefix wouldn't become bored with him, or impatient, or simply abandon him? He would never be able to find his way home again. Sooner or later he would lose his focus; fall asleep; and, for all he knew, that shark was continuing to follow him, angry over having lost its opportunity and anxious for another chance.

He rubbed furiously at his eyes lest they tire and betray him, and when he lowered his hands, he was surprised and gratified to see sunlight creeping up over the horizon.

"Morning," he whispered.

The morning came up literally like thunder, for Paul heard a distant booming sound that he thought to be thunder...although it was, in fact, cannon fire. For that matter, the thunderous noise barely registered on him, for he was far too captivated with the land that was spread out before him. If one has ever looked at a globe, one has seen imaginary lines of longitude and latitude crisscrossing it. In the case of the Anyplace, the lines themselves were visible, giving the waters around it a checkerboard appearance. There were also large arrows pointing from four different directions, like a vast compass, all aimed directly at the Anyplace so that any passing fancies would be able to find it with minimal difficulty.

Paul recognized the land immediately, even though he had never actually seen it with his waking eyes. It may sound odd that one would be able to identify instantly something he had never seen as if he had always known it. The very notion makes no sense. The fact that it makes no sense should tell you that it is true. Truth usually makes no sense. If your desire is for everything to make perfect sense, then you should take refuge in fiction. In fiction, all threads tie together in a neat bow and everything moves smoothly from one point to the next to the next. In real life, though, in real life... nothing makes sense. Bad things happen to good people. The pious die young while the wicked live until old age. War, famine, pestilence, death all occur randomly and senselessly and leave us more often than not scratching our heads and hurling the question *why?* into a void that provides no answers.

So if everything in your life makes perfect sense, then make no sudden moves and do not allow anyone to pinch you, for you are likely dreaming and you would not want to spoil it.

Headlong into the unreal reality of the Anyplace did Paul Dear fly. He gazed in awe at the island where all four seasons transpired simultaneously in different sections. He wondered if they remained in their relative climatic states all the time, or if the seasons rotated so that each part of the island was visited by snow, sunshine, and falling leaves at alternate times. Paul wanted to ask Fiddlefix about it, but the pixie was suddenly buzzing around his head. There was excitement in her voice but not the pleasant kind. Instead it was the sort of thrill that one possessed when one was eagerly anticipating revenge most dire upon someone who had done one wrong. "He's there!" said the splendidly angry Miss Fix.

"He? You mean The Boy?"

"Who else?" Fiddle said. "There's no one else in the entirety of the Anyplace who matters."

"I suppose that's true."

"And now we're here, and you can help me get my revenge."

Although talk of revenge was all well and good when the Anyplace had been something in the abstract, being discussed in the security of his bedroom, now that Paul had arrived, the impending reality of the situation was beginning to drape its uneasy cloak around him. "How, exactly, are we going to go about getting it?" he said.

"It? You mean revenge?"

Paul nodded.

Fiddle floated in front of his face, her fluttering wings keeping her moving backward even as Paul angled toward the Anyplace. "You'll kill him for me, obviously."

Paul stopped in midair. "Kill him?"

Not realizing that Paul had ceased his forward motion, Fiddle fluttered several yards away from him before darting back toward him, a frown on her tiny face. "Of course. Why, what else did you think?"

"I don't know!" Paul said. He was starting to drift toward the water without realizing it. "I thought we'd . . . taunt him or something."

"Taunt him." Fiddlefix sounded less than enthused. "He wishes me to death and you think the appropriate response is a severe taunting? You silly ass."

"Stop calling me that!"

"Then stop being it!" Fiddle said, who really was a most rude little thing.

"Why don't you kill him, if you're so upset with him? I was coming here in hopes he could find me a new baby sister. You're the one who apparently wants to see him toes up. What do you need me for, if blood is all you desire?"

"Because I can't kill him," Fiddle said impatiently. "Pixies don't kill. It's not allowed. If I could kill, I wouldn't have needed the Vagabonds to try to rid me of the Gwenny."

"Why isn't it allowed?"

"Because it's wrong."

"But then if it's wrong, why do you want *me* to do it?"

"Why should I care if *you're* doing something wrong?"

"But if you're encouraging me to do it," Paul said in exasperation, "then that's practically the same as you doing it yourself!"

"Practically isn't the same as exactly. By the way, you're about to be eaten."

"*What . . . ?*"

So involved in his discussion with Fiddlefix had Paul been that he had drifted too close to the ocean. The soles of his feet were dangling directly above a couple of sharks, patiently waiting with their mouths open. With a yelp, Paul immediately rebounded heavenward while Fiddlefix flew in a circle around him, laughing in that ringing way she had. Under other circumstances he might have found it charming, but these were not those circumstances.

"You could have warned me!"

"I did," she pointed out when she stopped laughing.

Before Paul could respond, there was another resounding noise, and this time Paul recognized it for what it was. "Was that . . . a cannon?" he said.

"Pirates," Fiddle said with rising excitement in her voice. "Where there's pirates, The Boy will undoubtedly be. Come on." When Paul hesitated, she tugged him firmly by the front of

his shirt with even greater strength than he would have credited
her with. He could not be certain, but it seemed that the light
she generated was growing brighter the closer she drew to the
Anyplace.

"But . . . when we find him—am I still supposed to . . . ?"

"We'll sort it out," Fiddle said, brimming with a confidence
that Paul did not feel.

He gave up trying to direct the path of his flight, for Fiddle was hauling him along like a child dragging a pull toy on
a string. They angled around and down; and, sure enough,
there was a pirate ship floating offshore. Paul felt an unde-
niable thrill, witnessing firsthand the sort of thing that had
previously been confined to books or motion pictures: an actual, genuine pirate ship, sails fluttering in the breeze, smoke
rising from the recently discharged large guns pointing over
the side.

Fiddle's bell-like language chimed in his ear, and even
though she sounded as musical as always, he could discern the
shock in her voice. "It's The Boy at the guns," she breathed.
"He's firing at the Gwenny. I—I thought he . . ."

"You thought he what?"

"I thought," said Fiddle, "that he . . . some part of me thought
he wanted me gone because he desired only the Gwenny. But if
he wants her dead as well . . ."

Paul thought she actually sounded quite cheerful at the
prospect, but he chose not to comment upon it since he considered it rude. Far more rude, though, was the prospect of the
heroic Boy aiming and firing upon a helpless raft filled with
youngsters not all that different in age from Paul himself.

He had been daunted at the prospect of taking arms against
The Boy, but Paul was—above all—a young English gentleman. The lad who was daunted by the undertaking presented to

him immediately gave way to the bristling, offended sensibilities of a young Englishman witnessing a lopsided battle.

"Right!" Paul said, and angled downward like a missile.

No one had taken notice of him, for they were all focused upon The Boy's target and even more particularly on his apparent inability to hit it. One of the pirates was shouting at him in bewilderment, "Captain, they're right there! How can you continue to miss them?"

"If I sink them with the first shot, the game is over!" The Boy said, sounding defensive. More than that: There was a strain in his voice, as if he were being subjected to some great inner struggle. "Who is captain here, anyway?"

An elderly lady stepped forward and, snatching the match from The Boy's hand, lit the fuse. "You are so right, my dear one. And because you're the captain, you shouldn't be bothering yourself with this!" She cranked the gun, angling it, as the fuse burned down. "I'll attend to it."

The fuse was nearly to the powder, and the children on the raft were madly paddling, trying to get out of range, knowing they would fail. At that moment, before disaster could befall, Paul dropped from on high, feetfirst, driving them into the muzzle. The cannon angled sharply downward and discharged a heartbeat later. The cannonball blasted into the water not five feet from the raft, and the resulting gout of water came close to swamping the small craft. It did not quite succeed, and the passengers coughed and sputtered but managed to hold on.

"Who are you!?" said the old lady.

"Who cares?" said The Boy before Paul could answer, and shoved down as hard as he could on the rear of the cannon. The abrupt movement catapulted Paul high through the air. He soared with the weightless grace of one upon whom gravity had only limited sway, and that agility was not lost upon The Boy even as Paul landed in the rigging above. "You've been taught to fly!" The Boy said, pointing in an accusatory fashion. "Who taught you thus?"

Unsure whether he should reveal Fiddle's presence to her would-be murderer, Paul said, "You did!"

"I did not!" Then The Boy paused, for he was well aware that his memory was not always the most reliable. "Did I?"

"Did you?" said one of the pirates.

The Boy shrugged. "I might have done. If I did, what of it?" He studied Paul with a cocked eyebrow. "He seems familiar, now that it's mentioned."

"You spoke to me through a mirror," Paul reminded him from above. "You told me to catch you if I could."

"Then do so!" The Boy said defiantly. He thrust out a hand and shouted, "Sword!" Seconds later, a pirate cutlass had been thrust into his left hand. With his right hand, he yanked out his own sword and, quick as the wind, hurtled heavenward toward Paul. He tossed the cutlass with an easy motion toward Paul. It spun end over end, and Paul flinched back from it, prompting a derisive laugh from The Boy. The sword lodged in the rigging just over Paul's head. "Best have it, my lad," The Boy warned him, "before I have you!"

Paul grabbed the cutlass. He'd been worried that it would be too heavy, but it felt light enough for him to wield as he swept it back and forth through the air.

"Boy!" It was Gwenny's voice, floating to him from the water. "Don't hurt him!"

"Are you Gwenny's new husband now?" The Boy said. He floated back and forth before Paul like a pendulum, and Paul was sore afraid but determined. "Is that the way of it?"

"I'm just someone who wants to make my mother happy," said Paul, trying to keep his sword steady. It seemed his arm trembled more and more violently even as he worked to steady it. "And I don't like bullies, which is what you've become. So I'm here to stop you!"

This prompted a chorus of derisive laughter from below.

"Then your efforts are doomed to fail," The Boy said darkly, "as are you. You cannot defeat me."

"Yes, I can. For I am the hero, and you've become a villain, and my father told me that heroes always win."

More laughter from the pirates, and choruses of "Oooo, his daddy told him that," and more cries and pleading from the young people on the raft. The Boy's eyes narrowed, and he no longer looked amused or even youthful. A terrible aura hung around him like a shroud, and he said, "Proud and insolent youth, prepare to meet thy doom."

"Dark and sinister Boy," Paul said, "have at thee!"

Mustering all his courage, Paul threw himself off the rigging and came straight at The Boy. The Boy looked surprised for a moment, and barely brought his sword up in time. The blades clashed, and Paul kept to the attack. The swords clanged and crashed, sparks flying from the metal; and for every move that The Boy made to subdue Paul, Paul was a hair quicker, a shade faster.

His confidence began to build as he drove The Boy down, down. The pirates' initial laughter and derision fell into bewildered silence as this young flying upstart went toe-to-toe with their captain and, by all appearances, was winning quite handily.

The Boy's movements were slow, confused, desperate. He seemed unable to deal with the increasing speed of Paul's blade, and was even gasping and breathing heavily as if with great effort.

The pirate crew was wondering: Could this be the great Boy, slayer of pirates, the most respected blade in the Anyplace? By all rights, Paul should have been wondering as well. But he was not, instead growing overconfident in his own prowess and convincing himself that The Boy's reputation was exaggerated. Would that you and I could warn him, but we must instead be confined to mute witnesses as Paul sees an opening and drives his blade home, hoping not to kill The Boy but to wound him grievously enough that his immediate threat would be ended.

And there is The Boy's blade, as we might have expected, but Paul did not. With a speed he had not displayed earlier, The Boy easily turned aside Paul's attempted coup de grâce. Their blades skidded against each other, locking at the hilts. The Boy smiled a wolfish smile, displaying those perfect first teeth; and his face was bare inches from Paul's.

"Was this a good game for you?" he said, his solicitous tone at odds with the darkness of his expression. "Did you enjoy my pretending you were a threat? Personally, I've grown bored. Time for a new game."

That was when Paul realized that he had woefully miscalculated. The Boy shoved him back hard; and he hurtled across the deck, evil crewmen throwing themselves to either side like tenpins to clear his path. He rebounded off the forecastle, and there was The Boy coming straight toward him, blade extended. Paul realized in a heartbeat that meeting the thrust, trying to deflect it, was a hopeless cause. All he could do was avoid it. He backflipped out of the way, The Boy just barely missing him. The Boy promptly pivoted, kicked off the deck, and came at Paul once again, cackling and swinging his gleaming blade.

Paul parried once, twice, a third time; but each time he did it was as if a powerful shock ran the length of his arm, for The Boy was just that strong. It wasn't that he was remarkably muscular, but there was formidable power in his wrist; and in swordplay, that was what was required.

The full truth rapidly became apparent to Paul. The Boy had been toying with him. It really had all been a game. The Boy could have done him at any time, but instead it had amused him to let Paul believe he was providing a challenge. This realization dawned upon the pirate crew as well. Reinvigorated, they cheered on their leader and roundly catcalled and hissed the upstart.

The Boy drove him backward, and the tip of his sword began raising small cuts on Paul's arm. Paul wanted to cry out but bit it back, resolved not to show vulnerability even in the face of overwhelming odds. But his movements slowed, and as his confidence waned, even his ability to fly started to diminish. The increasing weakness that The Boy had only feigned, Paul now genuinely experienced. His feet were no longer airborne, instead grounded upon the deck. The Boy did not even bother to continue flying, instead matching him step for step, driving in faster and faster, wounding Paul at will now. Then Paul tripped over some coiled rope and fell backward. The Boy stood over him, ready to plunge his sword into his defeated challenger.

That was when the bells sounded; and if chiming was ever angry, it was then. The Boy looked up in confusion, and Paul in relief, as a glowing ball of light hurtled toward him like a streaking comet.

"Don't I know you?" said The Boy.

"You killed me!" the outraged pixie said.

"Did I?" The Boy said carelessly. "I've killed so many, it's hard to keep track."

"I'm Fiddlefix! I was your pixie! You saved my life!"

"Well then, if I saved it once, that entitles me to take it now, doesn't it?" But there was something in The Boy's voice that was perplexed, as if he were trying to justify things he had done that he knew he should not have.

"Get away from him!" said the crooked old lady.

Fiddlefix began to glow more brightly, and The Boy shielded his eyes, stepping back. Her incandescence was directly related to her mood; and the more outraged Fiddlefix became, the greater her illumination. "I will not get away from him!" Fiddle said. "He was mine before he was yours! Before he was any of yours! And I will have him, and be avenged for his betrayal of me!"

Paul wasn't sure if the crooked old lady understood what Fiddle had said. He did, however, see that she was going to attack the pixie, for there was a sword attached to her left wrist and she was clearly about to come at Fiddlefix with it. Paul was not certain if something as down-to-earth as a sword could hurt Fiddlefix, but he was not about to take a chance. Thinking fast, he grabbed up the rope he had tripped over and flung it quickly. By lucky chance it looped around the old lady's foot, and Paul yanked as hard as he could. It pulled her off balance and sent her tumbling to the deck.

The rest of the fearsome crew tried to attack, but the light from the angry Fiddle continued to grow until she was nearly a floating sun. They fell back, crying out, unable to keep looking at her.

"Bad form!" The Boy said, and Paul noticed that The Boy's voice sounded very unusual, far more petulant than the bravado that usually pervaded his tone.

And that was when Fiddlefix cried out, and what she said was, "His shadow! Look at his shadow!"

"Curse you, you meddling sprite!" said The Boy, swinging blindly with his sword. "You should have shown the good taste to stay dead!"

Paul looked where Fiddle had indicated, and what he saw caused him to gasp in astonishment.

The bright light that Fiddlefix was providing caused The Boy's shadow to stand out in stark relief against the deck. And Paul, even though he was squinting against the brilliance that Fiddle was generating, was still able to make out what she had already observed.

The shadow cast by The Boy upon the deck was not The Boy's own. The general outline of the clothing was there, but the body was longer, the head more angular and, most significantly, the shadow had a slim, curved hatchet instead of a right hand.

It was the shadow of Captain John Hack.

Chapter 8

Hack and Slash

It is now time to explain to you the truth behind the crooked lady with the hooked nose. It is not an especially long tale—barely long enough to serve as a diversion—but it is an important diversion nevertheless, and it must be told somewhere. So best it be here, especially since it informs much of what is to come.

There are certain things you know, and as I mentioned to you earlier, the main reason for the knowing of things (not to mention the telling of things) originates in the Anyplace. Everything that happens, or did happen, or will happen in the Anyplace reflects back and through to reality.

"Common knowledge" and "common sense" were both developed in an area called the Anyplace Commons, a central meeting point and neutral territory where all Anyplace denizens congregate from time to time just to shake hands and explain that, yes, they may have hunted one another and tried to kill one another but, really, no hard feelings and it was nothing personal.

Or consider if you will legends of a Great Flood that pervade many civilizations unconnected with one another. How was that possible? Because there was, or is going to be, a Great Flood in the Anyplace. The "when" of it doesn't matter all that much since the Anyplace is timeless. When it does happen, it will bounce forward and backward through all the memory of man, like a rubber ball. If it already happened, same thing.

For instance, you've certainly heard combinations of words so routinely that you simply take them for granted as having meaning without truly wondering why. "By hook or by crook," for instance. Most believe it to mean that something will be accomplished through whatever means necessary, be they fair or foul. They believe it so firmly that they don't pause to wonder why "hook" is equated with "fair means." "Crook" taken to mean "evil doings" is sensible enough, we suppose, but what is fair about a hook? Nothing in particular, as many a chagrined fish would tell you.

You did not realize, very likely, that a pirate team called Hook and Crook once traversed the outer seas of the Anyplace. If they came upon you, and Hook failed to kill you, then Crook would certainly attend to whatever unfinished business Hook had left behind. That's where it comes from.

Always beware of a meaning that is common knowledge, for "common knowledge"—as befits anything invented in the Anyplace—can be treacherous.

"Crash and Burn," "Vim and Vigor," these and many others were team denizens of some renown in the Anyplace.

Which brings us to "Hack and Slash." They, too, were a pirate team, not dissimilar from Hook and Crook. The difference was that Hack was the formidable foe of The Boy, as you well know by now. But who, then, was Slash? His first mate? A trusted (or distrusted) lieutenant?

No. Slash was Hack's piratical sister.

I notice some of you shuddering in outrage at the thought, or saying dismissively, "A female pirate? No such thing! Why, women on a ship are bad luck. Any seaman worth his salt would tell you that!"

What say you, then, to Anne Bonny or Mary Read, eh? Tremble in the presence of Gunpower Gertie, the Pirate Queen of the Kootenays, or Honcho Lo, a determined supporter of the Chinese revolution who took command upon her husband's death.

No, no, there were many females who did as much mischief on the seas as their male counterparts. But all of them paled in comparison to Captain Slash. Most of them, having encountered her, would have backed away and left quietly lest they find themselves in a battle they could not possibly win.

"Slash" was no more her family name than Hack's was his. What we do know of Captain Slash is as follows:

Her first name was Mary. Her education was not as impressive as her elder brother's. Nevertheless she did mirror him in several key aspects, such as his Eton-bred obsession with matters of good form. And she was untrustworthy and blackhearted as they came.

She absolutely adored her brother, and followed him everywhere and anywhere he went. When piracy presented itself as his most promising future trade, she followed him unhesitatingly into his mercenary endeavors. Technically speaking, Hack was the captain and she was his first lieutenant.

However, as time passed upon the *Skull n' Bones,* the captain and his sister came to follow very different patterns. Hack preferred to roam the deck and the seas by daylight, for he was very much into strutting and preening and being admired by all who saw him; and it was quite simply easier to see him in daylight.

The sister embraced the night side. With only a few of the

hardiest of the pirates up and about, Hack's sister would be at the wheel, keeping a wary eye out for danger or plunder, as either presented itself. Other ships that might have thought that night was a safe time for travel, since the pirates themselves no doubt slept, occasionally encountered a very rude surprise, thanks to the female pirate's nocturnal vigilance.

Since their activities thus did not overlap all that much, the crew tended to refer to her as "captain" as much as they did her fraternal counterpart. If the great man himself knew of it, he did not voice any objections, since it represented no undermining of his authority.

Curiously, she did not have the effete mannerisms that her brother occasionally displayed. She was, in that odd respect, more manly than the man who meant so much to her. She walked with a determined swagger, a squaring of the shoulders, and had a fondness for hard rum that garnered her the instant admiration of other pirates. It was not unexpected. In any field of endeavor that is dominated by men, a woman could not settle for being as good as the least of the men. She had to be better than the best of them. Unfair, perhaps, and unjust, but the way of things nevertheless, even in the Anyplace.

Nor did she share her brother's oddest phobia: the sight of one's own blood. She was less squeamish about such matters, if you will; and that was never more evident than this particular time that I will now share with you.

You know, of course, that The Boy severed Captain Hack's right hand from him and fed it to the formidable serpent, the one that would then continue to pursue Hack until that famed pirate's eventual demise.

What you do not know of are the minutes immediately after that legendary initial dismemberment.

There lay the great captain, sprawled upon the deck, moaning loudly and flitting into and out of consciousness (mostly out of). The right sleeve of his frock coat was bisected, and the material that remained was becoming thickly stained with his strangely colored purplish blood.

Pirates tend to take their cues from their captains, and so as the pirate captain wailed and moaned over the loss of his limb, so too did his crew take up the cry. The delighted laughing of the arrogant Boy floated above their heads even though he himself had taken leave of the place. None of them even noticed that the serpent was already endeavoring to haul itself up the side of the boat, anxious to devour the rest of the tasty morsel presented it.

Out from below deck stormed the sister of the great man. She held an alarm clock in her hand, shaking it angrily, sleep still blearing her eyes. It was early in the morning, and she was about to take out her frustration on the whole of the crew for making such an ungodly hullabaloo when she had so recently gone to bed.

Imagine her shock, then, at seeing the following: her brother lying bleeding; the crew in disarray; and a serpent with jaws wide open, perched halfway over the rail and about to insinuate its entire massive body onto the ship's deck.

You might well have heard the expression "throws like a girl." That most definitely did not apply to the lady pirate. Seeing the situation laid out before her, she addressed the most immediate problem by slinging at the serpent the only weapon she had at hand—namely, the clock. She hurled it with such precision and force that the clock struck the serpent directly between the eyes, sending the animal off balance. The serpent flipped backward while the clock ricocheted straight up. As the serpent slid down the side of the boat toward the water, it let out a roar of frustration and protest.

I'm certain you can anticipate what happened next. Say it. Go ahead; we can wait. Yes, there it is, as you most assuredly have predicted: The clock dropped from on high and skidded down the serpent's throat. The serpent was dimly aware it had swallowed something but wasn't entirely sure what. Then it hit the water, sank, and began to choke on the unexpected obstruction. The only thing that saved the animal was the onrush of water into its still-open mouth that pounded down and through and shoved the clock the rest of the way down the serpent's gullet.

Shaken and confused, the serpent swam away.

Mary took a cloth and fashioned a tight bandage around her brother's maimed arm. The rest of the crew was shouting, crying of their own very likely doom, for if their mighty captain could be so treated, what hope had they of surviving?

With a great swelling of anger, Mary said, "Stop your barking, you dogs! It's just a hand!"

"Easy for you to say!" lamented her brother, coming briefly out of his swoon. "You have two!"

Without a word, Mary released the pirate captain, allowing his head to thud to the deck. She turned, picked up an ax with her right hand, slammed her left arm upon the rail, and did not so much as cry out as she—

I see you flinch. I do not blame you. I flinch as well. If you are young enough that you need to ask what precisely happened next, then very likely your mother or father is reading this to you and can take this opportunity to explain it as delicately as your sensibilities will allow. Likewise, your older sister, if reading aloud, will be careful in her description. If your older brother is reading this, then I fear you are out of luck. He will likely describe the fate of Mary's left hand in as brutal and gory a fashion as he can muster, just to watch you squirm, because . . . well, because that is what brothers do. Our apologies in advance, and we hope it does not make you dislike The Boy for having cut off the pirate captain's hand and thus set this tragedy into motion in the first place.

Anyway . . . onward.

It was Mary who suggested the ax to replace her brother's lost limb, and he, in turn, recommended she sport a sword where her hand had once been. Thus did he acquire the name Captain Hack. By all rights, she could simply have gone with the name Captain Sword, but her devotion to her brother and desire to emulate him in all things was monumental. It would even have been touching if it were not all in the interest of evil doings. So she dubbed herself Captain Slash in order to emphasize that they were a team; and for a time, they were.

But familiarity can breed contempt. Not only that, but pirates can breed mistrust. Indeed, they excel at it. One of the crew, Starkly—whom you've met—began fomenting dissatisfaction among his shipmates. Their noble captain, now Captain Hack, may have endeavored to bounce back from the trouncing he had taken from The Boy; but nevertheless there was clear, physical evidence that their captain was far from invincible. Had not a mere laughing boy gotten the better of him? Had not that boy's actions resulted in the ship's being perpetually followed by a ticking serpent? What sort of man had they trusted their fates to, if he was displaying this sort of ineptitude?

Later in his career, Hack would have had a quick answer for these sorts of mutterings, content to gut Starkly from belly to collarbone along with anyone else who might actually give weight to his words. But Hack was still smarting from the encounter that had maimed him; and he even felt a small degree of shame, if such as he knew shame. Whenever one is a cowardly custard such as that, one inevitably looks for someone else upon whom blame may be assigned.

In this instance, Hack blamed Slash.

It was not difficult to do. She was a woman, first of all, and that alone is a great crime in the eyes of many. Plus, if she had not been a slugabed, she might well have aided him in warding off The Boy's assault, thus averting the tragedy. The more the crew thought about it—or the more Hack told them what to think—the more blame they were able to lay at Captain Slash's doorstep.

So it was that the angry Hack banished his sister from the crew of the *Skull n' Bones*. He might well have killed her but did not consider himself totally without feeling, and so he and his crew settled for putting her ashore and instructing her never to darken their deck again.

Mary Slash, as you may imagine, was stunned. She slunk away into the greenery of the Anyjungle, and there she hid. She did not blame her brother in the least for his actions. She worshipped him so much that she simply accepted as truth all the disparagement of her that he and his crew had said. Her inner turmoil became reflected on her outside, as is so often the case. When afflicted with some great sadness, some of us get fat, others of us get skinny, still others lose their hair or the luster in their eyes.

In the case of Mary, the ex-Captain Slash, she began to age very rapidly. Very rapidly. Within a remarkably short time she was nigh unto unrecognizable, a shriveled and bent lady with an oddly shaped nose who tended to stick to the outskirts of the Anyplace.

Captain Slash would have spent the balance of her withered life in loneliness and despair had not events transpired that she could not possibly have expected.

For her brother, Captain Hack, eventually went to his end within the mouth of the serpent.

He did not elude that demise, as some might have you believe. He did not trick nor treat his way out, or otherwise elude the jaws of death through some wave of an authorial hand.

Dead is dead, even in the Anyplace, although the Noplace is another matter—but we shall speak of that much later.

However, the serpent—in its eagerness to make certain that Hack did not perform some miraculous escape—snapped shut those powerful jaws just a hair sooner than it really should have. As a consequence, although it devoured the man deftly enough, the man's shadow was severed from him by those razor-sharp fangs.

This was about as disorienting as you might imagine it to be. Hack's shadow floundered around in the air for a moment, unable to see, for it was in fact quite blind, as newly freed shadows generally are. Unsure of what had transpired, the shadow flung itself toward familiar haunts and solidly attached itself to the individual standing in his customary place. That person, of course, was The Boy, dancing a jig at the helm of the pirate ship and reveling in his new position as captain.

So if you have been wondering why, in tales you doubtless heard before this one, The Boy had been—shortly after Hack's death—strutting about demanding clothing that was a duplicate of Hack's and slicing his hand downward in imitation of an ax, now you know.

But here's an odd thing about shadows: Like spirits who are condemned to haunt the areas in which they passed on, so, too, are shadows restricted to the area where they were loosed from their flesh-and-bone partner. In the case of Hack's shadow, it could not depart the Anyplace. So when the *Skull n' Bones* initially sailed beyond the Anyplace's borders to return Gwenny and her brothers home, the shadow of Hack remained behind.

Alone. Adrift. Afraid.

In its miserable state, with its pirate crew scattered or dead and its greatest foe triumphant, it sought out the only creature in the Anyplace who it thought might tend to it.

Imagine ex-Captain Slash's surprise when the shadow of her late brother came slinking to her late one Anyplace night. Word of Hack's demise had reached her ears, for nothing remained secret for long in the Anyplace, and she had been deep in the depths of mourning when the shadow presented itself. By that point, the shadow had acquired enough of Hack's impeccable good form to bow deeply in Slash's presence.

Do you think for a moment that Mary Slash reveled in her brother's state or considered for half a heartbeat the notion of tossing the shadow out into the cold? If so, then clearly you have not been paying attention. She welcomed her brother's shadow as she would a prodigal son. She provided it darkness and a place to huddle and grow in strength and power. Mary would continually whisper to it, tell it great tales of its former owner's deeds, and scheme along with it to plot its next move.

The simplicity of it was such that, since you now know of the events directly preceding the events of this tale, you likely have once again divined what I am about to tell you. That is because modern children are so much cleverer than parents, who require that things be spoon-fed to them and are not even much good helping with mathematics homework. So if we roll our eyes at their ineptitude, surely we can be forgiven our impatience with them; for we love them as they love us, but they are not always the brightest of creatures.

One night, when The Boy was sleeping deeply, the shade of Captain Hack insinuated itself within his shadow. The first attempt had been in a state of panic and confusion and during daylight to boot. At nighttime the shadow was far more powerful, drawing strength from all the surrounding shadows. How tragic that The Boy habitually slept with a flickering candle nearby! Without that night-light, his shadow would not have been present for Hack's shadow to invade. But it was and it did.

Very slowly but steadily this time, the shadow of Hack took control not only of The Boy's shadow but of The Boy himself. "Control" might be overstating it, actually. What it did was influence him in directions that it desired him to go. It encouraged him to gather a band of Vagabonds who were, for the most part, of far more dubious moral fiber than their predecessors. Captain Slash was welcomed back aboard the *Skull n' Bones,* introduced to the newly christened Bully Boys as The Boy's mother. They, knowing no better, accepted the explanation. With the aid of Captain Slash, the daunting band of cutthroats that was to constitute the new crew was gathered from all around. Hack's shadow, having firmly attached itself now to The Boy's shadow and gaining strength with every day, was even able to depart the Anyplace when the pirate ship's journeys took it out of the area.

An early victim to Hack's influence was poor Fiddlefix. It was the shadow that cajoled The Boy, all unknowing, to declare his lack of faith in pixies that nearly expunged Fiddlefix from the lives of men and boys.

So now you know.

And here is the most interesting bit: The Boy now knows as well.

How? Because I have told you, and The Boy is watching over my shoulder as I explain all of it to you. (He does not read words on paper, but thought is as clear as sunlight to him; and for you and I to think, it is the same as The Boy knowing it.)

Even as you digest that kernel of information, The Boy is busily telling the other players in our drama about the true nature of things. Imagine, if you will, Gwenny shuddering in dread at the realization of how The Boy's very personality has been usurped by his most repellent of opponents. And Fiddlefix... ah, she is sobbing great, racking tears, filled with relief to learn that The Boy had not, in fact, forsaken her in a devastating act of cruelty. Paul is much relieved, for he did not relish the notion of The Boy as villain, nor was he taken with the idea of acting the part of hero when he wasn't entirely certain he was up to the job.

We will spare you the reactions of the others except to say that they were similar in some ways and different in others.

Here is what happened next.

Chapter 9

What Happened Next

Foul villain!" Paul cried out, for it was because of Hack's scheming that he had been forced into a battle with The Boy and so felt extremely ill used.

Likewise did Paul see that The Boy's rage was a mighty and terrible thing. The Boy's compact body was fairly trembling with indignation. Its charade now revealed, the shadow made no effort to mimic The Boy's movements but instead simply stood there mockingly, thumbing its nose at him.

As this was happening, Gwenny and the Vagabonds clambered up the anchor chain and landed on the deck. The pirates and Bully Boys paid them no mind at first, so entranced were they by Paul's and The Boy's antics.

Paul lunged forward, attempting to stomp on The Boy's shadow. The Boy quickly followed suit, bellowing "Get out of here!"

"I'll get him!" Paul said, and sword in hand, he slammed it point down squarely into the middle of his shadow's chest.

This had precisely the effect that you could reasonably presume it would have: namely none at all. Actually, in the interest of full disclosure, we will reveal that he did manage to chip some wood off the deck of the *Skull n' Bones*. In comparison to Paul's intentions for the efficacy of the blow, however, it would have to be considered a tremendous letdown.

It did, however, cause a deal of guffawing among the pirates who were looking on at the spectacle; and Gwenny and the others felt great chagrin on Paul's behalf. The Boy, however, firmly lined up behind Paul's intentions.

"Get out! I said get out! I command this ship and I order you to go!" He then proceeded to make matters worse by embarking on his own attack at the shadow again and again with his blade. That was the difference between Paul and The Boy. Paul, having tried something once and finding it had no effect, ceased. The Boy, oblivious, kept on doing it in the hope that, sooner or later, it would succeed. Unfortunately it continued to have no effect on the arrogant silhouette, although it did prompt the pirates and the Bully Boys to laugh all the harder. This might have actually worked to the benefit of our young heroes, if their enemies had laughed so hard that they collapsed and dropped down dead from an excess of merriment. At least to Paul, however, that certainly did not seem the best strategy to pursue insofar as taking the day was concerned; and he was starting to feel a degree of embarrassment on The Boy's behalf.

"Boy!" he said, trying to keep his voice low. He took a couple of steps toward him and whispered again, "Boy!"

"I'm busy!" The Boy said, continuing to stab at the deck.

"No, you're really not," said Paul. "I mean, yes, you're occupied, but 'busy' means that you're accomplishing something; and regrettably that's not happening here."

The Boy paused in his assault and assessed the damage he

had inflicted upon his enemy ... which was to say, of course, none at all. He also became aware that the pirates and the Bully Boys were laughing at him. This rankled him more than his ability to express. Despite the fact that the Hack-infested shadow had been meddling with his mind, he remembered all too clearly that he had been in command of these men and boys and they had snapped to at his every order. To see now the sneering, the derision on their faces made him feel as if there had been some grand joke going on the entire time to which he was the punch line.

His cheeks flushed bright red. It was almost too much for The Boy to comprehend. It was bad enough that he felt personally violated by his greatest enemy's infusing himself into something as personal as his own shadow. But now he was being subjected to something that he had never experienced in his life: humiliation. He had known danger of all manner; he had known threats upon his life and had nearly been stabbed to death on more than one occasion. Never, though, had he been laughed at, and there was a thudding deep in his head as blind rage crept in behind his eyes.

It was because of all that—combined with the fact that, in the final analysis, he was still a boy—that he allowed his emotions to take over rather than common sense.

Some time previous—a lifetime it seemed to some—The Boy's shadow had become severed from its master. It had happened during one of The Boy's journeys into the nursery in which Gwenny and her brothers had dwelt; and Gwenny's father had attempted to impede his abrupt departure upon discovering The Boy's presence. The Boy had fled out the window, but Gwenny's father had slammed the window shut quickly enough to snag The Boy's shadow. Gwenny had undone her father's action by stitching the shadow back onto its master's feet, reuniting them. Those stitches had remained in place all this time. They were not like medical sutures that eventually dissolve into the body; they were merely normal thread, holding the shadow in place through Gwenny's deft stitching.

Now, seized with a desire to divorce himself from the humiliating shadow as quickly as possible, The Boy swung his sword—not at his umber opponent—but at his own feet where the shadow was joined to him. He proceeded to slice deftly through the threads that kept his shadow a part of him.

This struck Paul as a marvelously clever solution to the problem, for he sympathized with The Boy and understood the embarrassment he must be feeling, being held to such derision by the pirates and Bully Boys. But Gwenny was far more mature, being a girl and all, and thus intuited instantly that The Boy's actions were staggeringly unwise. "Boy!" she said. "No! Don't!" Hearing her say that, Paul realized the danger and lunged forward shouting, "Boy! Wait!"

Too late. Alas, too late.

In a heartbeat, The Boy's deft manipulation of his blade parted the last of the threads that kept his shadow attached to him. The instant he did, a fearsome wind washed over him, chilling him to the bone. He had no idea whence the wind originated. It was as if a door had been swung open that led to somewhere that The Boy had never explored and had no desire to. There was loud, fiendish laughter, and The Boy shouted for it to stop immediately.

"What laughter?" Paul said, which did little to quiet The Boy's unexpectedly and unusually jangled nerves.

It was Mary Slash who said aloud that which Paul was already beginning to surmise. "That," she said, her voice sounding curiously youthful, "was a mistake."

The shadow of The Boy slowly peeled itself up off the deck

and stood upright. It remained completely flat, as slender as a piece of paper. It was already holding a sword in its hand, since it had been mockingly imitating The Boy, and now it assumed a perfect fencing pose.

"En garde, Boy!" called Mary Slash triumphantly.

"Get away from him, Boy!" Paul said in alarm, his attitude the exact opposite of Slash's.

Ironically . . . and yet, not surprisingly . . . it was the urging of Mary Slash to which The Boy attended. He lunged at the shadow of Hack, which eluded his thrust through the simple expedient of standing sideways, presenting nothing except its wafer-thin edge toward him. The Boy thrust this way and that, and was utterly unable to make contact. The shadow made no riposte, seeming to enjoy The Boy's frustration.

Switching tactics, The Boy swung his cutlass in a sweeping arc. It made no difference. The blade passed harmlessly through the shadow, not slowing in the least. The Boy brought the sword back, and once again it did nothing against the shadow. It did, however, provoke even more laughter from the pirate crew.

"*Stop it!*" said Paul. "Stop that laughing at once!"

The Terrible Turk ceased his chortling long enough to fire a dangerous glare at Paul, and his mighty beard bristled as he said, "Or what?"

"Or . . . it will go badly for you," Paul said, mustering his nerve.

The Terrible Turk laughed curtly, and then drew his sword. It was everything that Paul could do not to tremble in its presence, considering that the Turk's scimitar was practically as big as Paul himself. Irregular shouted out a wholly unnecessary warning as the Turk came in fast at Paul. Paul did the only thing he could: He vaulted over the Turk's head, his power of flight carrying him safely onto the rigging. With a roar, the

Turk turned and started hacking at the rigging, trying to knock Paul from his perch.

The Boy, meantime, was having no success against his opponent. Nor did matters improve as the shadow, apparently becoming bored with just standing there and letting The Boy make futile thrusts at it, moved to the attack.

Paul, concerned with his own predicament, still found the time to cast glances in The Boy's direction to see how he was faring. He was assuming—and we cannot blame him for this—that the shadow would be as helpless against The Boy as The Boy was against him.

So Paul was much shocked to see such was not the case.

Instead the Hack-shaped shadow glided forward, light as air, and swung its sword in a leisurely arc that was evocative of The Boy's. But the outcome was completely different. The Boy turned sideways automatically to avoid the thrust, and that was what saved him, for the tip of the shadow blade sliced through The Boy's upper arm. The result was wholly unexpected: a loud, pained yelp from The Boy, clutching at his arm as his eyes widened in pain. There, on his forearm, was a visible wound, with a trickle of blood welling up from it.

There was no whooshing of air to alert The Boy that the sword of his enemy was coming back at him. His warning was an alarmed cry from Paul, and The Boy backflipped, arcing upward in a lighter-than-air somersault.

The shadow watched him for a moment . . . and then, with even more grace than The Boy had displayed, went airborne and bounded upward after him.

"He's running away!" said Mary Slash, and she began laughing uproariously. "The Boy is running away!"

"I am not!" said The Boy, and indeed he had not been. Instinctively the young warrior had been seeking the higher

ground, and now he turned to face his pursuer. He tried crossing swords with the shadow, which was hovering just below him.
His sword passed right through the shadow blade, but then the
hatchet upon shadow Hack's wrist came around quickly. The
Boy had never realized how much he had counted upon
sound—the swish of air, the rustling of clothing, the scraping of
boots upon the ground—to warn him of the direction or speed
of attacks. He realized it now, though, for the hatchet cut across
his face, and another gash was raised. If he had moved a hair
slower, his head would have come tumbling off his shoulders.

There were gasps from the youngsters, seeing The Boy so
easily scored upon. Once had seemed a fluke, but the second
touch was extremely disheartening.

Paul was helpless to come to The Boy's aid. Instead it was all
he could do to clamber out of the way of the Turk, who had
given up cutting at the rigging and was instead climbing up
toward him.

The other Bully Boys and pirates, seeing an opportunity,
moved toward Gwenny, Irregular, and Porthos. Gwenny and Irregular looked ready to defend themselves, but it was Porthos
who was the most daunting of them all. He was holding a sword
in one hand and a belaying pin in the other, and there was a
look of quiet determination on his face. Big Penny and Yorkers
tried coming in from either side, and were surprised to discover
themselves flat on their backs moments later. Yorkers had been
slapped across the face by the flat of Porthos's blade; while Big
Penny's head was swirling, thanks to being bashed in the skull
with the belaying pin.

Pirates and villains in general are cowards by nature. So,
even though the pirates outnumbered the young people, they
were hesitant to press their advantage, since no one wanted to
be the first to be smacked around by Porthos. Plus the fact that

Yorkers had a face left at all meant that Porthos had issued a warning. If he had used the edge of his blade rather than the flat, Yorkers would have had a bare grinning skull staring out at his shipmates rather than the bewildered look he was sporting.

To Fiddlefix, everything else was irrelevant. Only The Boy mattered to her. To that end, the pixie soared toward the shadow, spitting out a string of profanity that all sounded like the chiming of bells. To say there was a stark contrast between what she was saying and the way that it sounded would be to understate it: It was akin to hearing a ballerina cursing like a sailor.

But before she could get near enough to have any effect on the situation, she was knocked off her course by a well-thrown belaying pin from Mary Slash. Fiddlefix tumbled toward the deck, her glow flickering.

"Fiddle!" called out Paul, and his impulse was to go after her. But he had his own problems to deal with. Nor could The Boy intervene, for the shadow did not slacken its attack. It came at him again and again, pressing its growing advantage.

Mary Slash was dancing. It was an odd thing to see in such an old woman, but her movements belied her age. Her feet were moving deftly, and she was up on her toes, bouncing to the right and left, back and forth, and then in a small circle. Her arms stretched over her head, the sun glinted off the curve of the blade upon her wrist. As she spun, the hem of her garment spiraled outward so that she looked like a twirling bell. And her laughter, which had at first sounded crackling and elderly, became lighter and airier with each thrust of the shadow's weapon toward The Boy. The more The Boy found himself unable to attain any sort of advantage, the more the shadow struck at him with impunity and the more deliriously happy Mary Slash became.

Paul, from his vantage point, saw the whole thing. Saw

Gwenny and the boys mounting a valiant defense, but defense was all it was. Saw The Boy trying again and again to inflict some sort of damage upon his opponent and getting nowhere, while there were now half a dozen cuts upon him. Individually none of them was fatal, or even daunting. But they were accumulating, and soon it would have to wear him down, leaving him open to a killing stroke. Plus there was his own predicament, as the Turk clambered closer and closer to him.

"Boy! Gwenny! We have to get out of here!" Paul shouted over the melee. "We have to leave now! *Now!*"

Paul's words struck to the very core of The Boy's pride, which was boundless. The notion of an open retreat was anathema to him. But he looked around and saw the same situation that Paul perceived, and knew in his heart that Paul was right.

The most stunning sight was Mary Slash. She was youthening, the ravages of age melting away from her in the light of her joy. Her gray-white hair was now almost entirely raven black. Her warts and liver spots had disappeared. Her movements became lighter by the second; and with one fast slice of her sword, she cut away the long flowing garment she'd been wearing. Beneath was now revealed a dazzling piratical ensemble: Trousers and a greatcoat, both made of crushed red velvet. A crisp white shirt with a ruffled tie, and classic black buccaneer boots. A wide sash across her middle completed the ensemble, and there was a single-shot pistol jammed into the sash. And her eyes blazed with a singular hatred directed entirely at The Boy.

And still The Boy hesitated, his pride making it impossible for him to withdraw. Seeing that hesitation, Paul called out to him, "Boy! There's too much going on here that we neither know nor understand! If we fight and die, then we die ignorant, and what purpose will that serve?"

Knowing that Paul was right and despising him for being so, The Boy called out the word that was bile in his mouth: "Re-treat!"

He ducked under a desperate slash from the shadow's sword, hurtled through the air like a projectile, and snagged Paul from the uppermost section of the rigging. It was at that moment that Paul remembered he could fly . . . an understandable lapse in memory, since he had a lot on his mind and the notion that he could defy gravity was still quite novel to him.

Paul shook loose of The Boy's grasp and floated there for a moment, regaining his equilibrium. The Boy glanced in surprise, for if Paul's awareness of his airborne abilities was new-found, The Boy was quite simply notorious for forgetting new concepts from one moment to the next. His battle with the shadow of his enemy had so consumed him that not only had it slipped his mind that Paul could fly, but also he had quite forgotten who Paul was.

"I'll get the boys!" Paul said. "You get Gwenny!"

The Boy nodded, a rare instance of accepting orders at all, much less orders without question. He dove like a streak toward Gwenny, while Paul angled down toward the outstretched arms of Porthos and Irregular. The pirates started to converge on Gwenny, but The Boy easily got to her first. He snagged her wrists and lifted her up, high out of reach. Then he called, "Bully Boys! With me!"

The Bully Boys laughed.

It was the most cutting noise that The Boy had ever heard. He froze there for a moment, and Paul—who was holding Irregular by one hand and Porthos by the other, and was marveling at the fact that they seemed to weigh nothing to him—noticed that The Boy appeared to be sinking slightly.

"I am your captain!" The Boy reminded them.

This drew even more laughter of a most contemptuous nature, and then a female voice soared over their hilarity.

It was Slash, and she pointed her sword hand defiantly at him. Next to her, the shadow of Hack was visibly shaking with mirth. "You were a figurehead, Boy!" she said, trying to contain her amusement and not being terribly successful. "No different than the wooden skull that sits at the prow of the ship! 'Twas the noble Hack who truly guided your hand...and 'tis I, Captain Slash, who is running matters upon this ship! Now fly!"

The Boy, out of defiant reflex, started to head back toward her, and suddenly Agha Bey was swinging one of the deck cannons around at him. The fuse was already burning down, and Paul realized instantly that it was about to detonate. "Boy! The cannon!"

Seeing the source of Paul's warning, The Boy—given no choice—dropped back, Gwenny clutching desperately onto him with all her strength, her legs thrashing about in the air. The cannon went off, and The Boy twisted to the side, just managing to avoid the cannonball as it hurtled past him. It arced out over the ship's stern, down, and crashed through the raft that Gwenny and the boys had so carefully manufactured. The raft was shattered to splinters, no longer identifiable even as separate planks of wood, much less a vessel.

As fast as they could, Paul, The Boy, and the others flew away from the pirate ship.

Caveat sidled over to Captain Slash and said in a low voice, "A hit. A palatable hit."

"Indeed," said Slash.

"They'll retreat to the tree house."

"Oh, they'll try to," Slash said. "They will not, however, be especially successful."

"Why not?"

"Let us just say that I've attended to it," she said with a smile.

"Well, if they're not successful at returning home," Caveat said aloud, "they will surely seek other means to come after us. I don't think any of us truly believes this is over."

"Oh, I know it's not over," said Slash. She was reaching into one of the copious pockets in her greatcoat. "But when it continues, I shall have . . . certain advantages."

"What sort of advantages?"

She withdrew a small tin box from her pocket. With a grim smile, she shook it and was rewarded with a frustrated and slightly frightened ringing from within. It was the sound of a very mortified Fiddlefix, slamming about within the box and getting absolutely nowhere.

"A small one," she said. "Wouldn't you agree?"

Caveat leaned forward, stared at the box, and grinned. "Indubiously," he confirmed.

Chapter 10

Slash and Burn

Paul had never seen The Boy looking more lost.

The Boy stood on the ground, looking up, side by side with Gwenny, Paul, and the others; and the anguish on his face was plain for Paul to see. If nothing else, it mirrored their expressions.

There were the smoldering ruins of the tree house. Where there had once been a comfortable domicile, all that remained was a charred husk. Wisps of smoke were still rising from it; and glowing embers wafted away from it, looking like pixies in the lengthening twilight.

It was that realization which suddenly prompted Paul to look around and say with alarm, "Where's Fiddle?"

The Boy didn't answer. He was too busy looking woefully at the remains of the tree house. "Gone. All gone. I built it with my own hands."

"Did he?" Paul asked Gwenny.

"Yes," said Gwenny, "if one defines 'own hands' as standing

around or floating around and barking orders while everyone else does it."

"I suppose being in charge counts for something," Paul said philosophically.

"It must have been Slash," said The Boy, his anger beginning to escalate. "I don't know when she did this—"

"Not that it matters," said Irregular tragically.

"—but she will taste my wrath. She will learn that she cannot do this and get away with it," continued The Boy, as if Irregular had said nothing, which, as far as The Boy was concerned, was probably the case.

"Where's Fiddle?" Paul said again, this time with some more force behind it.

It was sufficient to grab The Boy's mild attention, and he afforded Paul a brief glance before saying indifferently, "She's around somewhere, no doubt."

"But what if she was captured?"

"Far more likely that something else caught her attention."

"That much is true," said Gwenny. "Sprites are most transient in their nature, and sometimes . . ." She stopped, stared at Paul as if seeing him for the first time, and said, "*Who* are you again?"

"It doesn't matter who he is," said The Boy brusquely.

"Boy! You've no excuse for being so rude . . . ."

"At the moment, he's right. It doesn't matter," said Paul. "There's more pressing problems." He was busy looking upward, and saw dark and fearsome clouds rolling toward them. Indeed, it seemed as if the clouds had targeted them specifically and were bearing down upon them. "We need shelter. We need it quickly."

They took shelter in a dark and dank cave some distance away. Paul, Gwenny, and the others huddled close to one another for mutual warmth as the storm shattered the skies over-head, rain thundering down. The Boy, by contrast, huddled by himself at the far end of the cave. There was no source of light other than the dimness filtering in through the cave opening. So the only things visible from the rear of the cave were The Boy's eyes. They could have been floating there by themselves, and they had the grim appearance of a trapped and angry beast.

"What are you doing here?" The Boy said abruptly.

The others in the cave looked at one another in confusion, and then all gazes settled on Paul. "Oh. You mean me." When The Boy nodded curtly, Paul said, "Well . . . actually . . . I'm here because of my sister."

He then proceeded to describe all the events that had brought him—and them, as it happened—to this particular point. They listened with rapt attention, even The Boy, since he was always partial to a good story. When Paul got to the part on the ship, he began to taper off since everyone had been there and thus presumably knew what had transpired. But Porthos egged him on with, "What next?" and so, with a shrug, Paul continued until he arrived at their taking shelter within the cave. At which point Porthos, like a large eager puppy, prompted yet again, "And what next? What happened next?"

"Well, I . . . don't rightly know," Paul said.

This drew The Boy forward a bit, so that his silhouette was visible in the darkness. "What sort of story is that?" he said. "It doesn't have a proper ending at all. Not even a 'And they lived happily ever after.' "

"But the story's not complete," Paul tried to explain. Even as he did so, he was seeing that as a very poor excuse for an incomplete story. The other boys quickly confirmed that, imploring him to stop holding back and please, oh please, tell them everything that happened next. Gwenny patiently tried to point out to them that their expectations were a bit excessive, given the givens; but they paid her no mind, which was often the case with boys and their mothers.

His mind racing, Paul suddenly said, "And so ... The Boy decided he needed help—"

"I never need help!" The Boy said defiantly, standing now and placing his fists firmly on his hips. "I mean, he—The Boy—never needs help."

"Well, he does in this story."

"What kind of story is that?"

"Mine," Paul said firmly, for he knew that he was in the mode of storyteller and thus had the final say in all the important matters. "And you wanted to hear it. You insisted. So now I'm telling it, and, by your own rules, you have to listen."

Caught in a web of his own credulity, The Boy made a rude noise and then flopped down to the rocky cave floor. "From whom did he seek help?" There was a hint of challenge in his voice, just enough to remind Paul that The Boy had a sword tucked in his belt and might well not hesitate to use it if he did not like how the tale was unfolding.

Paul was ready to continue, though, for The Boy's resistance to the tale had given Paul enough time to conceive of where it was to go. "And so The Boy, most splendid and wonderful as he was, sought out the aid of the Picca tribe. For the Piccas had a vast warrior army, capable of canny maneuvers in their canoes. The Piccas were happy to join The Boy in an attack on their mutual enemy."

The Boy was nodding slowly; and naturally the others took their cues from him, so they nodded as well. Thus emboldened, Paul continued: "And so the Piccas, in the company of The Boy and his stalwarts, snuck up on the pirates, attacked, and destroyed them utterly."

"*Hurrah!*" crowed the boys.

"What of the Bully Boys?" Gwenny said worriedly. Although she had no hesitation to see the pirates done for, she still could not help but feel that the boys left behind upon the pirate ship were merely misguided and not deserving of the ultimate penalty.

"They . . . saw the error of their ways, swore fealty to The Boy, and became family once more."

"*Hurrah!*" they all said again.

"And what of your quest?" Irregular said. "To find a new sister to keep your mum from being sad."

"I . . ." Paul tried to come up with something, but his own future was a blank wall to him. He could not begin to imagine what would happen. So he settled for saying, "I . . . found a sister. And my mum, and dad, and all concerned, including you lot, lived happily ever after."

This inspired yet another cheer from the listeners, who had quite forgotten about their plight as they had become engaged in Paul's history. "Well!" said The Boy, slapping his hands on his thighs. "At least that's all settled! On to the next thing!"

"It's not all settled!" Paul said.

The Boy looked puzzled. "It's not?"

"No, Boy, it's not," Gwenny said, understanding faster than the lads what Paul meant, since girls are traditionally far more clever than boys. "You haven't actually done any of these things yet. Nothing is settled. The pirates are still running about, we have no home, and Captain Hack remains in possession of your shadow. None of these things are going to change until you take the steps to change them."

The Boy gave a lot of thought to that. He was accustomed to stories being presented to him in a completed manner, described after the fact. Here he was apparently in the middle of the tale and needed to do whatever was necessary to be able to write "Happily ever after" himself... preferably in blood, for he was a rather sanguinary youth. Finally he smiled and nodded and said, "It shall be so! On the morrow we go to the Piccas, enlist their aid, and defeat the pirates... and then have lunch!"

Gwenny clapped her hands in approval, as did the rest. "And what will we do *after* lunch, Boy?" said Porthos with typical enthusiasm.

"Something exciting, I fancy," he said. Then, slightly cautious, he looked at Paul and said, "Right?"

"Absolutely right," said Paul, although honestly he did not see the entire campaign as something that would be wrapped up before lunch. In the past weeks, Paul had come to realize that matters rarely proceeded as smoothly and without fuss as he would like them to. He had a dark suspicion that this would be no exception.

And as I think you have already figured out—considering that there are far more pages remaining in this book than would be reasonable for a quick "We've won, let's have lunch, and they lived happily ever after"—the sad fact is that Paul was very much correct. There would be much more arguing, fighting, mistrust, betrayals, natural and unnatural disasters, and one or two more deaths of individuals we'd much rather see survive.

So now you know this. And I've said it in a very low voice so that The Boy, Paul, and the others won't overhear. Otherwise they might remain in the cave indefinitely rather than launch themselves into situations that could prove overwhelming. Besides... no one should know too much of what is to happen, or too much of the details of his own demise.

Chapter 11

Betrayal

It would be an understatement to say that the Piccas did not warmly greet Paul and his companions. The tragic truth is that our heroes showing up at the Piccas' camp (which the Piccas had hastily relocated after seeing the pirate ship below ready to blow the cliffside to bits. By the time Mary Slash had taken command, the Indians had already moved inland) did not go remotely as expected.

The Boy was not expecting a trap of any sort, although he had thought to divest himself of his pirate garb so the Piccas would see him in his more familiar green tunic and leggings. He reasoned that was all the Piccas would require to accept his change in attitude. Gwenny, however, voiced definite concerns. "My understanding, Boy," she reminded him as they trekked through the underbrush, "is that the last encounter the Picca tribe had with you, you were doing them some mischief."

He waved it off dismissively. "That means nothing," he said with confidence. "They will know that something was amiss.

What better, greater, more splendid friend have the Piccas ever had than I?"

Suddenly an arrow was poking out from the brush, aimed squarely at The Boy's face. He took a step back, his eyes wide—not in fear but in surprise.

Gwenny let out an involuntary shriek and then another as she saw she had her very own arrow aimed at her very own head. Paul, Irregular, and Porthos reacted with their own exclamations of surprise, although thankfully none of them shrieked like a girl, for The Boy would never have let them hear the end of *that*.

Sensing that they were surrounded, and wanting to avoid a battle that would likely not end well, Paul called out, "Do nothing! Make no attempt to fight them!" The Boy chafed under this pronouncement but—somewhat to Paul's surprise—he made no move.

"Good plan," said Gwenny.

"I can do that," said Irregular.

Porthos's mouth was moving, but nothing was coming out.

"Show yourselves!" Paul said in his most commanding voice, hoping that valor would carry the day. "Or are you braves so lacking in bravery that you have to hide from people who are unarmed?"

"What 'unarmed'?" came a rough voice from the underbrush. "Boy have sword on hip."

The Boy glanced down at the sword, then looked up at Paul and shrugged. Thinking quickly, if not well, Paul said, "It's purely for style."

There was a pause, followed by a confused "Oh." Then, slowly, the braves emerged from the underbrush. They were fiercely decked out in war paint, and their bare torsos glistened in the early morning sun.

One of the Picca braves stepped forward . . . presumably the leader of the war party. He was the one with his arrow leveled squarely at The Boy. Like all Picca males, he had been named for the first thing that his mother saw outside her wigwam after he had been born. "What you do here?" said Pouring Rain. "Boy now enemy of Piccas."

"You have no enemy in me," The Boy said with considerable command and remarkable calm. One would never know he was one slightly twitchy finger away from an arrow splitting his face in twain.

"That news," said Pouring Rain. "Boy attack braves. Boy command pirates."

"Do you see any pirates anywhere around?" Gwenny said.

The Picca warriors glanced around suspiciously. "Could be hiding," another brave said. "Could be trick."

Pouring Rain said, "Dog Licking Self speak truly. Could be trick."

"Look around," said Paul. "Take your time. Search the entire area. We're not going anywhere. We're here looking for you, so why would we?"

Pouring Rain considered, then said brusquely to The Boy, "If Boy so much as twitches . . . arrow will go into eye."

"I'm not moving. You have my word," said The Boy. And, true to his word, he remained precisely where he was, without moving so much as a muscle, while the Picca braves spread out through the woods and sought some sign—any sign—that an ambush was afoot.

None was, of course, and when Dog Licking Self and the other braves reported back that they were alone in the woods, Pouring Rain slowly lowered his arrow, although suspicion still radiated from him. "You attack braves. With guns. With sword."

"It wasn't him. Well, not exactly," said Paul and he quickly described the circumstances that had brought them to this situation.

The Boy listened and nodded with approval. "You're getting very good at telling that tale," he said. "I would like it if next time I could sound more heroic, though."

"Well . . . you *were* the villain. Or at least possessed by the villain."

"I suppose," said The Boy, "but it stings."

"How so?"

"Because," The Boy said with a bit of his sauciness reasserting itself, "nothing happens in the Anyplace that I don't want to have happen. That's the way it has always been. Ultimately the realm is subject to my imagination."

Now there was some truth to that, but also some falsehood, as is typically the case with The Boy. We shall go into it in more detail later when matters are not quite as tense, for the Picca are liable to become trigger happy—or bow happy, as it were—if we compel them to wait much longer.

"You have opportunity to tell story again," Pouring Rain informed him, caring nothing about either The Boy's pride or existential angst, "to Princess Picca." He paused and then added curiously, "You know story about princess in tower with long hair?"

"Rapunzel? I do, yes."

"You tell later," Pouring Rain said so firmly that one would have thought it a dictate from on high.

Again The Boy nodded, and he patted Paul on the shoulder. "Keep doing what you're doing. You tell stories better than Gwenny. I wonder why she stopped telling us stories."

"Because you flew off to be a pirate and left me behind," Gwenny reminded him, sounding not a little annoyed.

"Oh. Well, yes, there's that, I suppose," he said carelessly.

In short order they were brought to the Picca camp. Somehow word must have been sent ahead, for the Piccas were waiting for them and looked none too happy to see them. Princess Picca was foremost among those waiting, standing with her arms crossed and her savage expression fixed upon The Boy. Paul did not think she was even paying attention to The Boy's companions. Perhaps they simply were not important enough for her. It was hard for Paul to get a fix on her age. She might have been as young as fifteen or as remarkably ancient as thirty, for her physique seemed youthful but her bearing added many years. Her hair hung in girlish black braids, but her face was stern and unforgiving, her round chin defiantly outthrust and her dark eyes like the storm before a calm.

"You," she said, and pointed at The Boy, "betrayed Picca. Betrayed us all."

"Actually, I didn't. He'll tell you"—and he indicated Paul. "He's a storyteller."

Princess Picca turned and looked at Paul as if seeing him for the first time, which she probably was. "You know story of girl with glass moccasin?"

"Cinderella? Why . . . yes, actually."

"Always like that one. You tell later. Now speak of Boy's betrayal."

So Paul did. By this point he had gotten down the pacing of his story so that it flowed smoothly. There were no hesitations or stammers or pauses as he tried to figure out the best way to describe what happened next. He was rather pleased with himself over his accomplishment.

As it happened, it was the worst thing he could have done.

When he finished, Princess Picca—rather than smiling and nodding with interest as others had—scowled fiercely and fearsomely. "You," she announced, "too smooth of tongue. Spin tale like spider spins web. Seek to ensnare us as well. Devour us, per-haps."

"No!" Paul said with alarm. "No, that's not the case at all. Tell her, Boy!"

"It really was a good story. Do you know the one about—"

"It wasn't just a story! It's what happened!"

The Boy looked at him wide-eyed. "Aren't all stories?"

Paul was not at all sure how any of this was coming across to the Piccas. He was aware, though, that there was a good deal of scowling among them, and he was not certain how to address it.

The Boy, however, did not hesitate. He stepped toward Princess Picca. This prompted a number of the braves to bring their bows and arrows to bear as quickly as they could. The Boy paid them no mind at all. Instead he threw his arms wide and said, "If you choose to disbelieve our storyteller . . . if you reject our tale . . . then you reject me as well. If that is the case, then do with me as you will."

"Even if it mean you must die?"

As amazing as it seemed to Paul, The Boy really, truly ap-peared indifferent to the prospect. To underscore his laissez-faire attitude, he added an apathetic shrug.

Princess Picca frowned at his lack of more dramatic re-sponse. As long as she had known him, one would have thought that his history of bravado combined with his devil-may-care at-titude would have prepared her for his daring the braves to fill him full of arrows. The trick was, she and her tribe had been al-lies with him for so long that they had quite forgotten what it was like to face him as an opponent. The Anyplace tended to do that to all people, not just The Boy. When you get down to it, the Anyplace very much existed for the now that reflected the children from whose imagination it was torn.

Think on it: How often do youngsters thrust themselves

into situations that they know are wrong for them? Their parents warned them many times that they should not get involved in such endeavors. And they know that if and when they are caught out, certainly there will be swift and terrible punishment brought down upon their heads ... provided, of course, that they survive the experience in the first place, which is not always a guaranteed thing.

But they care not for what was said to them earlier, nor do they dwell on what is to come. They live for the moment, for the now. And in that heartbeat—or, more precisely, in between each heartbeat—is where The Boy resides, egging them on to greater and more monumental disasters. In that way does his fundamentally tricksterish nature overlap with the fundamentally self-destructive nature of children.

So, parents, be a bit more understanding of your children, now that I have told you not only what I know but also what you probably already knew deep down. The Boy can be most convincing, for that is part of his charm. Therefore, whenever you are inclined to shake your head in despair and wring your hands and muse aloud, "What in the world gets into children's heads?" the answer is, like as not, The Boy. Which is why young boys are more susceptible to his blandishment than girls, the latter tending to remain more sensible, while the former hurl themselves headlong into danger.

We have wandered from the point. As we recall, Princess Picca was saying, "Even if it mean you must die?" and The Boy was delivering an apathetic shrug in reply.

Princess Picca frowned at his lack of more dramatic response. In the intervening silence, as she considered allowing her braves to release their pointed ambassadors of death, Gwenny decided that someone had to do something that would not result in a quick and brutal demise. She did not step forward, concerned that any movement might trigger the itchy fingers of the archers. She did, however, say in a calm but firm voice, "Princess. There must be another way. Some means by which The Boy can prove his trustworthiness and usefulness to the Picca tribe."

"Are you sure, Gwenny?" The Boy said, one elegant eyebrow arched. "I mean, certainly the death business is much quicker and far less involved."

"Yes, I'm sure," she said, making no effort to hide her annoyance. "You'll find in life that, more often than not, the easiest way to solve a problem isn't the best."

"It *isn't?*" The Boy looked thunderstruck.

"That's what my mother often says," Paul said, prompting an eye roll from The Boy, who thought that it was quite simply the silliest thing he had ever heard, but he also knew that arguing with mothers was a futile endeavor.

Princess Picca, meanwhile, was considering Gwenny's words. "Must speak with braves," she decided, for she was a wise and thoughtful ruler, and did not like to reach decisions in a precipitous manner if it could be at all avoided. The braves promptly lowered their weapons once more and gathered in a circle around Princess Picca. Not having to make their sentiments known to the outsiders, they reverted to their native tongue. It sounded rather a bit like pig Latin to Paul, but he said nothing about it since he did not want to risk doing anything else to annoy the Indians.

Finally the circle of braves separated and Princess Picca strode forth. She gave The Boy a look that Paul considered a rather challenging one, and said, "How anxious are you, prove worth to Piccas?"

"I don't know," The Boy said, which might have been an annoying answer as far as both Gwenny and the princess were con-

cerned, but at least it had the merit of being an honest one. The
Boy really had not given it all that much thought.

Wisely choosing to ignore what The Boy had just said,
Princess Picca continued, "For if you want prove worth . . . we
have dangerous task give you."

"Dangerous?" Clearly The Boy's interest was piqued. "How
dangerous?"

Her face darkened, and her voice dropped to a tremulous
warning. "Could mean . . . your life."

"*Excellent!*" crowed The Boy. "That being the case, I'm most
anxious indeed!"

He started jumping about enthusiastically. He had removed
his sword from his belt, whipping it around artfully. It was fortunate for him that he was pointing away from the Piccas as he
was doing so, lest they consider it a threat and fill him with arrows, thus aborting the mission before it even got started.
"What needs to be done?" The Boy said. "Does it require
killing?"

"Yes."

This prompted The Boy to bound into the air and ricochet
off several tree branches. When he landed, his lips were pulled
back in a feral snarl, displaying his perfect ivory teeth. Paul
could not help but feel a twinge of pity for whoever it was that
The Boy was to go up against. "Bring him here!" said The Boy,
making a couple of thrusts with his blade for good measure.
"His day is done!"

"Not a 'he.' An 'it.' "

Curiously, this pronouncement gave The Boy pause. Paul
had a feeling that he knew why. According to what his father
had told Paul in his tales, The Boy supposedly had a superstitious streak about him. True, he had no fear of death, but he
had a healthy wariness of anything that returned from the dead.

He misliked monsters of any ilk and things that went bump in the night. Not that he would have admitted such to anyone. He had far too vast an ego for that. Still, as noted, it gave him pause . . . in this case, the pause being about three seconds. "What sort of 'it'?" he said finally, although he tried to add a careless toss of his head at the end of the question so he could appear casual.

Princess Picca looked at him oddly, since the answer was self-evident to her (what with her being a girl and not at all superstitious). "An animal," she said.

Realizing how painfully self-evident that should have been, The Boy strutted about momentarily saying "Tut-tut. Of course an animal. What else could it be *but* an animal?"

"An undead zombie?" said Paul, who felt that the aptly named Anyplace was the perfect territory for just about anything the mind could conjure.

The Boy fired him an annoyed look, but he was saved from having to respond when Princess Picca said dismissively, "Nonsense. Although may wish for zombie when see animal. Great murderous beast it is. Kill several of my tribe. Many braves try to hunt it. None return."

"Make ready your cooking fires," said The Boy, "for I am on the hunt now, and I always return! What sort of beast do I seek?"

Something within Paul knew. Before the princess even spoke, he knew the words that were about to tumble from her mouth, like a story that is suddenly coming back to you after not having heard it for many a year.

"A tiger," Princess Picca said. "A tiger—"

"With fur white as a drift of snow," Paul said, as if speaking from very far away, "and eyes that glisten with power, and a tail that snaps like a whip. And where he treads, everything around him stops and listens, even the trees and the bushes and the smallest mushrooms. He is the mightiest predator in the Any-place."

"Not mightier than I," The Boy said with confidence.

"Mightier than anyone or anything," Paul shot back, feeling unaccountably as if his pride had been stung.

"How do you know that?" said Irregular, feeling a bit forgotten in all the proceedings.

"Because he's mine."

"Yours?" The Boy looked at him askance. "What mean you by that?"

"I mean he's mine. In my dreams, I run with him. I ride on his back and feel his powerful muscles and silken fur. And he would never hurt me, and he would never hurt any of you. I asked him not to hunt humans, and he told me he wouldn't."

"Then he has lied to you," Princess Picca said with quiet certainty, although she did look a bit sympathetic. For some reason, that very sympathy outraged Paul all the more, for he did not feel as if he needed her sympathy or anyone's for that matter. Moreover, the way she was staring at him, it was as if she could see straight into his uncertainties. For, as you may recall, Paul suspected even at the time that the snow tiger's claims of never hunting humans might well be slightly false. Paul had glossed over it in his mind, wanting to give his beloved friend the benefit of the doubt. Now those doubts were no longer beneficial.

"The beast hunts my people," said the Princess. "The beast kills my people. For hunger. For sport. Matters not. Must be stopped. If Boy stop the killing, then will be great service to Picca. We will be in debt. We in debt, we can be allies."

"You don't have to kill my tiger!" Paul said. "This is a mistake! A misunderstanding! I'm telling you, if it's the same tiger—"

"Only kind like it in the Anyplace," said the princess.

"—then he can be reasoned with! He's . . ." Paul thumped his chest with his fist. "He's a part of me. A part of who I am. He always has been. I'll talk to him. He's not the one attacking your people. I know it. I just know it."

Once again Princess Picca felt the need to confer with her people. This conference, however, took a good deal less time. "Very well," said the princess. "Storyteller go with The Boy. You see for self. And when you see, then you help Boy kill snow tiger."

Privately, Paul was convinced that that would never happen. He knew his snow tiger. He knew the greatness, the nobility that pounded beneath that glossy fur, and was positive that he could get the entire matter sorted out. If it required the tiger to return with him, bound, to the Picca camp, so that he could explain it to them himself, then he was certain he could talk his tiger into it. They just didn't know the tiger the way Paul did.

Paul said none of this. Instead he simply bowed and said formally, "I will do whatever is necessary."

"What about us?" Irregular and Porthos piped up in unison. And even Gwenny queried the prospect of joining them on this big game quest.

But Princess Picca shook her head with finality. "No. You stay here. Only Boy and storyteller leave."

"But why?" Gwenny said pleadingly.

"Because," Princess Picca said as if it were the most reasonable deal in the world, "If Boy and storyteller have not returned before the rising of the sun"—she pointed to Gwenny, Irregular, and Porthos—"you three will die. Executed by braves."

This piece of information landed upon the youngsters like the metaphorical sack of bricks. "Ex-executed?" Gwenny managed to stammer out.

Princess Picca nodded gravely.

"Executed...if he fails to return?" When Princess Picca again bobbed her head in the affirmative, Gwenny said with some alarm, "Boy? Did you hear that? All our lives depend upon you accomplishing this mission!"

The object of her admonishment was paying no attention. He was far too busy thrusting his sword and dodging the attacks of imaginary opponents.

Paul watched him gallivant about, and then turned to Princess Picca and said hopefully, "Is it too late to accept your offer to kill The Boy?"

"Yes. Too late."

"Bugger," said Paul.

Chapter 12

Tiger, Tiger Burning White, in the Forest at Midnight

Paul had not truly thought that murdering The Boy was a viable option, although he could not say for sure what he would have done if he had been informed that, yes, the possibility of that solution remained.

They set off from the Picca camp that very day. The Boy and Paul were both armed with swords, Paul still holding the one that he had swiped from the pirate vessel. Princess Picca seemed of the opinion that The Boy's blade would be inadequate protection against the savage teeth and slashing claws of the snow tiger, but The Boy's confidence was boundless. He dismissed any such concerns out of hand, loudly announcing that he could handle whatever was thrown at him. Paul noticed, but did not comment on, the fact that The Boy said "I" at any opportunity, rather than "we." Obviously he considered Paul a tagalong at best, a burden at worst, and fully anticipated that the success or failure of the mission was wholly on his shoulders.

Paul knew otherwise. For Paul was certain that the mission's success depended not upon The Boy's flashing blade but rather on Paul's ability to communicate with his great tiger and convince him to change his ways. That was presuming that the tiger, *his* tiger, was truly responsible for the slaughter that the Picca tribe had laid at his door . . . an accusation that Paul was not fully prepared to accept. Between you and me—and it really is necessary to keep it *entre nous,* since Paul might well feel a bit hurt by this sentiment—Paul was in his own way as unbearably overconfident as The Boy. There were just different reasons for it. As you well know, pride goes before a fall, and both lads were bristling with their own sorts of pride. Thus even the casual observer could foresee that matters would not end well . . . and I am telling you this in advance so that, when matters do not, in fact, end well, you can be prepared for it to some degree.

They made their way into the forest. From the outset Paul felt as if all his nerve endings were on fire. Every rustle of brush, every bend of a tree seemed to hide a hundred different menaces. The Boy, by contrast, whistled in a carefree manner. He did not relax his guard. He had his sword at the ready the entire time. But he did not carry it in an en garde position. Instead he held it casually by his side, like a suitcase or handbag. All he was doing was eliminating the time that would be required to draw the blade.

Still, Paul felt it prudent to follow suit, so he likewise held his sword. If nothing else, it was convenient for chopping away whatever brush managed to get in their path.

The Boy watched Paul's excessive wariness with great amusement. He even chuckled whenever Paul would jump at some new and unexpected sound. This began to wear on Paul, who saw nothing funny about the situation at all.

"Do you truly think he's going to attack us now?" The Boy finally said.

"I don't think he's going to attack *me* at all," Paul said. This was mostly the truth, although there was some niggling part of him that insisted on reminding him this was a tiger they were talking about: a wild animal. What made such creatures wild was their unpredictability. So although Paul expected that he was safe from a fierce charge by the creature, he was keenly aware that the possibility of such an assault remained. "You, on the other hand...that's a whole different matter."

"Not during the daytime," The Boy said. "He's a hunter. It's daytime. He won't be out and about until night. There's an off chance that we might stumble upon his lair in our meandering, but the real confrontation will likely come once the sun has set."

Paul was not thrilled about that prospect. The looming trees seemed filled with menace even now. The notion of stumbling about at night, with nothing save moonlight to give them guidance, was quite daunting.

"How will we find him?" Paul said.

"We'll hunt him."

"But what if we don't find him?" he said again.

"We will."

"You can't know that for sure...."

The Boy stopped in his path and turned to face Paul. There was excitement glittering in his eyes, the prospect of facing a tornado of claws and teeth kindling an almost savage glee within him. "A great hunter, which by all accounts the snow tiger is, knows when he's being hunted."

"How?"

"Any one of a hundred ways. He just knows. That's what makes him great. And a *truly* great hunter—which, again, de-

scribes our target—will endeavor to turn the tables and trans-
form the predators into the prey."

"You mean . . ." Paul said with a gulp. "You mean, while
we're hunting him, he's going to be hunting us?"

"Exciting, isn't it?"

"Not as much as you seem to think it is."

The Boy turned out to be right about one thing: For the balance of the day, they saw not the slightest hint of the tiger's
whereabouts. Conversation was sporadic and mostly consisted
of The Boy launching into some recounting of his previous adventures. Paul found them interesting enough, since he was
rather enamored of stories of adventure and derring-do. He did
not bother to press The Boy about their previous encounters
through mirrors and such. He had tried a few preliminary
queries along those lines, but The Boy answered in that offhand, careless manner he used when he plainly did not recall
the subject being discussed.

At one point, Paul's stomach was growling so audibly that
The Boy ordered him to stay where he was. He vanished into
the undergrowth, and just when he had been gone long enough
that Paul was starting to worry, The Boy reappeared. He held
up the point of his sword proudly, and Paul gasped. A dead rabbit was dangling helplessly from the end of the sword.

The sight made Paul a bit sick, although he did have to ad-
mire the amazingly efficient way that The Boy skinned the
creature in mere seconds. The Boy went about it so matter-of-
factly that the very absence of effort made it all the more remarkable. Then The Boy briskly gathered some brush around a
stone and struck the stone with the edge of his blade. The single blow was all that was required to send sparks leaping onto
the brush, and a few gentle gusts of breath from The Boy
fanned the flame higher. Shortly, The Boy was roasting the rab-

bit over a small but impressive fire. Paul was so taken with the expert display of forestry and woodsmanship that he didn't even take note of the sun setting until it was well below the horizon. By the time he did notice, his mouth was filled with roast rabbit and so he wasn't in a position to comment.

He found it curious that The Boy ate nothing. When he attempted to offer some to the strange lad, The Boy shook his head and waved it away. He was about to query as to why that was and how The Boy was not remotely hungry, when The Boy spoke first. "How long will you be staying?"

Paul was surprised that The Boy would ask. Indeed, it was the first thing The Boy had posed to him that was not related to The Boy himself in some way. "I . . . suppose until I've done what I came here to do: to find a new little sister for my mother, so she won't be unhappy anymore."

"You want to make your mother happy." He sounded unenthused.

"Well . . . yes."

The Boy shook his head. "No point in trying. Mothers are always unhappy; and no matter how much you do for them, it won't ever be enough. Be best for you if you gave up on that idea and just remained here for good."

"Best for me? Or best for you?"

"I don't see the difference."

"I don't suppose you would," Paul said with a small laugh. "You are marvelously adventurous and fear nothing. For that I can only envy you." He tossed the remaining bit of rabbit onto the ground, where a small creature of some sort ran up and carried it off in its teeth. "But you aren't one of the world's deepest thinkers."

"Thinking is a waste of time. It keeps you from action." The Boy, who had been crouched nearby in imitation of a frog, now leaped to his feet and thumped his chest. "We should get moving. The sooner we find the tiger, the sooner it finds us."

"But...don't you ever wonder...? No," Paul corrected himself, "no, of course you don't. But I wonder..."

"Wonder what?" The Boy blew air across his teeth with impatience.

"I just...I don't understand why you've no desire to grow up. That's all."

"That's *all*?" The Boy's delicate features twisted into a sneer. "If that's all you don't understand, then you *do* understand *nothing.*"

"Then explain it to me." Paul wasn't considering the time constraints or the snow tiger hidden somewhere out there, perhaps watching them from a safe distance even as they spoke. "I mean, don't you see that there's something wrong with being the way you are? Explain why you've no interest in growing up."

"Explain why you do."

"Well, because..." Paul gestured helplessly, trying to find the words. "Because there's so many great things to experience as you get older."

"Greater than that which I live every single day? Honestly now."

"I...suppose not," Paul said. He tried to rally, but The Boy overspoke him.

"There you have it," said The Boy, as if the entire matter were settled...which, as far as he was concerned, it was. Yet, strangely enough, he continued to speak with a heaping dollop of disdain. "I used to spy on old Hack just for fun, and once I overheard him when he was in his cups. He was talking about how he felt the absence of his hand and upper arm. A faint ghostly tingling for a missing part of himself. What they do to you, Paul...you have no idea. As you grow up, they're not satisfied until they cut the very heart of your childhood out of you. And you spend the rest of your life feeling the joys and freedom of your youth—the cut-away part, the best part of you—with that same phantom tingling that Hack felt. But it is gone, and no matter how much you wish it so, will never come back, because it's been devoured.

"None in the waking world seem to know what they want. Children desirous of nothing but to become adults. Adults who have no desire but to recapture their childhood. The entire human race doesn't know whether it comes or goes, and you think that I—who may well be the only one who knows precisely what he wants and doesn't want—have something wrong with *me*?" He tugged on his hair. "My locks will never be unlocked. My teeth"—and he pointed to them—"will never be rootless." He placed his arms firmly akimbo. "I will always crow but never have crow's-feet. My forehead will wrinkle in thought, but never remain that way. My body will never die a hundred little deaths, and I will never know what it is to grow up and spend the rest of my days running about trying to find forms of amusement that will be nothing but pale imitations of the entertainment to be found here in the Anyplace. And, best of all, I will never have to count on people."

"For what?"

"For anything. If Gwenny, if you and the others flew away tomorrow, I would be just fine on my own. I was betrayed once in my life already, thank you very much, and by adults. I'm damned if I'll ever trust another, and double damned if I am to become one."

"You're referring to your parents barring the windows, preventing your return."

"I am," said The Boy icily. "That's why your mother is not worth the fuss you're making over her wants and needs, Paul. I guarantee you that, were the situation reversed, she wouldn't be doing the same for you."

Paul drew himself up, and, although he made no motion to attack, there was stern warning in his tone. "I grieve that your mother did you such injustice, Boy," he said, "but dare not speak ill of mine. Is that understood?"

It is impossible to say whether The Boy understood or not. He had no sense of tact, no comprehension of boundaries. How could he know that he stood in danger of crossing a line when he knew not where the lines were?

What might have occurred between The Boy and Paul had The Boy continued his verbal assault on Paul's mother can only be imagined. And so I leave it to your imagination, with full confidence that you will be able to conjure it on your own time. For matters are now proceeding apace that will force us to leave their animated discussion behind.

A low growl emanated from the forest nearby. Paul froze where he was, all the blood draining from his face. It was impossible for him to determine exactly where the sound was coming from. It seemed to be everywhere at once.

The Boy had immediately assumed a defensive posture. He was holding his sword in an entirely different manner from the lackadaisical way he'd been handling it before. His grip was tight, but he wasn't choking it, and his arm was loose and limber. Unlike Paul, who was trying to get some idea of where the creature was, The Boy was instead watching Paul to see how he reacted. Paul's momentary panic seemed to amuse him.

"Is that it? Is . . . that him?" Paul whispered.

"I should think so," said The Boy. Paul hadn't noticed it before, but the tips of The Boy's incisors were slightly extended, so it almost looked as if he had fangs. Or perhaps they simply got that way for special occasions such as this. Paul wouldn't put anything past him. The Boy's nostrils flared and he nodded once in approval. "I smell him. He's upwind of us. That was a mistake."

"You think he made a mistake?"

"Either that or he simply doesn't care."

Paul barely had time to take in that bit of information. Suddenly the underbrush crashed apart in either direction, and the snow tiger fairly exploded into the clearing. It was not a huge clearing, perhaps ten feet by twenty, with tall trees lining the edges. To Paul it seemed microscopic, barely enough room for the tiger himself, much less for the tiger, Paul, and The Boy.

The snow tiger landed in a crouch, his head whipping back and forth, his tail snapping around. His teeth were bared, and a rumble like a thousand freight trains emerged from his throat. It was at that moment that Paul realized just what a degree of safety his dreaming had provided him when it came to encounters with the snow tiger. After all, if anything had gone wrong, he would simply have woken up. That was not an option this time.

"Ho, creature!" said The Boy. He was not on the ground any longer but instead floating several feet in the air. His sword was at the ready, and he looked prepared to make short work of his growling opponent. "Now thou shalt pay for thy murderous pursuits! At least take some solace in that you are to be killed by the finest hunter in the land!"

If the tiger understood anything of what The Boy had said, he certainly gave no hint of it. Instead he pitched his head back and roared defiance. It was so loud that Paul thought he might go deaf if the tiger did it too much. It was so powerful that the sheer blast of it caused The Boy to bounce about like a cork bobbing in the ocean. He recovered quickly, though, and swept his sword down. It nicked the tiger's right ear, and the tiger lunged upward at the levitating Boy. The Boy barely got out of the way in time, but Paul quickly realized that that was the entire point. The Boy was trying to stay as near the tiger as possible, to court death, to stay just that far out of reach but no farther. It was either to give the beast a sporting chance, or else to display his own wonderfulness by providing the tiger every opportunity to catch him and then fall short.

The Boy ricocheted from one side of the clearing to the other, and the tiger pursued him. It was amazing to watch the pure white tiger in action, sharing so many similarities to small cats that Paul had seen wandering about the streets of home any number of times. But the snow tiger was so much larger, so much more dangerous, that despite the resemblance, it was hard to credit that they were part of the same biological family.

The tiger pivoted, getting closer to The Boy with each thrust, but The Boy continued to jab at him and remain just out of reach, laughing the entire time. His laughter infuriated the beast all the more, and finally Paul said, *"Leave him alone, Boy! Let me talk to him!"*

Paul's outcry stopped the tiger in mid-lunge. He fell back to all fours and his eyes narrowed, studying Paul with a curious tilt to his head that made him almost look like a large canine. His tail, which had been sweeping about with such force that it was almost a weapon on its own, promptly dropped to a lazy, slowly swishing manner that suggested polite curiosity on the part of its owner.

"Paul?" said the tiger.

A grin split Paul's face, and instantly he felt all the tension seeping out of him. "You remember me?"

"Of course I remember you. I didn't recognize you at first because you had a scent. I'm not used to you having a scent because usually you're dreaming when we're together, and dreams have no scents...except to pixies. They can smell anything, anywhere."

The Boy was looking from one to the other, his brow furrowed. "Are you talking to him? Is he talking to you?"

"Yes. Can't you tell?"

"I can tell what *you're* saying. He just sounds like growling to me."

"But you taught me to talk to animals!"

"I taught you how *you* could talk to animals. I can't do it myself."

Paul didn't understand the difference, but The Boy did; and as always, that was all that mattered to the Boy. "What did he just say?"

"There's no scents in dreams."

"Well, *I* could have told you that." The Boy sounded a trifle put out, and I think you know the reason quite readily: An individual with such a monumental ego as The Boy could scarcely tolerate the notion that there was someone in the Anyplace who could do something he himself couldn't do. And Paul's facility at talking to animals certainly fell under that category. The Boy was just going to have to deal with it as best he could, which is to say, not particularly well. He was, in fact, so annoyed that he forgot to fly and moments later his feet were resting on the ground. He waited for the snow tiger to notice this and make a run at him. But no: The tiger was too busy chatting with Paul. This meant that The Boy was no longer the center of attention, and this galled him deeply.

Paul was oblivious to all this. He was too busy speaking with his tiger. He walked cautiously toward the great beast and ran his fingers through his fur. He was amazed at the totally different sensation when he was awake. The texture was the same, but there was also the warmth from the pulsing blood that flowed through the beast's hide. The snow tiger felt so much more alive, rather than just a fantasy construct.

"How came you here?" said the snow tiger.

Paul summarized it as best he could. The Boy, who already knew this and might even have forgotten it by now, yawned loudly. The tiger nodded thoughtfully, taking it in, while Paul scratched the tiger's chin.

"A worthy goal," the tiger said finally. "A worthy quest, finding a new sister. I hope you don't turn away from it, or that death doesn't overtake you in your pursuit, leaving your quest unfulfilled."

This was a startling notion to Paul. "I didn't think that was possible. I mean...don't quests always succeed? Isn't that the nature of quests?"

"Oh, not at all," said the snow tiger. Looking utterly unthreatening, he had curled himself up on the ground and was resting his great head upon his fearsome paws. Paul had shifted to scratching the top of the cat's head just behind his ears, and they flattened in response. "Most quests end in failure."

"Are—are you sure? I mean, in every quest I read about, good triumphs over evil."

"Those are the rarities. The exceptions. Why else do you think those are the ones that are written about? No one wants to write about the failed quests. There's far too many of them, and all they do is reinforce what everyone already knows deep in their heart: Evil tends to triumph over good, and a hero is someone who rushes headlong to death while singing hosannahs." The tiger looked up at him, puzzled. "You stopped scratching my head. Why?"

"I just...I was surprised, that's all. All the times I've run with you, all the times I've known your strength...when I was with you, I always felt like there wasn't anything I couldn't do. And now the things you're saying—"

"You've seen me in dreams," the tiger reminded him. "Dreams are for the sleeping mind to tell lies to itself. To make of the world what it wants. Now you're awake, and I am still your friend and devoted tiger. But I will not lie to you. Not ever. That's how you know I'm your friend."

"This is boring," The Boy said, not having understood anything the tiger said. "Remind him that I'm here to kill him, and the night is not getting any younger."

"You're not going to have to kill him," Paul said, and then turned back to his tiger. "The Boy thinks he's going to have to kill you."

"Why would he think that?" said the snow tiger.

"Because the Piccas believe that you've been hunting down their braves and killing them."

"Oh. Yes. That's right."

The tiger replied so matter-of-factly that Paul didn't comprehend at first. "What do you mean . . . ?"

"I mean, yes, that's right, I've been hunting down and killing Picca braves. And then eating them," he added as an afterthought. "I wouldn't want you to think that I was just doing it for sport."

Paul started to feel short of breath, and there was a pain in his chest that he realized with some amazement was his heart breaking. "But—but I don't understand! Why? Why would you do such a thing?"

"Because I am a hunter. I do what I'm created to do. Just as you do."

"But the Piccas are afraid of you! They sent us to kill you!"

"I cannot blame them," the snow tiger said, sounding unconscionably reasonable about the whole matter. "If I were the Piccas, I'd probably want to do something about me."

"What's going on?" The Boy said. "Is he the one we want or isn't he?"

"He's not," Paul said immediately, instinctively, but his inability to meet The Boy's level gaze betrayed his pathetic attempt to dissemble. "Okay, yes, he is . . . but he doesn't understand—"

"What is there to understand?" The Boy once again had his sword at the ready. Noticing the gesture, the snow tiger turned to face the threat that The Boy represented. "He's a killer, Paul. A man-eater. However . . . there may be another way. A way that will not involve killing him."

"Truly?"

"No, not truly. I am tricking you, for I am grandnephew of Loki and cannot help myself. The truth is that his death will be a brave and magnificent one at my hands, but die he must. There's nothing else for it."

"Shut up, Boy!" Paul said as he darted around, placing his fragile body between the crouching form of the tiger and The Boy who was preparing to do battle with him. "I don't accept that!" He pivoted and faced the snow tiger. "Look . . . maybe . . . maybe we can still fix this. You can go with us to see the Piccas . . . . I can help you explain that you won't do it anymore."

The tiger pondered this, and then said, "Tell me, Paul: Know you the tale of the scorpion and the frog?"

"Yes, yes," Paul said impatiently. "But this isn't the time—"

"Tell me."

"But you can't—"

"*Tell* me," repeated the tiger, this time with such force that it caused Paul to jump slightly.

Paul gulped once, feeling as if there was a great blockage in his throat. "There was a scorpion, stranded by a rising river. He asked a passing frog for help. For a ride to the shore. The frog was naturally worried that the scorpion would sting him. But the scorpion pointed out that he'd be foolish to do so, because he was depending on the frog to save him. So the frog, convinced, allowed the scorpion to ride on his back. As the frog swam the river, halfway across, the scorpion stung him. The frog, drowning and dying, asked the scorpion why he had done such a foolish thing, since he had doomed them both. And the scorpion said, 'I couldn't help it. It's my nature.' "

"Well told. Very well told," said the snow tiger approvingly. "It's the same with me, Paul. I would never hurt you because I belong to you. But it is my nature to hunt and kill. I could tell you that I will never chase down Picca braves again. Perhaps I would even mean it at the time. But I know myself and my nature, and sooner or later—probably sooner—I would do as my nature commands me to. So I know now that I would be lying to you, and I won't do that anymore."

The Boy, meanwhile, was at the end of his tether. His body was practically vibrating with anticipation over the pending battle, and watching an ongoing conversation—only half of which he could comprehend—was more than he could handle. *"Enough!"* he finally said, and stood defiantly with his sword pointed straight at the tiger. "Have at you, beast!"

"My pardons, Paul," said the tiger politely. "I have to go kill your friend."

And then, with no hesitation between word and action, the snow tiger spun and lunged directly at The Boy.

Fortunately The Boy was ready for it, or he would have been done for right there. Instead he leaped skyward, laughing and delighting in his own cleverness, as the tiger's lunge came up short. The fearsome claws raked the air, missing The Boy clean. The Boy then returned the thrust, jabbing with his sword, hoping to get a clean stroke at the tiger that wasn't impeded by teeth or talons.

But The Boy missed the tiger as well, and that initial encounter set the pace for much of the battle that followed. Jab and thrust, bob and weave, attack and retreat—a cruel dance between boy and beast, each trying to seek out the slightest weakness or hesitation that they could quickly, fatally exploit.

Paul tried to shout to both of them, but neither was paying attention. They both knew what Paul had yet to admit to himself: The time for talking was past, if it had ever existed at all.

Down came The Boy, and he would thrust quickly, pinking the tiger's hindquarters or outthrust paw before bounding upward again. He never strayed far; part of the amusement for him was staying as close as possible to his prey, just out of reach, thus frustrating and angering him all the more.

There was nothing in the snow tiger's bearing or actions that remotely reflected the calm, discerning creature that had spoken so eloquently to Paul. Nor did he even resemble the occasional tiger that Paul had seen when his parents had taken him to a zoo, lying docile and bored and wondering when its next meal was going to be served. This was pure, undiluted ferocity that shook Paul to his core. He felt a swell of pity for the Picca braves who had been faced with this fearsome creature and gone to their deaths beneath his claws. At the same time, unaccountably, Paul also felt a tinge of pride. This was, after all, *his* tiger, and was he not magnificent in his ferocity?

He ceased his efforts to talk the two opponents away from each other, and instead simply stood there and watched the delicate dueling ballet. He lost track of how long it went on. Minutes, hours, all much the same in such a struggle; and over that period of time The Boy made some mistakes, and so did the tiger . . . an increasing number as their fatigue grew. The tiger was bleeding from a dozen small wounds, and was visibly slowing. The Boy had claw marks on his legs, and the upper portion of his tunic was badly shredded from a moment when he had gotten too close to his opponent.

The moon—the only possible measure of time—continued to climb in the night sky. It reached its zenith, midnight, the witching hour; and it was at that exact moment that the snow tiger apparently decided to run away.

The Boy's breath was ragged in his chest, and the snow tiger sounded as if he had a locomotive straining in his torso. In all the battle, though, the two of them had never dropped their gaze one from the other. Their eyes had remained locked in a struggle that was as much mental as it was physical. Suddenly the tiger broke that locked gaze, turned tail, and ran as hard as he could for the outer rim of the clearing.

"*Coward!*" said The Boy, startled for a moment, but only a moment, and then he flew in pursuit of the snow tiger.

Paul had no idea what to make of this sudden turn of events. If there was one thing upon which he would have staked his life, it was that his tiger was incapable of pusillanimity and would never flee a battle save as some sort of trick.

As it so happened, Paul was absolutely correct.

The tiger reached the edge of the clearing at full speed, but he did not exit it as The Boy had expected. Rather than running between the trees to escape, the snow tiger instead ran about halfway up the nearest tree. The tree bent back, elastic like a palm tree rather than rigid like an oak. The tiger, using both his own momentum and the tree's flexibility, catapulted himself backward, twisting in midair and angling upward.

The Boy, meantime, had headed downward, anticipating having to get below the tops of the trees in order to keep an eye on the snow tiger. Consequently, he was caught completely by surprise when he found himself looking straight at the oncoming teeth and outstretched claws of the snow tiger. The Boy hesitated a split instant, not sure which direction to go, and that was all the opportunity the snow tiger needed. He collided with

The Boy in midair. The Boy, knowing he was in dire straits, thrust hard and true with his sword. The point glanced off one of the tiger's ribs, leaving a cut and a trail of blood, but otherwise doing the tiger no serious harm.

The tiger thudded to the ground, The Boy directly beneath his paws. The impact was so bone jarring that Paul felt it from where he was standing a short distance away.

The tiger roared in triumph. The Boy tried to bring his sword around again, to drive it into the tiger's throat. But the tiger whipped his head around, catching the flat of the blade and sending the sword tumbling from The Boy's hand. The Boy tried to squirm out from under the tiger and grab for his weapon; but he had no chance. The tiger brought his left forepaw down hard on The Boy's chest, immobilizing him. The Boy looked straight up into the wide-open mouth of the tiger, the mouth that would—within seconds—close upon his face and likely tear his head from his shoulders. Not once did The Boy cry out, and there wasn't a hint of fear in him. Instead he seemed almost fascinated, as if he were wondering what it would feel like to be eaten alive by a raging tiger.

But if The Boy was mute, Paul was far more vocal. "*Get away from him!*" he screamed at the tiger. Acting completely from instinct, with no other goal than to get the tiger's attention, Paul threw his sword as hard as he could toward the tiger's head. His intent was to bounce the weapon off the beast's skull, in the increasingly vain hope that he could distract him. Perhaps even talk sense into the beast and salvage the situation.

His aim was both terrible and providential.

The blade came nowhere near the tiger's skull, nor to striking it with the flat of the blade as had been Paul's admittedly meager plan. Instead, the sword pinwheeled through the air and, with the blind luck that had not been accorded The Boy's more seasoned thrust, embedded itself in the snow tiger's side. It slid between the third and fourth ribs and skewered the mighty creature's heart.

Never in the whole history of the animal kingdom had any creature looked quite as surprised as did the snow tiger. He lifted his paws clear of The Boy, who lay on the ground and appeared as stunned as the snow tiger himself over the turn of events.

The tiger looked up at Paul, who was stricken by what he had done. "I'm—I'm sorry," said Paul softly. He had read any number of times that one should never get near a wounded animal; that that was when they were the most dangerous. That didn't stop him from approaching the snow tiger. "I—I was just..."

"You've killed me," rumbled the snow tiger, sounding hurt and confused but also somehow resigned to the fact. He slumped over. "I've run with you...since before you remember. You've killed your childhood."

"I didn't mean to...."

There was a low noise in the tiger's throat that sounded almost like a laugh. "No one ever means to. That's usually how it happens...by accident."

Paul reached for the tiger's great muzzle, and there were tears rolling down the lad's face. The tiger's head was heavy and Paul sank to the ground. The tiger rested his head in Paul's lap, and Paul started scratching him behind the ears. "You were a good tiger," he whispered.

"You were a good friend," said the tiger, and then he closed his eyes.

The Boy was about to airily inform Paul that he had never truly been in any danger. That he had a handle on the situation and was simply trying to lure the tiger into a false sense of security so that he could make the decisive strike at exactly the moment when the tiger was certain of his triumph. In short, in order to salve his ego, The Boy was prepared to lie through his pearly white teeth.

But he did not do so. Instead he simply stood there in silence.

Nothing stirred in the Anyplace for some time, and the only sound to be heard in the entirety of the island was the soft sobbing of Paul Dear.

Chapter 13

Slash on the Rocks

In order to accord Paul a respectful mourning period, let us draw a curtain upon the previous scene and instead shift our attentions to the schemes of Captain Slash and her tormenting of Fiddlefix.

Pity poor Fiddle. The torment resulted in her betrayal of The Boy, but we must not upbraid her overmuch for this. All of us like to believe that—were we to have torment inflicted upon us in order to encourage our turning upon those whom we love or are loyal to—we would remain steadfast in our convictions. Everyone is the hero of his own personal story. But I think we are all honestly aware that no man (or pixie or sprite, for that matter) knows his true measure until confronted with the reality. To that end, we again ask that you extend some degree of compassion to Fiddle rather than judge her harshly, since you never know when you might find yourself in a similar situation and crave the indulgence of others after the fact.

Fiddlefix had been through an emotional roller coaster. First she had thought that The Boy had betrayed her. Then she had been restored to the land of the living, burning for revenge against he whom she had loved more than herself. Then she had learned that the betrayal was a false one and that he himself had been a dupe . . . only to be left behind when The Boy, Paul, and his companions fled the *Skull n' Bones*.

Now we know that the others were unaware that Fiddlefix had been captured by the evil Slash. Had they known, they would have returned for her straightaway. But as you saw, there was a great deal of hugger-mugger involved in the retreat (a word that, even now, The Boy bristles over) and, well . . . the Anyplace tends to play tricks with the memory of its residents. Consequently, The Boy, Paul, Gwenny, and the others were so caught up in their immediate need and their involvement with the Picca Indian tribe that Fiddlefix had—temporarily—slipped through the cracks of their attention.

Given enough time, surely they would have realized that her absence was far too prolonged to be chalked up to the flighty nature of pixies. They would have put their collective deductive power together. It would have been insufficient to— for instance—capture the Napoleon of Crime. But it would have been enough to make them realize that Fiddlefix was very likely in the hands of the pirates and needed immediate succor.

But events conspired to overtake our heroes, as events often do.

We are, however, getting slightly ahead of ourselves.

Let us focus, instead, on Fiddlefix in her prison.

The prison was a simple metal box, with no light and only a tiny hole drilled in the top to allow air to seep through. So stale was the atmosphere within the box itself, even with the ventilation hole, that Fiddle was reduced to pressing her tiny nose right up against the hole in order to try and take in a few draughts of fresh air. She repeatedly choked back sobs over her situation, while at the same time angrily pounding on the interior of the box with her fists. Fiddlefix's strength was formidable. But the box was quite durable and easily able to withstand her pounding, even though she kept hitting it until her knuckles started to bleed. Once that happened, she sat there with her legs curled up, miserably sucking on the wounds and lamenting her lot in life.

But that wasn't the worst of it.

The worst was the shaking.

With no warning, at random times, whether she was awake or asleep, Fiddle's box would suddenly be lifted and shaken violently. The poor pixie would be thrown around inside; slamming up, down, and sideways; helpless to do anything about it except cry out in protest. Her protest was, naturally, ignored by her tormentor. And her tormentor, as you've undoubtedly surmised, was Captain Slash.

Fiddle completely lost track of time. Her life had been reduced to darkness, confinement, stale air, and violent shakings. So, as strange as it may seem, the unexpected sound of Captain Slash's purring voice was something Fiddlefix actually welcomed. If nothing else, it was a break from everything else.

"Poor thing," cooed Slash. "Trapped here by pirates. Helpless to control your destiny. Not much of a life for you, is it?"

Fiddlefix uttered some relatively foul curses in pixie language. Either Captain Slash didn't understand them or else she simply ignored them.

"You know you're at my mercy, don't you?" Slash said. "The Boy has forgotten you, as he tends to do. Gwenny never liked you in the first place."

"Paul . . ." Fiddlefix managed to say.

"You mean that other lad?" said Slash, who, as it happened, was quite conversant in pixie language. "He'll do what the rest of them tell him to do. He was just as eager to fly away as any of them. You're on your own, my dear pixie. They're not coming back for you."

Fiddle slammed her open hands against the interior of the box, and she was trembling with indignation. But she was also as helpless as Slash claimed her to be, and she knew it; and, worse, Slash knew that she knew it.

She barely had time to ponder her situation before she was being knocked about all over again. She tried to grab something to hold on to, but it was purely instinct. She knew that there was nothing there upon which she could seek purchase.

Then the shaking stopped. The box was being held sideways, so Fiddlefix had slid down into a far corner of it. Her legs were drawn up tightly to just under her chin. She was trying not to cry because she didn't want Slash to hear her sounds of despair, and she knew that Slash was still holding the box.

"I could, of course, just toss you over the side," Slash said. "That little hole I'm sure you find so inadequate for air will be more than adequate to let water through. It would take a while, although not quite as long as you probably think. And then you would drown, down in the briny deep, alone and lost and forgotten. Farewell to Miss Fiddlefix. Not exactly the end you had in mind, is it, my pretty pretty? Or would you just like me to keep repeating 'I don't believe in you know whats' until you drop dead once more . . . this time forever, I assure you?"

Fiddlefix clapped her hands over her ears, not wanting to even chance hearing the forbidden phrase. As a result she didn't initially hear Slash's next comments, but then took the chance and lowered her hands just enough.

"—have to be that way," Slash was saying to her. This

caught Fiddle's attention. "If you help me," Captain Slash continued, "I would be happy to help you. Just tell me what The Boy fears. What is his weakness?"

"He fears nothing. He has none. Now let me go."

"Then let's take it from another angle," Slash said, making her voice sound sweet as honey. "Who hates The Boy? Who would ally with me to dispose of him for good? Who would stop at nothing, care about nothing, if it meant ending him?"

"Well, that would likely be everyone in the Anyplace," Fiddle said. "After all, you and your despicable brother turned him into a pirate. He's likely feared and loathed by the entire population."

Captain Slash laughed at that. "I think you underestimate The Boy, pretty pretty. I would venture to guess that, even now, he is reforging old alliances with such former friends as the Indians. Once he has recaptured their goodwill, it's only a matter of spreading word to everyone else on the island that The Boy was treated ever so badly by cruel, heartless pirate folk. Cast us as the villains once more. We're used to it."

"You *are* the villains."

"Eye of the beholder, pretty pretty." She shook the box once more, more violently than ever, and was rewarded with more squeaks and squawks; and she didn't cease doing it until she actually heard Fiddlefix beg for mercy. Even then, she kept it going for a few moments more, just to drive home the point that she was completely in charge of the situation. Then she stopped, although she heard Fiddlefix's body rattling around for a short time before it rolled to a stop. "You know The Boy better than anyone. You know the island of the Anyplace better than anyone. Your wings, your tiny size give you free rein to move about as you see fit. And now I'm asking you to tell me: Who will help me destroy him?" She paused and then added,

"There's no point in loyalty, you know. He's not coming back for you. None of them are. None of them care."

We will condense this back and forth for you, for in fact it went on for quite some time. We don't want you to underestimate Fiddlefix's resistance to Slash's words or to think that the pixie gave in so easily to the pirate queen. But we don't want to belabor matters either, or dwell excessively on poor Fiddle's torment. It will provide excessive stage time for a nasty egg such as Captain Slash and certainly diminish your enthusiasm for the tale we have to tell. So, without telling you how long it took, except to say it was a long time, Fiddlefix finally broke down and told Captain Slash exactly what Slash wanted to know. Fiddle did this in exchange for a promise of her freedom. That should give you some idea of just how desperate the beleaguered Fiddlefix was that she capitulated to Slash on the basis of a promise from a pirate . . . a promise that was worth about exactly, not one farthing more or less, what you would think it was worth.

Consequently, Fiddle and her locked box were set safely back in storage in the captain's cabin. The captain then set sail for the far side of the island, heading straight for the individuals whom Fiddlefix had named.

She stood upon the forecastle, the wind whipping past her, and she saw her brother's shadow stalking the deck. Big Penny was giving the shadow a wide berth, as were the other Bully Boys; and even the fiercest of the Moriscos seemed disconcerted by the disembodied silhouette's presence. This didn't surprise Captain Slash all that much. Pirates were generally averse to the unnatural. So although the shadow of their former captain had been initially welcome, particularly when it gave them leverage in the battle against The Boy and his cohorts, the shadow's continued presence tended to discomfit them.

It might have helped if the shadow had had voice to accompany it. If it had stalked the ship being verbally abusive, that would have seemed a more customary state of affairs. But it just hung about, eerie in its silence. Captain Slash, however, felt no need to address the matter. As long as her crew got its job done, it was all she required.

Caveat, the craftiest of the Bully Boys, approached Slash at one point and said in a lowered voice, "Captain . . . begging your pardon, but . . . I know this particular route. It puts us in severe peril of drawing too near the Seirenes. Their nests are—"

"I am very aware of that, Caveat," she said. "That is where we are heading. I have it on"—and she smiled that terrible smile—"good authority . . . that they would be willing to aid us."

"But their song . . ."

"I know that as well. It does not concern me, though, and I have made allowances." She had a pumice stone and was calmly sharpening the curve of the blade upon her arm. She looked askance at Caveat. "Are you doubting the wisdom of my decisions?"

"No," Caveat said quickly, as she knew he would, for he was far too craven for any sort of direct confrontation. Quickly he scuttled off toward the far part of the ship, leaving Slash smiling to herself.

Some minutes later, she ordered the ship to drop anchor. She was sure she could hear sighs of relief from the crew, since the word had spread that they were coming within range of the Seirenes and no man aboard was ecstatic over that prospect.

Once the ship was anchored, Captain Slash ordered a longboat to be put into the water. What with her being the captain, it would have been unseemly for her to row herself. But bringing any male within proximity of the Seirenes represented unconscionable risk. Fortunately, there was an easy solution. Remember that there are some pirates we have not yet named.

We will name one of them now: Fearless Earless, a buccaneer who had the misfortune to run afoul of the East India Trading Company early in his career. His ears had been severed in punishment for his piratical practices. It didn't make him entirely deaf; just mostly deaf. So the only way he was able to hear orders was if someone walked up and practically shouted them into the side of his head. Since that was far too much effort, mostly he was left alone to sit around and deal hands of solitaire.

He was particularly useful in hand-to-hand assaults, since he was usually unable to hear shouts of "Retreat!" As a result, he would keep on fighting beyond all sense of reason, and had single-handedly turned the tide on several occasions simply because he literally didn't know when to quit. Thus had "Fearless" been tacked onto the more obvious sobriquet of "Earless."

In this case, though, force of arms was not going to be required. Instead, Fearless Earless simply served as oar master for Captain Slash as the longboat set course for the nesting area of the Seirenes.

The longboat bobbed atop the water as Fearless Earless drew the ship closer to the shore. The sun was rising high. At that moment elsewhere in the Anyplace, the Piccas were having a grand celebration at which Paul was looking rather morose while The Boy and the others danced and gyrated around the Piccas' blazing campfire. So Captain Slash's assessment of The Boy returning to the good graces of the Anyplace's other denizens was being proven quite correct. But that was of little moment to her. Only her business with the Seirenes concerned her now.

There was an outcropping of rock that blocked her immediate view of the Seirenes, but the splashing of the longboat in the water undoubtedly alerted them to her presence. That was how the Seirenes always knew of the approach of potential victims. If unwary mariners happened to see them before they were in range of their voices, they would know enough to turn aside. But if they were upon them without knowing the dangers that awaited, then the Seirenes could lure them close with the summoning call of their song.

Fearless Earless had a bit of a time maneuvering the longboat around stray pieces of wreckage that dotted the area from previous unfortunate travelers. Directly in front of the Seirenes' lagoon was a shoal of devastating rocks, hidden beneath the water's surface. Directly in front of the rocks was a gargantuan drop-off. As a result, ships drawn toward the lagoon courtesy of the Seirenes' song would strike the rocks, take on water, and then sink into oblivion, down and down into the drop-off never to be seen again. But a few random pieces of masts and such had caught on stones, and those were what Fearless Earless had to attend to as the longboat approached the lagoon. The fearsome rocks were too far below the surface to be of concern to the smaller, lighter boat, although naturally they were fatal to any of the far heavier sailing vessels that dared draw near.

Nevertheless, Captain Slash had no desire to draw too close to the Seirenes themselves, for who knew what additional obstacles might present themselves as traps? The outer shoals might prove no danger, but Slash wasn't overlooking the possibility that there might be more jeopardy within. That was why Fearless Earless was essential to her endeavors: Any other man at the oars would have felt compelled to keep right on rowing toward the Seirenes, no matter what orders to the contrary Captain Slash might issue. For that matter, had it been Slash's brother at the helm, he would have been perfectly willing to order the longboat speeding forward to its likely doom. But since Fearless was largely deaf and Slash was female, neither was at risk.

The Seirenes were singing their alluring melody at full strength now. It was light and airy, but at the same time there was a sense of timeless sadness about it, like something that might be produced by a lark that had seen its mate and off-spring torn to shreds one by one. Captain Slash could sense the attraction that the song might provide in the same way that a sober judge could, upon sipping a glass of sherry, comprehend in a distant manner the glorious wonders that excess imbibing might provide. But the sober judge would feel no personal compulsion to partake, and Slash was no different in her disposition. The blue water was astoundingly clear, and she could see the drop-off and shoals that provided her line of demarcation. She put up a hand, gesturing to Fearless Earless that he should cease his forward motion. He did so, putting up the oars. The water was flat and motionless this particular day, with not a shred of wind to gust it, so the longboat maintained its position easily.

From this vantage point, Captain Slash could easily behold the Seirenes. Their nest was elevated far above the waterline, with cliffs stretching high above and behind them. There were three of them: One with blond hair, one blazing red, and a third dark as the heart of the foulest villain. They shared one nest, and their long hair hung down and around their naked torsos, covering their bosoms discreetly. From the waist down, they had no need of hair covering: Their plumage more than sufficed. As human as their torsos were, from hip to toe they were a bizarre combination of human female and bird. Their legs were festooned with wild purple feathers, and they ended not in normal feet, but in three-toed talons—two forward, one reversed—as a parakeet might have. Although they had human hands, their arms were covered with feathers, these overlaying one another and with a skeletal structure that gave the arms the distinct likeness of wings. Their eyes had an avian look to them, with gleaming yellow irises.

Their nest was extremely large to accommodate the three of them. They had brought their heads close together, perhaps the better to harmonize. But when they saw who had drawn near, and that it was a female at the helm and a man who for some reason was immune to their musical blandishments, they promptly ceased their song and merely looked irritated. The raven-haired one, whom Captain Slash had correctly intuited was the leader, flapped her wings in irritation and then drew them around herself like a bat. She tilted her head slightly. When she spoke, there was still a musical, singsong quality to her voice that reminded Slash of a Jamaican lilt.

"Who are you?" said the Seirene. "What brings you to this place?"

"I am Captain Slash, a humble pirate. I seek your help."

This brought a good deal of twittering from the Seirenes, who thought this was simply the funniest thing they had heard in many a day. But their chorus of birdlike laughter abruptly ceased when Captain Slash said, "I seek your help against The Boy."

The Seirenes cried out as one then, in a combination of fury and pain; and then the black-haired one stilled the outrage of the other two as she perched on the edge of their nest. "What know you of The Boy?"

"I know that you both despise him and covet him," said Captain Slash. "I know that you have wanted him to remain with you forever and always."

"Who told you such things?"

Captain Slash thought of the trapped pixie and yet again smiled her awful smile. "Someone who would know."

"He flies!" said the Seirene, as if the source of the information was no longer of interest. "The Boy flies! And he sings pretty songs. Why should he not be with us forever and always? We have begged him and pleaded with him to remain with us and be ours, and we would love him if he would only love us, for we are so very similar. But he denies us! Refuses us! Will not give himself over to us! Instead he prefers to laugh and play and remain a boy always in the jungles of the Anyplace."

The redhead spoke up. "And every so often, he flies near us and calls down taunts over how foolish we are. If he remained with us, we would sing for him and only for him. No sailors need ever fear us again. But does The Boy care? He does not!"

"How does he remain immune to your song? Could you not force him to remain with the allure of your song?"

"His head is far too full of himself to become filled with us," said the blonde sourly. "We sing to him, and he whistles back a mockery of our song before flying away while laughing."

"Evil boy. Inconsiderate boy," said Slash in her most sympathetic voice. "And how long has this state of affairs been the case?"

"For as long as we can remember," said the raven-haired one. Naturally, since all three of them were somewhat birdbrained, it is impossible to determine exactly how far back that "as long as" really was.

"And you have allowed it to remain thus?" Captain Slash stroked her chin thoughtfully and shook her head. "I am frankly astounded, my deary dears. To think that beings as formidable as you would be satisfied with such a situation . . ."

That comment truly ruffled the Seirenes' feathers; and the black-haired one lifted high into the air, her wings beating furiously. She let out an angered cry. Fearless Earless was taken aback and was glad he couldn't hear her screeching protest.

Captain Slash winced and shook her head slightly to clear out her ears.

"*How dare you!*" said the black-haired one. "How dare you come here and presume to— Who are you to judge us?"

"Captain Slash," she told them again, but then added, "sister to Captain Hack, who suffered at the hands of The Boy to a legendary degree. The woman who wants to see vengeance taken upon The Boy even more than you do."

This reply seemed to appease the black-haired Seirene, and she slowed the beating of her wings, allowing herself to drop back to the nest. She cocked her head once more and said, "And what would you of us?"

"You," Captain Slash said, "can help me achieve it, and help yourselves as well. Satisfy your anger against The Boy and the Anyplace, where he hides and frolics and ignores you."

"How?"

"You know how," Captain Slash said. "You are Seirenes. You are daughters of Father Ocean, sisters of the storm, and they will all attend to you. You've had the ability forever and always, and you've simply never chosen to use it."

"We know not whereof you speak," the redhead said quickly, but too quickly to be convincing in her protest.

"I think you do," said Slash. "I think you know precisely whereof I speak, and you need only screw your courage to the sticking place in order to accomplish it."

The other two exchanged looks, and Slash knew at that point that they were considering it. But the raven-tressed one still looked very uncertain.

And so Captain Slash kept talking to them. She cajoled and complained and convinced; and whether it took longer or shorter than it did to convince Fiddlefix to cooperate, again we cannot tell. Know, though, that Captain Slash had something of a silver tongue, coated by Satan himself, and thus could eventually talk almost anyone into doing almost anything. In a way she had her very own Seirenes' song at her command.

It took her much of the day. Not until the sun began to sink into the sea did she finally convince them of the rightness of her beliefs and also of what she was asking them to do. Indeed, so persuasive and insinuating was she in their minds and hearts that, by the time she was done, the Seirenes were convinced that the entire notion she had proposed to them was, in fact, their very own.

Never has there been a more clear underscoring of the difference between men and women, at least as far as their villainous methods are concerned. The difference was exemplified in the very weaponry of the piratical siblings. Captain Hack believed that the solution to all problems was to chop away at them. If it was a living opponent, cut it to pieces until it ceased movement. If it was an obstruction, try to batter it out of the way.

The sword was a far subtler instrument than the hatchet. It slipped and slid into its opponent and could cut to the quick before anyone even knew they were under attack. That exemplified the tactics of Captain Slash, who insinuated herself into people, getting under their skins before they even realized that the blade had penetrated to its target. The late Captain Hack preferred to battle with his own "claws" barred; Captain Slash preferred the many advantages of cats' paws.

Now, having spent much of the day with the Seirenes and feeling it was time to leave them to their work, Captain Slash had Fearless Earless row her back to the *Skull n' Bones*. It was probably fortunate she returned when she did, for the crew was beginning to get concerned by her extended absence. So there was much pointing and cheering from the deck when Big Penny was the first to spot the two of them steadily rowing toward them. "Yo ho and view halloo!" said the brawny second in command.

"Prepare to weigh anchor!" Captain Slash said, even before the longboat got within range of the pirate vessel. Fearless Earless was rowing as hard as he could. "We need to bring the ship around to the leeward side of the island!"

"Aye, Captain! Expecting a turn in the weather?"

As the longboat drew aside the *Skull n' Bones,* with the ropes being lowered to haul her back up, Captain Slash grinned and said, "Oh, yes. A major turn. We're in for quite a blow . . . and, by the shadow of my brother, it's going to be The Boy who bears the brunt of it!"

Chapter 14

Foul-Weather Friends

For Paul Dear, the events following the death of his great and mighty companion of a thousand dreams were as blurred as any dream might have been...except, of course, that they were really happening. Long after the tiger had passed away, Paul remained curled up in its embrace, trying to will the warmth in its body to remain. Instead it ebbed away into nothingness. By the time it did, The Boy had already returned to the Piccas and informed them of what had transpired. A hunting party had been dispatched to follow The Boy. Initially there was some suspicion that The Boy was endeavoring to lead them into a trap. Since he claimed to be half brother to the trickster god Coyote, first cousin to Puck, grandnephew of Loki, it was certainly not beyond possible that he had schemed up some fatal prank to perpetrate upon the Indians. We know that was not the case, but the Piccas did not.

Still, when the hunting party was finally sent to follow The Boy, he brought them straightaway to the clearing that had borne witness to the death of something truly magnificent. They began to let out war whoops until they spotted Paul, and then they became uncharacteristically silent.

Paul didn't remember being gathered up into the powerful arms of Pouring Rain or being transported back to the Indian settlement. Nor was he aware that the braves were tying the snow tiger to a long pole and were carrying the dead beast to the camp as well. He wasn't asleep exactly, or even in shock. Instead, in a manner of speaking, he was hiding from and within himself, his spirit curled up deep within his mind and trying to tell all the world that he would very much prefer that they all went away, thank you.

It was smell that began to bring him out of his semicoma. Not all that surprising; smell is the most ignored of the five senses since we associate it mostly with animals, and yet it is also the most potent. Even the poor, pathetic sense that passes for smell in human beings (as opposed to the glorious olfactory prowess of just about any "lower" animal you could name) was an amazingly puissant force. So the aroma of burning meat wafted its way not only into Paul's nostrils but also his consciousness.

Slowly he became aware that it was daytime once more. He was no longer in the forest or even outside, but rather in a wigwam. Paul crept forward on hands and knees and peered out through the flap. Interestingly, he knew what he was going to see before he saw it.

There was a large carcass roasting on a spit in the middle of the camp. The appendages had been cut away and it was denuded of hide as well; and it was already cooked to such a golden brown that it could have been the body of a very large hog or an elk or just about anything.

But Paul knew what it was. He knew it was his tiger.

He was amazed how he was able to view such a sight with detachment. His tiger was dead. Nothing was going to bring it back. And everything that dies gets eaten, whether by worms in the ground or fish at sea or maggots or vultures. That was simply the way of nature, and one as attuned to nature as was Paul understood that fact better than most.

But although Paul understood it intellectually, he knew that he himself wasn't going to partake of the feast that was obviously being prepared. He couldn't eat his dear friend. He'd likely choke if he tried. That didn't mean he wasn't hungry, for he very much was, and his stomach was tying itself into mad knots of desire over the smell of the roasting meat. Paul was determined, though, and crossly told his stomach that it was just going to have to deal with the situation and that was all there was to it.

His rustling of the flap must have attracted notice, for a minute or two later Gwenny stepped in between the flaps and smiled at Paul. He hadn't had all that much time to take stock of her, and certainly no private time with her. He found her, on the whole, pleasant enough to look at. He had a sense that she was on the cusp of something, but couldn't quite guess what. Which was all right, because he was correct about the cusp bit; truthfully, even Gwenny wasn't entirely sure what was to become of her either.

She knelt down opposite him, her hands resting gently on her legs after smoothing her skirt. "Are you feeling quite all right?" she asked politely.

"Of course I'm not," Paul said. He wanted to shout at her, to demand of her how she could be a patient mother and friend to The Boy. How she could tolerate residing in this place of sadness and death that was cloaked in a false environment of abandon and adventure. But there was no point to it at all. She was just a girl, an older girl, trying to be polite and helpful to him; and even though she presented a convenient target for his distress, he couldn't bring himself to lash out at her. So he reined in all his vituperation and restrained himself to a simple, "I killed my tiger. I'm never going to be all right again."

"The Boy told us that," Gwenny said. "It was extraordinarily brave of you, I must say. And the most impressive thing of all is that The Boy gave you the credit for it."

"So?"

"So! That's monumental, that is!" Her eyes were wide with amusement. "No one but The Boy himself is the hero of his retelling of adventures. Even incidents that I know beyond question happened one way turn out an entirely different way when The Boy is involved. And he's so convincing in his oratory that I almost come to believe that it all occurred just the way he said."

"And that didn't happen in this instance?" Paul said, prompted by his curiosity in spite of himself.

"Oh, no!" Gwenny said. "No, not at all. He told us the whole thing. How he was about to deliver the fatal blow, but you thought that he was in dire straits and so you suddenly charged forward and, shouting 'This is the end of you, beast,' you drove home the point of your sword with unerring accuracy and..." She saw his change of expression and the truth began to dawn upon her. "It was nothing like that, was it?" she said.

Paul shook his head, and explained to her how his slaying the tiger was purely happenstance. How The Boy in fact *had* been in dire straits, with the tiger having him pinned and all, and how Paul had blindly flung his sword and a one-in-a-million chance landed the sword in between the tiger's ribs.

"Well," said Gwenny, with a shrug, "the Anyplace is a one-in-a-million land. So it shouldn't be all that surprising that one-in-a-million occurrences transpire here all the time. Still"—and she shook her head, making disapproving clucking sounds—"wicked, wicked Boy, to make it sound as if he was never in the slightest danger."

"Who knows?" said Paul. "The way his mind works, by this point he probably genuinely believes it. It's not wicked or a lie if you believe what you're saying, is it?"

"I'm not sure. That's always one of those questions that adults change their minds on, depending upon who's doing the asking and who's doing the lying." She paused and then said softly, "You should come outside. They're all done with . . ."

"Eating my friend?"

"The feast, yes," said Gwenny. "I hope you don't hold it against them."

"Did you . . . ?"

She looked down, her cheeks flushed. "Well . . . I didn't want to be impolite." When she saw his expression, she added quickly, "Besides, I never chatted with him."

"That shouldn't make a difference!"

"Well, it does. I mean, honestly . . . do you have any problem eating lamb chops?" Paul shook his head. "No? All right. Now how about if you knew the lamb before it was slaughtered? If you'd cared for it, or if it had been a pet of yours. Would you be able to eat it then if someone cooked it up and served it to you on a bed of rice?"

"Probably not," Paul said.

"There, you see? It's never a good idea to develop a personal relationship with a possible future meal."

Paul's chin sank into his hands and he sat there disconsolately. "I should never have come here. My parents say that some places are nice to visit, but you wouldn't want to live there. That's what this place is. The Anyplace. Nice to visit briefly, in your dreams. Pass through, see the sights, and then scurry back to your bed. But come and live here, and it does things to you."

"Oh, but we're not living here, you and me," Gwenny corrected him. "We're likewise just visiting—"

"Are we?" He gave her a piercing stare. "How do we know that? How long have you been here?" Now it was Gwenny's turn to shake her head, looking puzzled. "You lose track. Nothing is as it appears. For all we know, our homes are long, long left behind. We might only think that we've been here a short time. Maybe we've been here years. Or forever. Maybe it's our memories of our past lives that are the dreams. How do you know if you're truly alive?"

"Are you grieving for the loss of your tiger?"

"Yes."

"That's how you know," Gwenny said. "You don't feel grief in a dream."

"You don't know that for sure. You don't know anything for sure. That's the advantage of growing up. You know things for sure."

"I know," Gwenny said wistfully. "I wonder when that happens."

"What do you mean 'when'?"

"Well, I wonder if it happens all at once. Do you reach a certain age and suddenly everything comes into focus, like a camera lens? Or is it a gradual thing where you just become more and more sure until you realize belatedly that you're just sure of everything all the time?"

Paul shrugged. "Couldn't tell you." He chucked a thumb in the general direction of outside, indicating The Boy in a broad manner. "Do you think he ever wonders about such things?"

"No. He doesn't care. That's the joy of being him."

"I'm not sure if it's so joyful," said Paul, "or whether it's very, very sad." He paused, and then said, "What do you want to be? When you grow up, I mean."

Her eyebrows knitted. "A teacher, I think. Or perhaps a social worker. Maybe even a psychiatrist. Specializing in dream therapy... Wouldn't that be appropriate? Plus a mother, of course, with three children... two girls and one boy. Although, you know, a sports star might be nice. I do fancy skating. And dancing—I so love to dance." She paused. "Bother, you'd think I'd have it sorted out by now. What about you? What do you want to be when you grow up?"

Paul thought about it and then said, "Myself."

She looked at him skeptically. "Well... good luck with that. Pardon my saying, but I think that may be the hardest thing of all."

"You may be right."

There was a knock at the tent flap, which technically wasn't a knock since the canvas didn't allow for much of a true knocking sound. The flap peeled back slightly and Dog Licking Self peered in. "Princess Picca wish see you. Make present."

"I don't know that I'm in the mood to get any presents right now," Paul said.

Gwenny saw the expression on the warrior's face and turned quickly to Paul. "I think you'll find that when a princess says she wishes to see you, it's not the same as if you or I wish for something. You know, like when you blow out candles on your cake and toss out a wish in the hope that maybe it will happen, except maybe it won't. The wish of a princess is more of a command. And when the people who convey that wish carry sharp weapons, there really isn't a good deal of room for negotiation."

"Well then," Paul said, having no desire to cause problems with the Indians. "I suppose there's nothing else for it, is there?" He rose, shaking out his feet since they had quite gone to sleep while he was sitting cross-legged, and followed Dog Licking Self out into the center of the camp. Gwenny trailed behind.

The sun had long since set, and the full moon was already on the rise. It was at that point that Paul came to the realization the moon had been full ever since he had arrived. However long that was, it was certainly longer than a moon is typically full. He saw that the braves had formed a fairly large circle, and he was being ushered into the middle of it. He might have felt some faint tickle of alarm in the back of his head, but he was too morose about the entire situation to care. Torches were posted at the outer edges of the circle, casting illumination throughout the camp. That was fortunate, for large, dark clouds were moving across the moon, causing its light to be inconsistent.

The Boy was standing next to Princess Picca. She had her arms folded, as did he. She had a grave air about her, and Paul wondered what could possibly be going through her mind that she looked so serious. In looking around, he saw no sign of the barbecue that they'd been consuming, and for that at least he was thankful.

"Storyteller," she said with great intensity, "you help provide great service to Picca tribe. We prepare great honor for you in exchange."

"That's . . . very kind of you," Paul said, "but it really wasn't necessary."

"Was necessary. Is Picca way."

"I suggest you respect the Picca way," The Boy said, and there was something in his tone that seemed to carry a degree of warning.

Princess Picca raised one arm in a commanding fashion and gestured for something to be brought forward. Paul turned to see where she was pointing, and his jaw dropped, as several braves brought forward a large white bundle. He blinked several times, unsure that he was seeing what he thought he was seeing. "Is that...?"

"Tiger skin," Princess Picca said. "Prepared special for you. Wear mantle of tiger. Great honor. Greatest Picca can give. And new name. 'Storyteller' no longer best word for you. New name is..." and she paused for what seemed effect before thumping his chest lightly, "Tigerheart."

Paul's gut instinct was to run from the circle and hide back in the wigwam. He was utterly repulsed by the notion. Indeed, he was now remembering times when his mother would be wearing one of her furs, and he would nuzzle up against it and stroke it lovingly because it felt so soft and real. He'd never given a thought to the animals that had once been adorned by them. Now the previous owner of the fur was all he could think about.

And *Tigerheart?* A name earned at the expense of his oldest, dearest friend? What a terrible insult to the memory of his beloved snow tiger. It wasn't even accurate. "Chickenheart" would have been the more appropriate, for his own boy's heart had been thudding with terror against his rib cage during the entire encounter.

He was about to stammer out that he wanted no part of it— not of the skin and not of the name—but suddenly Gwenny was at his side, one hand resting on his shoulder. "Tigerheart thanks you for your gracious gift, and accepts it gratefully," she said in a loud voice. This response garnered smiles from the Piccas, and a number of the braves who were holding spears thudded the bottoms of the poles on the ground approvingly.

As the fur was brought toward him, Paul said to Gwenny in a low, desperate voice between clenched teeth, "I don't want it!"

"If you refuse it," Gwenny whispered back, "you will be insulting the Piccas. Worst-case scenario, they take such offense that they attempt to fill us full of arrows. The best-case scenario is that they simply refuse to ally themselves with us. Should that happen, not only do you never complete your quest but your tiger died for nothing. Now if any of those are acceptable to you, by all means, refuse it. But know the consequences if you do."

Paul trembled with indecision, guilt, angst, and a desperate wish that he was absolutely anywhere else than where he was at that moment. And while he vacillated, the Indian braves walked up to him and, with great ceremony, draped the skin of the snow tiger around his shoulders. They fastened it around his throat with a clasp. "Tigerheart, Tigerheart," they kept saying.

The instant the soft pelt was upon him, Paul felt an almost unnatural calm. More than calm, in fact. It was a sort of quiet inner strength, the type which he was quite certain his tiger had possessed. Although he knew that physically he hadn't changed, suddenly he felt taller. Stronger. The burning anger, the frustration, the despair . . . all of these melted away, leaving him quiet and confident in a way that he could only come up with one description: grown-up. He felt very grown-up.

Princess Picca walked toward him; and she was nodding, as if she understood what was going through his head. "You feel it, yes? You feel bravery. You feel greatness. You feel that which tiger felt. Yes, Tigerheart?"

"Yes," Paul said, not understanding why he was feeling that way or how Princess Picca could possibly have known.

"Was meant for you," she said. "You two sides of one rock. Same same. What was his, yours. Yours, his. Same same."

Her words made sense to him. Not only that—and he was fully aware that he might be imagining it—but he was certain he could hear the voice of the tiger in his head, telling him that this was all right and proper. That he had no use for the fur anymore and, if anyone was going to be wearing it, it should be Paul. That the tiger could now still feel the wind against him and continue to have just the faintest taste of what it felt like to be alive.

And more . . . if Paul had the heart of a hunter, the heart of a tiger, then wearing the tiger's fur gave him a sense of that heart and emboldened him in ways he would not have thought possible.

"I think maybe it happens all at once," he told Gwenny. She looked blankly at him at first, but then she understood and smiled.

"I thought it might," she said.

Paul turned to Princess Picca and bowed deeply. He was still somewhat uncomfortable with the fur and, particularly, the name, but at least he could acknowledge the Indians' good intentions.

The princess bowed in return, and then the Indians began the steady beat of their drums. Paul typically felt self-conscious when the prospect of dancing came up, but not this time. His feet began to move almost of their own accord. As the drumbeat increased, he bounded across the circle, spinning in front of The Boy, the edges of his tiger skin cape whipping out. The Boy grinned and vaulted toward him. The two of them began to do a mock version of hunter and hunted, each of them taking turns in which was which.

Other braves joined in, each leaping into the circle in turn. Princess Picca entered the dance as well, as did Irregular and Porthos and even Gwenny, who felt it wasn't really proper decorum to prance about with half-clad savages; but still she wanted to be polite.

The wind began to whip up far more fiercely, and the tops of the trees were shaking, but no one noticed. Or if they did, they simply took it to be an extension of the wild savagery in their hearts, and thus part of their celebration.

The entire circle was filled with gyrating bodies, slick with sweat and leaping about in a manner that seemed both chaotic and yet amazingly controlled, since they weren't crashing into each other willy-nilly.

So seized by his celebration of primal energy was Paul that he felt the very ground shaking beneath his feet and thought it merely part of the dance. It was The Boy who first began to sense that something was wrong. Smack in the middle of the celebration and its most enthusiastic participant, The Boy suddenly stopped dead center of it all, his feet planted firmly on the ground and his gaze riveted to the skies. Since he stopped moving, naturally this caused others to career into him. This could easily have been calamitous if they had taken offense at it. But when they righted themselves and glared at The Boy, they saw that his attention was fixed elsewhere and not upon them at all, not even in the slightest challenging fashion. Naturally they did what anyone does in such a situation: They looked at where The Boy was looking to see what it was that had so garnered his attention.

In short order, more people were standing still than were dancing, and finally everyone was looking up. Even the drummers had ceased their steady beat and were looking skyward.

They were staring at a full moon that had gone, for no apparent reason, blood red. If it were any more so, it would have been dripping.

"Is that . . . normal?" Paul whispered.

The Boy shook his head. "I've never seen it."

It was at that point that Paul realized something else, as everyone else did as well. Despite the fact that everyone had stopped dancing, the ground was continuing to shake. It had been mild at first, but it was beginning to increase in intensity.

The clouds had taken on the same sanguinary tint as the moon; and now the distant rumble of thunder rolled toward them, with flashes leaping across the sky. Paul had experienced many thunder and lightning storms in his life, and so had gotten into the habit of counting the period of time between sighting the lightning and hearing the thunder. The first time he saw lightning lash from the storm clouds, he rattled off a solid six-second count. But a couple of seconds later, when there was more lightning, he barely made it to three before he jumped from a crack of thunder. The storm was moving toward them unconscionably quickly.

And the ground was continuing to rumble.

"Something's coming," said The Boy grimly. "Something big." With that, he threw his arms to either side and rose into the air, soaring above the trees, trying to reconnoiter and get some sense of what was wrong.

There was the smell of both water and ozone in the air. Rain started to pour down upon the Piccas, first a few drops, but then a full-blown cascade. They began to run for their wigwams, but huge gusts of wind came roaring through. The wigwams were torn from their moorings, thrown about like leaves from a tree. Paul pulled the tiger skin tightly around himself, suddenly grateful for the warmth and security.

He looked up toward the treetops, trying to make out what The Boy was up to, and was shocked to discover that The Boy was nowhere to be seen.

The Boy, meanwhile, was soaring high above the trees, battling against the wind that seemed determined to toss him around like a ball skittering across a billiard table. The Boy was accustomed to battling enemies, but it was most disconcerting for him to be slapped around by what was essentially nothing . . . except it was nothing with the pounding power of a thousand hammers. The Boy flipped, flopped, boomeranged around, and fought to regain his equilibrium with every ounce of energy he possessed.

He managed to move beyond the edges of the island, his eyes searching for some hint of what was transpiring. And then he saw something in the distance; and the sight of it struck him cold.

The three Seirenes had relocated their nest to a very high point on an outcropping of a cliffside. They were singing, and even from the distance at which he was hovering, The Boy was able to discern the general tone and direction of the song. It was a song steeped in anger, jealousy, and frustration. He had heard them sing variations on the theme every time that he had taunted them into believing he would be theirs, only to bound away laughing at their foolishness for trusting him.

But that tone and direction were merely the melody line. There were grand embellishments now, a reedy tune transformed into a full concerto. Nor was the wayward Boy the target of their song, oh no.

The Seirenes were calling their parents.

Children of sea and sky they were, patron saints of the tempest tossed. The Boy was able to see vast, pounding waves reaching higher and higher, and in the folds of the waves he was able to discern a huge, bearded, scowling male face with black eyes and a beard of sea foam. And high above, the skies were black and terrible, and the rolling storm clouds bore a distinct resemblance to a woman's face. Lightning danced around where her hair would have been. The storm clouds and waves worked together too, feeding off their mutual energy and their mutual indignation over the story of woe and heartbreak being shared with them by their offspring.

Great gouts of water washed over the Anyplace, but The Boy knew those were merely precursors. Warning shots. He saw the true power of the Seirenes—or rather of their parents—building toward a frightening climax.

At that moment, his instinct was to battle his way through the air to the Seirenes. To try and sweet-talk them. Appeal to their better natures, presuming they had any. The Boy was very much a creature of the moment, and his solution for the moment was to tell the Seirenes anything they wanted to hear if it would put an end to the current siege.

He tried shouting to them, but the wind batted his words right back at him. He tried to fly toward them, to confront them, but the fearsome gusts shoved him away.

The Boy was helpless.

We must now take the briefest of side steps to address what we're sure has just occurred to you, in order to make clear that certain apparent inconsistencies are, in fact, not. And if these have not occurred to you, be not angry with us that we are interrupting our narrative for a short time to deal with them, but rather focus your ire on the quality of your education that you didn't notice what we are about to tell you.

The Boy had boasted earlier that nothing transpires in the Anyplace without his cooperation. Remember how we warned you that this was both true and false.

For all his abilities and bravado, The Boy remains a boy. Imagination is a two-way lane, and that which The Boy is able to convince is equally able to convince The Boy.

To put it as simply as possible: If The Boy believes that he is in trouble, then he is in trouble. If he believes he can be hurt, he is vulnerable. If he believes that forces are building that he is unable to deter, then whether or not he *could* stop them is beside the point. And if he believes he can die, then he is as mortal as any of us and will die.

If The Boy had been of sufficient resolve to believe that he could have used his boundless charm to talk the Seirenes out of their present course, then he might have been able to. *Might* have been. Nothing is for certain in the Anyplace, no matter how much The Boy might wish it otherwise.

Besides, if The Boy consistently engaged in such actions, then nothing would ever be a challenge for him. The Anyplace would be a realm of endless tedium and no fun. And The Boy, as you've gathered by now, places fun above all . . . even his own safety and the safety of others.

Thus is our digression ended, except to say this: Despite whatever influence The Boy may have over the Anyplace, at the moment, he is as helpless in the maelstrom of events as any leaf fallen from a tree.

The Boy saw not only the source of their troubles, against which he could do nothing, but also even greater difficulty and impending danger on the horizon, were there any horizon to speak of. Instead, the line at which the skies and sea came together had blurred, creating one great black mass. And from that great black mass was surging a great black wave, thundering in The Boy's direction and promising no end of grief once it arrived.

The Boy didn't hesitate. Instead he hurtled back toward the Indian encampment as quickly as he could. He arrived just as Princess Picca was urging her people to get to the caves for shelter, and then he swooped down and said, "No! Not the caves! We have to get to high ground! The highest ground there is! There's a tidal wave coming and the caves will be underwater!"

"Highest ground is Spire!" said Princess Picca, and she pointed to a great tower of rock that had been used for ceremonies long forgotten even by the elders of the tribe. "Only high ground there is!"

Paul looked where she was pointing. He didn't like what he was seeing. It was narrow and not easily climbable and quite a distance. He shouted up to The Boy, "Can we make it there before the wave gets here?"

The Boy surveyed the expanse to be covered and checked on the progress of the tidal wave. He realized that Paul had been right to express concern; they weren't going to make it. "No! The wave's coming in too quickly! You were right the first time! To the caves!"

"But, Boy," Gwenny said, "you said they'll be underwater!"

"They will! Don't worry. I'll take care of it! Hurry! Go, go!"

With the ground trembling fiercely beneath their feet, and sounds like a hundred charging elephants rumbling all around them, those on the ground wisely opted to heed The Boy's advice, self-contradicting as it was. They sprinted for the caves, practically tripping over one another in their endeavors to reach them before the unthinkable occurred.

The Boy sailed overhead, and he shouted down to them, "Whatever you do, don't look behind you!"

Naturally they all looked. Their eyes widened in shock and fear.

A wave, the biggest wave they had ever seen, was roaring up from far below. Higher and higher, until it seemed as if it were genuinely touching the sky in a dark lover's caress, before it started to thunder down toward them. The more imaginative of them might have sworn they saw a man's face, stretched and distorted but clearly filled with an elemental fury.

They ran into the caves, which were dark and dank but thankfully bereft of other occupants such as bears. Paul found himself in one with Gwenny, Princess Picca, and several of the other braves.

"We get flooded in here!" said one of the braves with a tremor in his voice that seemed to contradict the notion of his being "brave." "We all die!"

"The Boy will make sure that doesn't happen," Paul said, pulling the tiger skin more tightly around himself.

"You believe?"

"I believe," he said firmly.

"As do I," Gwenny piped up.

The water was coming closer and closer, and within seconds was going to come crashing down upon them. But Gwenny was facing the cave entrance with utter sangfroid, and Paul—who, despite his proud words, couldn't help but feel at least some degree of uncertainty over their imminent fate—tried his best to emulate her remarkable reserve in the face of impending disaster.

It was at that moment that they heard even more rumbling, this time from overhead. Paul looked up, his face a picture of misery. "Oh, *now* what?"

A few rocks fell in front of the cave mouth, and then a few more, and suddenly dozens were tumbling down, filling in the gap.

"An avalanche!" Gwenny said, realizing what was happening. "The Boy's created an avalanche!"

She was correct. The caves were set deep into the mountain, but there were plenty of loose rocks farther up the mountainside. The Boy had flown up to them, knocked some of the larger supporting boulders loose from their moorings, and seconds later had sent an entire cavalcade of stone tumbling down the sides of the mountain.

They had one last glimpse of the wave careening toward them, and then that view was obscured by the rockslide as it completely covered the opening of the cave. Seconds later the rocky "door" to the cave trembled under the staggering impact of the wave. Paul was terrified that the rock barrier would give way, but the opposite turned out to be the case: The wave hit the rocky barrier with such force that it compressed it, making it stronger rather than weaker. The makeshift barrier held.

They heard the water thundering past them, to the sides and above, and they clustered together for security. The cave was completely dark, the last bits of light extinguished as the rocks came together to form their shield. Paul had no idea who he was pressed up against until a soft but commanding voice said, "Watch hands there."

"Sorry, Princess. Can't even rightly see them," he muttered, repositioning his hands to a less personal area.

Finally the assault on their ears subsided. The sounds of the storm were still audible, but muted. Over time—although how much time, no one could possibly have guessed—even those sounds lessened until there was silence.

"Gwenny...do you think there's nothing but floodwaters around us?" whispered Paul.

"I don't know."

"What about The Boy? Do you think he survived?"

"I don't know."

"How are we going to get out of here if he didn't survive?"

"I don't know."

From the darkness, Princess Picca said in irritation, "Anything Gwenny-lady *do* know?"

"I know not to punch an Indian princess in the mouth for getting snippy. Especially when it's pitch-black and she could never prove it was me." Then she paused and added, "Then again, this is the Anyplace, and memory can sometimes be an inconsistent thing. So let's hope I don't forget that as well."

Princess Picca wisely said nothing more on the subject.

Chapter 15

The Boy Helpless

The Boy saw the gargantuan wave crashing down upon him, but that didn't deter him from his endeavors to save the Piccas and his friends. He pushed against the boulders that he knew would trigger a rockslide, but they seemed disinclined to move. He threw all his strength into it, and more besides, and the air hissed sharply between his pearly teeth as he pushed and prodded and cajoled and begged the huge stones to cooperate with him. Just when it seemed hopeless, he felt a small amount of give that quickly escalated into a good deal of give. He let out a triumphant howl, like that of a wolf, as the rocks tumbled from their perch and rolled violently down the side of the mountain. Within seconds, they were covering the entrances to the caves that lay at the bottom.

So pleased with himself was The Boy that he yanked out his sword and shouted defiantly at the oncoming tidal wave, *"I'm not afraid! Have at thee!"*

Now there is much to be said for confidence and determination in the face of an opponent. But there is also something to be said for overconfidence, none of it especially flattering. And determination is, again, quite laudable in its proper place. There is undeniably, though, a fine line between determination and ill-advised pigheadedness, and we would be dishonest if we did not say that The Boy's behavior tilted rather toward the latter.

Let us focus ever so briefly on the positive aspects of the encounter: The Boy managed to hold on to his sword. This was rather miraculous, and we would be remiss if we didn't acknowledge it with a brief "Well done, you."

That, tragically, covers the entirety of the positive aspects, leaving us with a considerable debacle for the balance. Certainly it was one of the low points of The Boy's otherwise remarkable and generally successful career.

The wave slammed into The Boy, sending him tumbling end over end. Ludicrously, he actually made several attempts to stab it, which turned out just about as well as you might expect. The Boy thrashed about, completely losing track of up and down. He tried to fly away from it, but there was far too much water all around him. He was trapped inside a vast wall of water, unable to escape. He shouted in defiance, which turned out to be another rather bad idea, since it simply resulted in his swallowing water.

He flipped around out of control, unable to hear anything except the flowing and churning of the water itself. For one such as The Boy, who relished being in thorough control of everything, this was a torture vicious enough to have been spit up from the bowels of perdition.

And the biggest problem of all was a fairly simple one: The Boy couldn't swim. That's not to say that if he'd possessed the skills of even an Olympic-caliber swimmer, things might have gone differently. Chances are they wouldn't have. Nevertheless, he couldn't swim, and he knew he couldn't swim, and that knowledge certainly didn't do much for his confidence level.

Like an insect endeavoring to outmuscle a spider's web, The Boy fought to pull himself loose from his imprisonment. He was busy choking on water and so drawing a breath wasn't really an option. Finally a surprising notion crossed his mind: He might die. Of all the ways he might have died, he would never, ever have envisioned this one.

They say that one faces impending death through a series of regularized steps: shock, disbelief, anger, bargaining, and ultimately acceptance. Since The Boy tended to be a bit mercurial, not to mention precocious, he went straight to acceptance. Not that he had a death wish, mind you. It's simply that death tended to hold a morbid fascination for him. Nor did he regard death as the life-ending experience that you and I would. Instead, when it came to the subject of demises, The Boy's attitude was very much along the lines of "If I die, I wonder what will happen next."

The Boy had just managed to reach that point of "I wonder—" when death was snatched from him unceremoniously. With no warning, The Boy was spit out of the wall of water. He tried to regain his equilibrium, to fly, but things were happening too quickly. Unable to control his forward motion, The Boy spiraled through the air, the Anyplace whirling around him. Then he felt a violent crashing, and something tearing up his skin. He was barely conscious enough to be aware that he was plummeting through the tops of trees, hurtling toward the ground, and then blackness overcame him.

Imagine, if you will, the pirates' delight when they found him.

The *Skull n' Bones,* which we have left unattended for long enough in our narrative, had indeed found safety on the leeward side of the island. This isn't to say that the ship didn't feel the effects of the storm that Captain Slash had been instrumental in unleashing. The seas were so choppy that, although the veteran pirates handled themselves with aplomb, the Bully Boys were leaning over the edge of the ship and heave-hoing their lunches into the water.

Nor were they immune to the vast tidal wave that had slammed into the island. Although the majority of the wave's fury was expended upon the upper shores, there was still enough to cascade down upon the pirate vessel, flood the decks, and come perilously close to sinking the ship. This caused a good deal of grumbling among the crew even as they worked like fiends to bail out all the water, since they well knew that Captain Slash was the one responsible for the debacle in the first place.

But Slash was a wise and wily individual, and she knew precisely what to tell the crew to buoy their spirits: that they would make an immediate excursion onto the island as soon as the storm subsided, to see what newly unearthed treasure they could find and what prisoners they could take.

A landing party consisting of Captain Slash and a half dozen of her more stout swarthies rowed to the Anyplace and made their way through the forest, finding whatever they could find.

The sky was still dark although the fearsome rains had let up, and the ground was moist and spongy beneath their boots. Simon the Dancer had taken point, vaulting over puddles and pointing out newly made sinkholes so the pirates could make sure to walk around them. Slash's gaze darted here and there, looking for some sign of potential booty. She had experienced tempest-tossed lands where various valuables had been washed away from their owners to wind up in the mud, ripe for the picking.

It was Suleyman who spotted the unexpectedly valuable treasure first. We should not be surprised that Suleyman was the one who did it. Suleyman was very aware of the evil and viciousness of his various deeds, and was perpetually glancing skyward to make sure that the gods had not tired of his evil and decided to dispatch him with a thunderbolt from on high. So Suleyman, in one of his standard looks heavenward, spotted a most astounding sight. "Captain," he whispered, and even whispering his voice came out in a low rumble. "Look yonder."

She followed where he was pointing and gasped in delight. There, with arms dangling limply and body swaying in the nighttime breeze, was the unmoving body of The Boy. His torso was entirely visible; from the waist down (or should we say "upside down") he was snarled in branches and vines. There were scratches over his face and upper arms. His eyes were closed, and a small trail of spittle was trickling from the edge of his mouth.

They had brought heavy netting to drag things along in. Squealing with delight, Captain Slash ordered the netting to be brought forward. Agha Bey, at his captain's behest, clambered up into the trees and cut The Boy down. The Boy tumbled toward the ground and, as he did so, the sudden motion awoke him. But he didn't react fast enough to go airborne, and seconds later the pirates had him completely entangled in the net. He lay there, arms pinned to his side, the weight of the net preventing him from lifting off.

Captain Slash strode forward, grinning. "Well, well, well . . . The Boy. Quite an honor, if I do say so myself."

"You do indeed say so yourself," he tossed back carelessly.

She swung one booted foot fiercely and connected with The Boy's side. He groaned in pain and tried to roll away, but didn't get very far.

"You were a foolish young man," she said. She was strolling around him, reveling in her power over him, her hands draped behind her back. "All you had to do was remain exactly as you were, living in my brother's shadow. Had you done so, you would still be in command of the most fearsome pirate ship afloat. My brother was more than content to be the puppeteer. But thanks to your foolish efforts, the two of you are separated when you were so effective together." She eyed him slyly for a moment. "I don't suppose you'd consider returning to the previous arrangement. If you reattach to my brother, then all will be as it was before. This"—and she gestured toward him, lying there helplessly—"would slowly fade away and be forgotten. Instead of memories of humiliation, you would know nothing but success and triumph."

"I'm no one's puppet," he said defiantly.

This drew chuckles from the pirates. Captain Slash simply shook her head, as if this were the saddest thing he could have said.

"In that case, you'll be no one's anything. A pity, too. I wonder how your beloved pixie will react when we bring her your head as a trophy."

Sadly (for such is the transitory nature of memory in the Anyplace) The Boy actually had to pause and think what Slash could possibly be referring to. But then it came to him in a lightning flash of recollection. "Fiddlefix!" he said, new energy flooding through him. "You have her?"

"Safe and secure in my quarters, under lock and key," said Captain Slash smugly.

"Don't worry, Fiddle!" he said as if the pixie could possibly hear him. "I'll save you!"

"You," the pirate captain reminded him, "cannot even save yourself. And if you think I'm going to allow you to live so that eventually you might trick your way into freedom and unseat me . . . well, you are sadly mistaken. Sadly for you, that is. For us, we are the gladder for it." And she strode toward him, bringing her sword arm back, preparing to thrust it forward squarely into The Boy's chest.

The Boy did not flinch. "You wouldn't dare," he said defiantly, and his show of bravado caught her by surprise.

"I wouldn't?" she said, lowering her sword, one slim eyebrow arched. "And why wouldn't I, pray tell?"

"What do you think would happen to the Anyplace without me?" The Boy said. "You, your ship, your dreams . . . they'd all dissolve. You'd be nothing without me. I am the be-all and end-all of this land. It exists because I want it to exist. It needs me far more than I need it. When I'm gone, everything comes to a stop, hanging there in a haze of nothingness until I return. Nothing happens here that I don't allow to happen or want to happen. Were I to go, the Anyplace would go with me. And where would you be then?"

"Why, I imagine I'd be right here," Captain Slash said, not the least bit impressed by The Boy's outburst, "chuckling over your dead body and watching with laughter while creatures large and small come scurrying out of hiding to sup on you." She shook her head and actually sounded pitying. "Ohhhh, my dear, dear Boy. How tragically typical. Every young lad foolishly believes the sun rises and sets upon him, or that he is the axis upon which the world turns. But I thought you were exempt from such delusion because it's a point of view invariably fostered by too-attentive mothers. You have no mother, and so I would have believed you to be devoid of the standard delusions. I wonder how it could be that you have them, especially considering your mother wanted nothing to do with you."

"You know nothing about it," The Boy said defensively.

"On the contrary," she said, walking around him and looking far too confident to suit The Boy's comfort level. "I know all about it. Some you told me while you were still in the shadow of my brother. Our Miss Fix filled in the rest. How tragic that you think you can control all that transpires in the Anyplace when you cannot even control your mother's love for you."

The Boy's eyes smoldered with fury, but Captain Slash knew that she had pinked him, drawing virtual (if not actual) blood. "Villain," he snarled, "if I were free right now, I'd—"

"You'd what? Stop me? In the same way that you stopped the assault of the Seirenes?" She laughed loudly. "Or the way my brother, even though he was dead, was still able to outwit you? Consider that again: You were outwitted by a dead man's shadow. And now you stand helpless before my men and me"— and she gestured with her normal hand at the pirates who had accompanied her. They roared in bawdy approval of her words, causing The Boy to flinch. Captain Slash shook her head in clear disappointment. "I have to say, I don't understand you, Boy. How can you be confronted with mounting evidence of your own ineptitude and continue to have such an inflated sense of self-worth?"

"There's nothing inflated about it," he said, but there was increased quavering in his voice, and the uncertainty was becoming so foul that it was generating its own stench. "One of me is worth twenty of you...."

"There is only one of me, Boy, and that one has captured the one of you, so whose worth has been proven while whose was left wanting?" She whipped her sword back and forth just under his nose to add emphasis to just who was in charge. Were The Boy faster off the mark, he would have held the net up so that she could have inadvertently sliced it herself. But he failed to do so. "Is that, ultimately, why you refuse to grow up, Boy? Because you think that once you do, you'll enter the adult world and lose control of your environment? Have you ever considered the possibility that your imagination is no longer the single greatest source of energy in the Anyplace, presuming it ever was? That the Anyplace is far more responsive to my manipulation, specifically because I *am* an adult? I know the way things work. I know the true order of the universe and am not afraid of it, nor afraid to exploit it." She leaned in toward him, driving home a sword so metaphorical that the one upon her wrist didn't come into play. "If—when—you die, Boy, the world will go on without you. That may be the single most difficult truth that all such as you must cope with. You will die . . . and life will continue. I'll not shuffle off this immortal coil, nor will my crew, upon your passing. I will have my triumphs and tragedies, and you will be wholly unable to stop me. You'll just watch helplessly from whatever 'beyond' will accept consignment of you. And you will have plenty of time—eternity, by my reckoning—to come to grips with the notion that you are no more important than I. Less important, actually, since I have command over your fate whereas you have none over mine."

She brought her sword forward and cut him lightly on the thigh. He let out a surprised, pained gasp, like a sleepwalker who has just been awakened via the timely application of a bucket of cold water.

"Imagine that you rule the Anyplace, for all the difference it makes," she whispered, and poked him again. "Imagine you can escape. Imagine that I am not about to sever your head from your shoulders with my sword. Use the full force of your imagination, by God, for all the good it will do you." She waited as long seconds stretched by, and nothing happened. It might have been because the defeated Boy was hanging his head in mortified shame, consumed by the idea that he was helpless to control his own fate, much less anyone else's, and feeling mighty foolish that he could ever have thought any other way.

Boys' egos are fragile things. It doesn't matter if they are run-of-the-mill boys or magnificent boys. In The Boy's case, he was a slave of his ego, and his ego had just gotten a royal pounding from the pirate queen. As always a creature of extremes, The Boy had gone from believing he was totally in control to being not in control at all, not unlike when he had been confronted by the wave. The newest tide of events was once again threatening to overwash him; and this time the outcome was going to be considerably more fatal.

I am helpless. As helpless as any adult, he thought miserably.

And then, an instant before she could administer the coup de grâce—with her sword arm poised and shaking with anticipation—Simon the Dancer suddenly said, "Captain! Look!"

She didn't see it at first, peering through the underbrush as she was. But then she did, and her heart nearly stopped.

"A tiger!" she said. "And not any tiger! The great snow tiger!"

Sure enough, there was the unmistakable fur of the snow tiger, stalking them along the periphery of the clearing in which they stood. It had been utterly silent, but now with its presence clearly known, it growled softly . . . a precursor, no doubt, to the thunderously savage roar that would tear from its throat the instant it leaped into view.

Captain Slash lived in fear of being eaten by some sort of savage creature. Her brother's arm had been given over as an appetizer to a fearsome beast, and eventually the rest of his body had provided the entrée. There were many ways in which Mary Slash wanted to emulate her brother, the formidable Captain Hack, but meeting her end in an animal's gullet was definitely not one of them.

Consequently, the impending attack of the famed and formidable snow tiger of the Anyplace was more than enough to have Mary Slash sound the retreat. Her crew offered not the slightest argument, what with being cowards as mentioned earlier, and seconds later the pirates were fleeing the area. "What of The Boy?" said Simon the Dancer.

"He's what will delay the beast coming after us!" Slash said. "Let it sup on that tender morsel! That'll keep it occupied so that we can get back to the ship and safety! A good day's work, lads, seeing our greatest enemy left tied up to become tiger chow!"

The Boy was not intimidated at all. His mind was barely on what was transpiring around him. He, like you, knew that the snow tiger had already met his fate. For that matter he also knew—as you no doubt have likewise intuited—just who, not what, was facing him now. But he felt nothing, even as the last of the pirate's footfalls faded away into the bushes and trees and Paul's fur-covered head popped up from behind the brush. "Are they gone?" he said with a lopsided grin.

What The Boy did not know, or care about, however, was how in the world Paul had come to be there. After all, the last he knew of it, Paul and the others had been trapped behind a rockslide. The Boy may not have cared about how Paul had escaped the dark recesses of the cave in order to provide a timely rescue, but certainly you have some interest in the process.

I would very much like to tell you that recounting Paul's miraculous escape will be a grand and exciting adventure in which Paul displayed great cunning, and all the disparate members of the group formed a bond that enabled them to overcome their last mutual prejudices. And perhaps one of them was forced to make the Ultimate Sacrifice so that the others might live to tell the tale.

In fact, even though that's all falsehood, I suppose I could still tell you that. How would you really know? But if I am to set an example to The Boy and the others, then nothing less than the truth will do. And the truth is this:

It was a tragically boring escape.

Our apologies. Even in the grandest of adventures, occasionally the staggeringly mundane rears its ugly head. Not all dreams are memorable and not all goals are soaring. Sometimes one simply goes from A to B and there's not all that much to tell of it. This is one of those instances.

Tragic, really, that we live in a time when there is so much fundamental mistrust in the world. If we didn't, I could simply tell you, "Take my word for it; Paul and the others escaped, but it's not a particularly ripping yarn, so let's just skip it." But you wouldn't take my word for it. You would start to think, *Why is he withholding the details from us? It must be an amazingly remarkable story, filled with secrets so monumental that perhaps Those in Power have decreed it cannot be disseminated.* Or else you might start thinking that I don't actually know, and am trying to cover it up. Or some other variant steeped in refusing to believe that, well, there's really nothing remarkable there, and we'd all be better served if we just skipped right over it.

However, we know that it will then just fester inside you, this not knowing. So in order to make certain your enjoyment of our little narrative isn't ruined by something relatively insignificant, we will tell you as briskly as we can how Paul came to be where he was.

Was his escape entirely without drama? No. There was a brief time during which Paul, Gwenny, and the others bemoaned their imprisoned state and expressed concern over when they were going to run out of air. This lasted until the point where Princess Picca said, "Could use exit in back."

Everyone stopped talking at once. Gwenny took a step toward the princess and said, "There's an exit out the back?"

"Yes," said Princess Picca.

"Well, why didn't you say so earlier?"

"You not ask."

Whereupon she led them, mostly through her sense of touch, to the rear of the cave where—sure enough—a narrow hole, but wide enough for them to squeeze through, presented itself in the back wall. They slithered through one by one, each gratefully gulping in air as they escaped from the confines of the cave. Princess Picca immediately set her braves to work on removing the debris that lay blocking the other cave entrances, since the other caves did not benefit from having a nature-provided means of rear access.

The damage done to the Indian camp was a devastating sight to behold. The simple wigwams and huts of the Picca tribe hadn't stood a chance. The ground was thoroughly saturated, and clothes, trinkets, and weapons were scattered everywhere. Not only that, but a number of large trees had been flattened.

"Had we been out here, we crushed," Picca said solemnly. "Boy saved us."

"He tends to do that," said Gwenny, a touch of unmistakable pride in her voice.

"Where is he?" said Paul, looking skyward. As it was still night, it was difficult to see. "Boy!" he called, and the others joined in, echoing his summons. But The Boy did not present himself.

Paul sensed something else in the air. Although he wouldn't have known it, his nostrils were flaring slightly. He wouldn't have been able to articulate the reasons, yet somehow Paul simply knew that danger was afoot.

"I'll look for him," he said.

"Yes. Let's all go and——"

It had been Irregular who had spoken, but Paul turned and said firmly, "No. I'll do it myself."

Irregular was about to offer up protest, as were Gwenny and several others. But there was something in Paul's face, his attitude, that stilled their protests. It made him seem different. It made him seem like someone whose statements should not be questioned. It made him seem like someone who would operate best on his own.

Perhaps it was the way he stood when he had the tiger's skin wrapped around him. Or perhaps it was the fact that he'd growled slightly when he spoke, even though he didn't realize it.

Still, Picca was the princess, and she felt the need to make her authority in the matter clear. "You go. We give you time. Take too much time . . . we come looking."

"I'll be fine," said Paul, and he turned and sprinted toward the jungle. He vaulted easily over several fallen trees and melted into the greenery.

He'd never felt more alive than he did that night. He'd narrowly avoided death thanks to the efforts of The Boy, and was now determined to make certain that his savior was, in turn, quite all right. He moved quickly, and more, he moved silently. He passed through brush without rustling it, stepped through thickets without snapping a single branch. Paul felt growing excitement as he blended in with the lush natural surroundings, as if he had come home after a lengthy departure.

He made an unerring beeline straight toward where The Boy was dangling helpless in the trees. Paul didn't know he was doing it. Tell him that he was tracking the scent and he would have given you a strange look, because he was unaware of anything except that he needed to head in a particular direction if he wanted to find The Boy. The hundred little pieces of infor-

mation involving scent, forest craft, and so on that he was drawing upon were coming to him so instinctively that he didn't
even know it.

What was the cause of this remarkable tracking ability? You
may well wonder about it, and may continue to do so if it
pleases you. As for Paul, he wasn't thinking about it at all, so—
for the moment—we shall instead defer to his priorities and
focus on the fact of his search rather than the means of its being
possible.

Faster and faster he moved, and then his ears twitched
slightly, detecting the voices of the pirates up ahead. He froze,
and we must tell you that unless you had been looking right at
him, you would not have known he was there. Then Paul started
to pad through the woods, proceeding with such caution that he
would have made more noise if he'd been a ghost.

He drew within sight of the pirates and saw Mary Slash
speaking to The Boy in a manner that was, to say the least, disrespectful. Paul counted a half dozen pirates, all armed with
fearsome sabers. Despite his newfound sense of aggression, Paul
wasn't foolish enough to think that he, like the true snow tiger,
could leap into battle and shred the pirates with fearsome teeth
and slashing claws that he didn't possess. He quickly realized,
though, that the pirates wouldn't know he was bereft of such ac-
coutrements. It would be easy enough to make that lack of
knowledge work for him.

The rest you know.

"Are they gone?" Paul said with a lopsided grin as he
emerged from cover. The Boy's sword had fallen from his grasp
several feet away when he'd been hanging unconscious from
overhead, and Paul picked it up, intending to cut the net apart.

Then he saw that something was terribly, terribly wrong.
The Boy was standing there, swaying slightly, and he had his fin-

gers in his mouth. He was fumbling with something. "What's wrong?" said Paul.

The Boy pulled his hand clear of his mouth and held something up. It was a perfect, white, shiny tooth, with a tiny dab of blood on it.

"You lost a tooth," Paul said. "I'm not surprised. The way you must have been slammed around by the wave, it's lucky they didn't all get knocked out." He started cutting at the rope.

"No," The Boy said tonelessly. "You don't understand. It wasn't knocked out. It just . . . came out."

The significance of this relatively mundane event didn't register on Paul at first, but then slowly it began to dawn on him. He was so stunned that he lowered the sword and stared into The Boy's soulless eyes.

"I'm growing up," said The Boy.

Chapter 16

The Indian Way

The pirate raiding party returned to the *Skull n' Bones* amid great hoopla and celebration. Naturally the Bully Boys (who had not been feeling well enough to accompany them) and the shadow of Hack (which was, by its very nature, restricted to the general vicinity of the ship itself) were waiting for them with a mixture of curiosity and eagerness.

Captain Slash was leading her crew in song, and it wasn't a bad song at all when one considered that she had written it en route to the ship. It's a surprising bit of trivia to reveal that pirates are actually quite good at learning tunes. It's a means of compensation they've developed as a group since they're not terribly good at reading anything save treasure maps; and thus songs are the only means they have of immortalizing their triumphs.

> *"The Boy who harried Captain Hack,*
> *Who took his hand to not give back,*

Was captured well by Captain Slash,
Who helped to cook his boasting hash.
A fearsome fight The Boy did get
Before he fell into our net,
Tormented him about his flaws
And left him to the tiger's claws!"

We should note that the words can't begin to suggest the quality of the catchy little tune that Captain Slash had come up with. Really quite hummable. Had she not been committed to piracy, she might have made quite a career for herself in musical theater.

They boarded the ship, still singing merrily, and Mary Slash strode toward the shadow of her brother, singing the last lines of the song. She swept her sword through the air with a flourish and said, "So! What think you, Brother? The Boy is done for! He is gone! Your revenge is—"

And to the utter astonishment of all onlookers, the shadow of Captain Hack swept his hatchet around and struck Mary Slash with the flat of the blade. Had he hit her straight on, he could well have opened up her throat and sent her lifeblood spilling all over the deck. As it was, she was knocked clean off her feet, and she lay on her back with a look of total shock.

Captain Hack was gesticulating wildly. Clearly he wanted to convey something to her, and even more clearly he was quite irate.

Mary Slash scrambled to her feet. Her cheek stung something fierce; but in the best pirate tradition, she didn't rub it or otherwise acknowledge the pain. Actually, the pain she felt was far more the emotional sort. She worshipped her brother, even in death, and such a violent reaction from him for reasons unknown was devastating to her. She was also all too aware that her entire crew was looking on, no less flummoxed than she. But it was unquestionably a stinging rebuke not only to her personally but also to her leadership. Pirate captains never fared well if challenges to their authority, from any quarter, went unanswered.

"How *dare* you!" Mary Slash railed in response, and there was such palpable fury from her that Hack paused in his mute diatribe. "How dare you, Brother, and here I thought so much better of you! I know what grinds your gizzard!" She pointed with her sword hand, waving it accusatorily. "You're incensed because I disposed of The Boy when you were not able to! You—with all your greatness and your swagger and your confidence—were unable to put paid to one slip of a lad. Whereas I not only had the run of him for a full season of buccaneering but also, when he became himself again, trapped him and got rid of him without breaking the slightest droplet of sweat!" Her voice rose so that her entire crew would be sure to hear. "It infuriates you that my accomplishments are greater than yours, and in a fraction of the time! The *Skull n' Bones* is now the premier force for villainy on the high seas, and your greatest enemy, The Boy, is currently working his way through a tiger's bowels! Don't you dare assail me again, and don't you be trying to challenge me in front of my crew! Not our crew, and not your crew, but mine! *My crew! My ship! My—!*"

Mary Slash felt her heart thundering in her chest, and her forehead was beaded with sweat. She tried to regain her composure but wasn't entirely successful. So she pivoted on her heel and stormed off to her cabin.

There she thrust her face toward a mirror and checked it on one side and then the other, up and down, back and forth. She looked for the slightest hint of smoothing out of any crow's-feet or wrinkles. There appeared to be none. Everything was as she remembered it. She let out a sigh of relief and reminded herself that she needed to control her outbursts lest tragedy strike. A tragedy she had once seen befall her own mother, and she had no desire to follow suit. (Not that she felt pity over her mother's fate. She just wanted to avoid it for herself.)

Meantime, the shadow of Captain Hack strode the deck in frustration. We will take the liberty of telling you that he was not, in fact, at all jealous over his sister's disposing of The Boy. Hack wanted his revenge, and he didn't care if it was done via proxy or via cat's-paw, or even if The Boy was simply minding his own business one day and a huge tree fell upon him. What upset Hack, what irritated him to the point where he had struck down his sister in ire, was the awareness that she had not remained to make certain the job was finished. Hack didn't remotely trust The Boy to do the decent thing and die. He was certain that if Captain Slash and her crew had not actually witnessed the tiger devour The Boy, then there was a chance that The Boy had in fact not been devoured. He could have escaped his fate in any number of ways. It never actually occurred to Hack that there had not been a tiger at all but rather a young lad sporting the hide of a tiger upon him. If it had occurred to him and he'd thought that his sister and pirate crew could be fooled by such a masquerade, his fury would have been beyond calculation. Not that he had never been fooled by such fakery himself, but one tended to forget one's own transgressions when one was dead.

Since he wasn't able to convey the reason for his anger to his sister, he chose instead to stalk about the deck in a fine stew. And when Captain Slash emerged from her cabin, she stood defiantly and glared at him, clearly waiting for him to issue some sort of further challenge to her authority. How she would have handled it if he had offered such a challenge, we couldn't say, for she was no more capable of launching a feasible offensive attack against Hack than The Boy had been. But Hack made no move against her, for he saw no real point to it. After all, it wasn't as if he could take back charge of his crew. The chances were nil that the pirates would be willing to take orders from little more than a ghost, even if he could figure out a way to convey his wishes. They tolerated his presence with a shiver of their timbers, but if he tried to assume command, they would doubtless abandon the *Skull n' Bones* at their first opportunity. This would have left the shadow of Hack as skipper of a ghost ship, and of what worth was that?

No, his fortunes were tied to his sister. He knew it all too well. So when they faced each other, the shadow of Hack made the slightest of bows in deference to her, and then turned away. Captain Slash nodded approvingly and then said, "Hoist the mainsail! With The Boy dead, his leftovers aren't worth bothering with! Let's set to sea in search of new victims!"

The pirates prepared to set sail to wreak new havoc and new evil upon the waters, certain that there were none to stop them or stand in their way.

And at that particular moment, they were exactly right, for the one person who might pose a threat to them wasn't posing a threat to anyone.

With the sun creeping up over the horizon, Paul had brought The Boy back to the Indian camp without the slightest idea of what to do. The Boy looked totally dispirited. More than that... The Boy was looking older.

It was not older in any way that getting older made sense. He wasn't getting taller or broader. There was no beard stubble growing upon his face, nor did his features appear any more mature. But his eyes were looking glassy and, even more puzzling, his hair was starting to gray. He hadn't lost any more of his baby teeth, although Paul had no doubt that that would be next.

Gwenny, Irregular, Porthos, and the Indian braves gathered around him as if they were looking in fear at a breathing dead man. "What's wrong with him?" whispered Porthos.

"He says he's growing up," Paul said. "Can that be?"

"If he says it enough, I suppose it can," Gwenny said. "This is the Anyplace. Anything is possible...especially when it comes to The Boy."

"Y'hear that, Boy?" said Irregular, crouching in front of the listless youngster and prodding his shoulder. "Anything is possible when it comes to you."

But The Boy simply shook his head, his graying hair hanging down around his ears. "I'm growing up," he said for what seemed the umpteenth time.

And Gwenny, beginning to feel a little frustrated, placed her fists on her hips and said, "And what is so wrong with that?"

He didn't seem to have heard her at first, but then slowly he focused his gaze upon her. "You need ask?"

"Of course I need ask. I mean—" She was about to say things that she should not, and so she pulled back and endeavored to phrase it in a way that would better serve her. "Let us say that I were to grow up. To become an adult. Would you want to hate me then?"

"No."

"Well, there you see—"

"I wouldn't want to. But I needs would."

Her cheeks flushed brightly, and she almost upped and departed the Anyplace right at that moment.

But The Boy said, "Don't you see, Gwenny? That's what being an adult is all about. Hatred."

"You're wrong," Paul said heatedly.

"Am I?" The Boy's voice quavered slightly. "There was a time when I was hiding in Kensington Gardens. I was watching a group of very young children. They had been running about the park and, quite by accident, had converged in one area, having come from different directions. One of them touched another, said, 'You're it!' and within seconds they were all playing tag. It was just a group of youngsters thrown together. They had different-color skin. Different-shaped eyes. The chances are that they all believed in different things, had different names for God. But they came together there, in the park, reveling in the joy of being with one another.

"Because they were children."

"And then their parents showed up. With their different skin colors and different-shaped eyes, and different names for God.

"And they looked at one another with suspicion and fear and anger. Then, very quickly, they went to their children and plucked them away from one another and pulled them back whence they'd come.

"That was when it was all made painfully clear to me. When you are a child, there is joy. There is laughter. And most of all, there is trust. Trust in your fellows. When you are an adult . . . then comes suspicion, hatred, and fear. If children ran the world, it would be a place of eternal bliss and cheer. Adults run the world; and there is war, and enmity, and destruction unending. Adults who take charge of things muck them up, and then produce a new generation of children and say, 'The children are the hope of the future.' And they are right. Children are the hope of the future. But adults are the damnation of the present, and children become adults as surely as adults become worm food.

"Adults are the death of hope.

"And you ask me why I would hesitate to leave my childhood behind. That shouldn't be the question. The question is, why wouldn't you? Why would anyone be glad about getting older?"

No one had an immediate response... and then very quietly, Paul said, "Because it's change."

"So?" said The Boy.

"So... change is good. Having everything being always the same—what's the point of that?"

"It's not a point so much as it is an end in itself," The Boy said.

"Yes. That's right. It's an end," Paul said. "And we're too young to have something be an end. Childhood is about new beginnings. It's about discovery. If you've found everything that you can do... why do anything else?"

"And that's where our great divide is," said The Boy. "Because you see that as a bad thing... and I see it as a good thing."

And so it went, back and forth, with Gwenny or Paul putting forward notions as to why adulthood was not the terribly revolting thing that The Boy believed it to be, while The Boy presented his point of view with steadfast sadness and a sense of abandoning himself to a fate he felt would doom him. Meanwhile the Indians worked on repairing their camp. Princess Picca's wigwam and several others had been rebuilt by the time the sun crawled high into the sky.

"I'm becoming more and more convinced that it's the absence of his shadow that's doing this," Gwenny said to Paul at one point.

Paul looked surprised. That had never occurred to him. "Why do you think losing his shadow would have this kind of effect on him?"

"You didn't see him the first time he lost it. He was practically frantic when he was separate from it. It's not like your shadow or mine"—and she held up her hand and watched as her shadow mimicked the gesture. "It isn't just a thing the sun makes. It's part of him, sharing lives with him. As strange as it sounds, I think it anchored him to this world. That's why he was so desperate to get it back. Without his shadow, he has no roots, nothing holding him down. His mind is wandering to places it shouldn't go, and his body is following him into that abyss."

Paul wasn't entirely sure he was convinced, but he knew that Gwenny certainly was, and that was good enough for him. "We have to reunite him with his shadow," Paul said firmly, "and find a way to get Hack out of it. Otherwise we'll just be back with the same problem."

At that moment, Dog Licking Self ran into the camp, looking out of breath and concerned. He ran up to Princess Picca and dropped to one knee, bowing his head, as was the custom when returning to her presence.

"Stand, brave," she ordered. When he did so, she continued, "You check on boats?"

He sighed heavily. "Boats destroyed," he said. "Bare frames. Shards. Enough pieces from all boats could make one."

"Pity," said the princess, glancing toward Paul and Gwenny. "We plan use boats, go fight pirates. Cannot fight pirates, no boats."

"Pirates leaving."

"*What!*" That startled exclamation came from both Gwenny and Paul. Gwenny then continued, "How do you know?"

"See them," said Dog Licking Self, "heading out toward open water."

"This is bad," Paul said, looking at the shriveling husk of The Boy. The Boy's hair was now thoroughly shot through with gray. Bizarrely, his face still looked relatively youthful, yet more underscoring of The Boy's lack of familiarity with proper aging. Granted, he knew the pirates well enough, and the pirates were adults. But he thought of them simply as pirates rather than grown-ups; and besides, it was the very prospect of growing older that haunted The Boy. So naturally his own version of aging would mirror his innermost fears. "If they depart with The Boy's shadow, he'll be finished."

"Not just that," said Gwenny worriedly, "but who knows what sort of destruction they'll do to—to everyone—if they're out sailing around and wreaking havoc with no one to stop them."

"They have Fiddlefix," The Boy said.

They looked to him with alarm. "They *do?*" Paul said. "She's a prisoner?" When The Boy nodded, looking rather indifferent about it, Paul was moved to anger over The Boy's attitude. He strode forward and grabbed The Boy by the front of his garment and shook him. "And this is how you rise to a challenge? By doing *nothing?*"

"I'm becoming an adult," The Boy said tonelessly. "Adults don't go on grand crusades against pirates. They read and write and spew their ABCs. What matter is it to me what becomes of Fiddlefix?"

That was the point where Princess Picca had had enough. "We waste too much time on this," said the princess. She pointed to the sun, which was down upon the horizon. "Entire day spent on convincing Boy to do what must needs be done. Boy complain that he not boy. That he man. That, as man, he useless now. Princess Picca not believe that. Princess Picca show him otherwise."

The Boy looked at her blankly and then cried out as she gripped him firmly by the ear. "Come with me," she ordered.

She pulled him upward, and he almost tripped over his feet as she walked him firmly in the direction of her wigwam.

"Where are you going with him?" Gwenny said. "What are you doing?"

Princess Picca did not deign to answer. Instead she hauled The Boy into her tent, closing the flaps behind her. Gwenny tried to follow, but two large braves stepped in from either side and blocked her passage, their arms folded. Each of them was holding a spear firmly in his hand.

This did not daunt Gwenny in the slightest, but it was more than enough to deter Paul. So when he saw Gwenny striding up to the guards with the clear intention of trying to push past them, Paul quickly came up behind her and took her politely but firmly by the arm. "I wouldn't suggest it," he cautioned her.

She looked from Paul to the scowling braves and back to Paul. "You don't know what she's doing to him in there."

"Do you?"

"Well . . . no," she said uncertainly.

"Then you don't know whether it's good or bad."

"No," she said again. "But—"

"There is no 'but' here," Paul said, trying to sound reasonable. "She is the princess. They are going to obey her wishes. And failing any sure knowledge that she's hurting him, I think we're going to have to trust her—especially since we're not really being given any choice."

Ultimately she had to agree that there was wisdom in Paul's words. So the two of them retreated to the debatable safety of the Vagabonds' company, where Irregular and Porthos asked what was going on with The Boy and Princess Picca. "I do not know," Gwenny said primly, "and, frankly, I'm not sure I care to know. Whatever it is, I suspect it's not very civilized, which would make sense since they are savages." She made sure to say this loudly enough that the braves heard, not particularly caring if they took offense. But the braves either didn't hear or pretended not to. It's hard to say with them, since Indians lean toward being inscrutable.

It was a long night, and both Gwenny and Paul, independent of each other and without having discussed it, kept an ear out for the slightest sound emanating from Princess Picca's tent. None was forthcoming. They might have been talking. They might have fallen asleep. They might have been playing board games. It was simply impossible to say. But Gwenny and Paul knew one thing, and that was that they were determined to stay awake until they saw The Boy emerge from the tent, so they could ask him what it was that he and the princess had been engaged in.

Naturally that determination played a distant second to their own endurance, and so it was that they fell asleep before the moon was remotely high in the sky. When they finally awoke, it was because the sun was shining in their eyes. Caked mud clung to their clothes, and they brushed it off as best they could. Stretching and yawning, they rubbed the sleep from their eyes, and then Gwenny noticed that there was no one guarding the tent of Princess Picca.

Before Paul could utter a word to warn her off, Gwenny scrambled to her feet and made a dash for Princess Picca's tent. In what could only be called a shocking breach of protocol, she threw open the flap and looked inside, not having the faintest idea what she was going to see but certain that she wasn't going to like it.

Princess Picca was lying on the ground, a blanket pulled up to her chin. She was awake and looking at Gwenny, and her eyes were sparkling with amusement and, perhaps, something else. It was difficult to say.

Braves were coming from either side, making angry noises, but Princess Picca called out something in her native tongue, and the braves slowed and then stopped. They made no further hostile move toward Gwenny but instead stayed several feet back, content to glower at her.

"You look for Boy?" said the princess. Her voice was soft and relaxed. When Gwenny nodded, the princess said, "He not here."

"And when he was here? What did you do? What did he do? What did the two of you do?"

"Boy feel like adult. So ... I help him feel like boy again."

"And how," Gwenny said tartly, "did you accomplish that?"

"Indian way," was all Princess Picca said, and smiled in a manner that seemed to light up her face.

"Look!"

It was Irregular's voice that had shattered the air before Gwenny could continue with a questioning that likely wouldn't have gotten her anywhere. Gwenny turned away from the wigwam and ran toward where Irregular was standing on the crest of the far ledge that was the outer perimeter of the Picca camp. The vantage point provided a decent view of the water, although any view of the lagoon itself was obscured by trees below. But the interfering trees weren't a factor at this point, for what Irregular was seeing and pointing at was high above the trees. The others came to his side and gasped.

The masts of a man-of-war towered over the trees. It was fully rigged, and the shining oak of which the vessel was constructed glittered in the morning sun. The deck was lined with cannons, more than fifty by Paul's quick count. And standing, perched high in the crow's nest, his sword extended and howling a wolf howl in triumph, was The Boy. Even from this distance, they could see that his hair was its normal black, and although his shadow was still missing, he had been restored to his youthful vigor.

"Come on, ya swabs!" he said. "Hack and Slash are getting away! They have a full day's head start on us! We have to catch them! All hands to deck!"

"How is it possible?" Paul gasped. "Where did that—that ship come from?"

"From his imagination."

They turned to see that Princess Picca had emerged from her tent. She still had her blanket wrapped around herself, and her feet were bare. "You know well as I... Anyplace linked to Boy's imagination. He believe it, it be true. He believe that remains of Picca canoes can be transformed into mighty sailing vessel... then they are. Simple as that."

"You mean he just..." Paul couldn't find the words.

Gwenny, however, was able to. "You're saying he just dreamt that up."

Princesss Picca shrugged. Her shoulders were as bare as her feet. "Something like that."

"So—so it's over? He's cured? There's no problem?"

But the Indian princess shook her head gravely. "Still problem. Happiness passing thing. Loss of shadow still strong. Sooner later... he feel years again. Feel old again. Must regain his shadow. Must become as he was." She turned away from Gwenny and Paul and started shouting orders to her people in that harsh native tongue of hers. The Indians snapped to at her instruction and began running hither and yon. Paul thought it was all at random, but he quickly realized the Indians knew what they were about and were busily gathering their weapons in preparation for sailing after the pirates.

"You're going to aid us, then?" Paul said.

Princess Picca turned back to him, looking a bit surprised

that he would even have to ask. "Gave word. Allies now. Be-sides, Boy must be made whole. Only so much princess can do."

"Yes, speaking of that," Gwenny said, looking extremely sus-picious while the Indians scampered around the camp following their princess's orders. Fortunately they'd been carrying some weapons with them when they'd fled to the caves, and they were gathering up whatever they could find that the storm had not destroyed. "You still haven't told us what exactly it was that you did do."

"Indian way," Princess Picca repeated.

"And what would that Indian way be?"

"Very old," the princess intoned. "Very sacred. Very much none of business of girl." Gwenny huffed at that as the princess shifted her gaze toward Paul. "You also going to ask about it, Tigerheart?"

"Actually," said Paul, "I think it's one of those things I'd rather not know."

Gwenny gave him an angry look, clearly feeling as if he had just cut the ground out from under her. But all Princess Picca said was, "Very wise. I get ready lead braves in battle."

This caught Paul's attention. "You're going to lead them? Yourself?"

"Of course," she said matter-of-factly. "What good leader if not lead men into battle? Should not send men in battle if not willing risk same dangers. Act of cowardice."

With that she headed off to her tent to prepare. Paul looked at Gwenny and said, "You know, I think if our leaders had that same philosophy, there'd be a lot fewer wars fought."

"You may well be right," said Gwenny, who still didn't look particularly happy with how matters had been left with the princess. But she wasn't in a position to pursue the matter fur-ther. Even she had to admit that there was something to be said for Paul's philosophy: Perhaps there are some things best left unknown.

And if several of our heroes are going to maintain that opinion, then I—who am also not sure of just what went on in the Indian princess's tent that fateful night that restored The Boy to youth and vigor, if even for a short time, although I do have some general thoughts that I won't share—am disinclined to pursue the matter further. So if you're going to desire more details, I regret to tell you that, like Paul, Gwenny, and the others, you are destined to be disappointed. Don't feel bad. Disappointments are suffered throughout life, and how you endure them will determine the measure of the person you're going to be. Besides, since it is not to be spelled out for you, it is left to your imagination to determine what happened and serve as your own explanation. Not only does this make this adventure unique to each and every reader who will have his own viewpoint of this key turning point but also it will be a nice exercise in training your imagination. After all, you've seen the power of imagination and what it can accomplish in the mind of a true master of it such as The Boy.

The slow, steady beat of war drums began to fill the air. Paul, Gwenny, and the others heard them; and they saw that there was much activity in and nearby Princess Picca's tent. For no reason that he could readily understand, Paul felt his feet starting to move in time with the music. Up and down, sideways, then up and down again; and within moments he was moving in a circle. Gwenny, Irregular, and Porthos were right behind him, although Irregular's feet weren't moving in exactly the right way and Porthos got stepped on more than a few times. It was as if the beat of the drums was appealing to something primal deep within them.

A figure dropped from overhead, and although it should

have been obvious that it would be The Boy, Paul was still momentarily startled. The Boy glanced over his shoulder and
grinned at him, his pearly white teeth glistening and looking as
clean and complete as they had ever been. A roaring fire had
been built in the middle of the camp, which was quite an accomplishment considering how much of the surrounding trees
had been thoroughly soaked. The blaze was reflected deep in
The Boy's eyes, or perhaps that fire was always there and Paul
could simply see it more clearly this time.

Then a transcendent howl soared above the thudding of the
drums, and Princess Picca leaped out of her tent. She was wearing leather covering her breasts and loins, and thigh-high doe-
skin boots with fringe hanging from the tops. The rest of her
body—stomach, face, legs, and arms—was covered with an astounding and fearsome array of images. They appeared to sym-
bolize all manner of hunting animals: Panther, lion, and hawk
were all painted upon her skin as if seeking approval from their
spirit totems. Paul also saw, plunging down Picca's bare back, a
reasonably recognizable outline of his tiger. He supposed it was
a gesture of respect from the Piccas, that, even though they had
so feared the tiger because he was striking them down, they nevertheless sought his spiritual blessing on their enterprise.

Other braves were joining the dance now, and they were
likewise smeared face and body with war paint. They didn't
have totemic symbols upon them but instead merely undefined
shapes. The energy that was being generated in this dance was
far different from that of the earlier one. It seemed the very air
itself was charged with energy that the Piccas were siphoning
into their gyrations. Paul wasn't sure if he was imagining it or
not. It might well have been a trick of light due to the flickering of the fire, but he could have sworn that the painted images
upon Princess Picca's body were actually coming to life and

moving themselves, leaping and springing across her skin in anticipation of a hunt.

Even Gwenny was letting herself be swept up into the intensity around the fire. As prim and proper as she was, with her hair typically up in a carefully coiffed bun, now she had let her hair down. It swept around her as she tossed her head back and forth, side to side. She had kicked off her shoes and had hiked the hem of her skirt up to a bit higher than what would have been considered acceptable in polite society. She didn't appear to care, though; and although she sported no paint anywhere upon her, that didn't deter her from joining the ceremony with as much ferocity as any of the Indians born to their savage life.

It was at that moment that, although naturally Paul considered the pirates to be a fearsome enemy that deserved nothing but extermination, he began to feel just the slightest twinge of pity for the buccaneers. They had no idea what they were in for.

Chapter 17

Confrontation

You might be wondering at this juncture just what significance there is to allowing the pirates to run about as they
see fit upon the high seas. The problem is this: nightmares.

The pirates are the source of all nightmares, of all dreams
that are unpleasant and fearsome. You may not recognize them
as such, for dreams are very personal and the sleeping mind in-
terprets the images of the pirates as befits the dreams. So in one
dream you may find yourself assailed by vampires or other
monsters; in another dream, you panic over the loss of your
loved ones; in yet another, you find yourself falling from a high
place, your arms and legs flailing about as you pray that you'll
awaken before you hit bottom.

In each instance, you have had a brush with the pirates.
You have set sail upon the sea of dreams, and the evil ship
Skull n' Bones has descended upon you to work its mischief.
Certainly the fearsome Suleyman or Agha Bey, coming at you

with their gleaming silver or gold teeth and their daggers in their hands, could be seen as monsters. Certainly if your loved ones have accompanied you on your dream voyage (a circumstance that occurs far more frequently than you would think, for dreams are routinely shared, and we simply don't like to admit it since there are privacy issues involved), the pirates may have scarpered away with your beloved in hopes of obtaining a healthy ransom. Fear of falling? You've been made to walk the plank. Yes, it's only a plunge into water, but drops routinely look much higher when you're standing at the top of where you're about to jump from, do they not? A fall of six feet looks like sixty when you're staring down nervously from up high.

What you would call "nightmares" or "bad dreams" or "night terrors," the pirates refer to as "a good day's work."

The thing is, typically the pirates have other things to distract them, most notably the activities of The Boy and his followers. But with The Boy having been disposed of (so they thought) and the Indians annihilated by the great tidal wave (so they thought), the pirates had decided to focus all their activities on nautical nastiness.

It was not unprecedented. There had been several times previously in the history of man when the pirates decided that they were going to put their rudder to the isle of the Anyplace and turn their attentions elsewhere. It is disturbingly easy to determine what periods of man's history existed during those times. The rank and file of people lived in greater fear than ever; and, worse than that, those leaders who were of a disposition toward conquest and villainy swelled with heretofore unknown confidence and embarked upon campaigns of terror that were merely reflections of what the pirates of the Anyplace happened to be up to. Even men of blind incompetence who merely aspire to world domination can be driven to make foolish and precipitous decisions that unleash all manner of destruction upon the real world. And as they do so, the pirates of the Anyplace can be heard laughing in the distance.

Now you may be wondering just how far back the pirates of the Anyplace might stretch in the consciousness of man. The answer is quite simple: There have always been pirates in the Anyplace.

There has always been a Boy, and his cohorts, in the Anyplace.

The names change. The circumstances of how they got there and who they might be are constantly in flux. But heroes and villains remain heroes and villains, for such will always be needed to be in conflict with each other. Suffice to say that The Boy and Captains Hack and Slash were merely the latest occupants of roles in the Great Scheme of Things that long predated their arrival in the Anyplace and will continue long after their departure, whenever and however that might be.

The *Skull n' Bones*, left to its own devices, would unleash a new wave of fear and, most likely, war upon the hapless waking mind of man.

Naturally, The Boy and his allies were unaware of this. For that matter, so were the pirates. All were doing simply what came naturally, with none of them truly comprehending the stakes for which they were battling except in the most general and obscure sort of way. But that's as it should be. How much pressure, after all, do we need to inflict upon our heroes? The fact that they were in pursuit of The Boy's shadow and the captured Fiddlefix was certainly of sufficient moment.

We resume our narrative with the *Skull n' Bones* sailing across a sea as clear as glass in search of new prey. However, since there were no immediate victims for the pirates to ply their trade upon, naturally their interests were turning inward and upon one another.

Caveat, the most intelligent of the Bully Boys, was at that moment endeavoring to unseat Big Penny, the main commander of those Vagabond offshoots. With the reported demise of The Boy, Big Penny had become more swaggering and insulting than ever before. He was given to cuffing the other boys on the backs of their skulls if they didn't snap to fast enough upon receiving his orders. This didn't sit well with Caveat; and he was in the process of cozying up to Captain Slash, trying to convince her with as many impressive words as he could muster that she should place him in charge of the Bully Boys. His main method was to try and persuade Slash into thinking that Big Penny coveted her position as ship's captain. Pirates being a basically fearful lot, it didn't require much on Caveat's part to make Captain Slash think that Big Penny was eyeing her captaincy.

Meanwhile, Roomer was working his evil doings from the opposite direction. He was going around, slipping carefully chosen words like darts into the ears of such likely targets as Simon the Dancer. Simon, always on the lookout for all threats, was a perfect person to convince that Captain Slash and Caveat were plotting to get rid of all the Barbary pirates, since Slash considered them a threat to her authority. Why? Because they were such better pirates than she. A cunning plan on Roomer's part, since it appealed both to pirate vanity and pirate paranoia.

Captain Slash sensed unrest in her crew, and she solved the immediate problem by summoning Yorkers, who hadn't done a thing to anyone, and, in front of the entire crew, stabbing him. Yorkers pitched forward without a word; and as blood spread beneath him on the deck, Mary Slash said loudly, "Let this be a warning to anyone who talks to anyone about any-thing that I don't like!" She didn't let anyone come near York-ers for quite some time, and even when she said it was all right to do so, no one did because they were concerned it was some sort of trick.

It was left to poor Yorkers to haul himself across the deck, leaving a most undecorative trail of blood behind him. He man-aged to pull himself forward and tumble through the hatch that led to below deck. They heard nothing more of him and thus as-sumed that he'd died.

This sequence of events would likely not have had much im-pact on the politics aboard ship in the long run; but in the short run, it was quite effective, as both Roomer and Caveat reined in their activities in hopes of a more opportune time presenting it-self.

Up in the crow's nest, Simon the Dancer suddenly shouted and pointed out the latest thing he'd spotted that looked a likely target for the pirates. Mary Slash grabbed her telescope and fixed it in the direction Simon was indicating.

There, out in the middle of nowhere, was a dinghy being pi-loted by a head of state.

The choice of the dinghy was an appropriate one, since he had been feeling quite adrift and alone lately in terms of his leadership. There was no one he really trusted, and he had no clear idea in what direction he should take his country.

Mary Slash licked her lips, seeing this as an opportunity for some genuine entertainment. Such a small vessel naturally wouldn't contain much in the way of booty; but pirates sought fun wherever they could, and this looked to provide some.

So that you understand the severity of the situation, this is what was about to transpire.

The pirates were going to descend upon the head of state.

They were going to go directly toward him and not slow their approach at all. He would be forced to abandon his vessel as the pirate ship crashed right through it, shattering it to splinters. He would splash about in the cold water, crying for help, at which point the pirates would fish him out and make merry sport of him. They would strip him to his undergarments, pink him with their swords—all the time with him wondering when the killing blow would strike—and then tie his hands and ankles and send him off the plank. The water would envelop him, and he would sink like a stone; then he would awaken (since, unlike Paul and the others, he had come to the Anyplace in a transitional dreaming state).

Upon regaining consciousness, the head of state would feel a sense of weakness and humiliation such as he had never known. It would darken his soul and he would seek to expunge this new and unwanted sensation by taking it out on his own citizens, reveling in their helplessness in order to feel better about himself. People would suffer and people would die, lives would be ruined or ended, with the pirates in the center of it all, like a pebble thrown into a lake and causing a vast rippling effect.

All that because of one bad dream. And it happens more often, and in more varied ways, than you might suspect.

"More speed!" cried Captain Slash as she watched their latest target take notice of his pursuers. He let out an inarticulate scream and tried to row, but it might as well have been a snail trying to outrace a puma. The sails of the pirate ship flared wide, caught by the strong wind that was driving them straight toward their intended victim. The image of the pirate ship had been small on the horizon at first, but it was picking up speed and getting larger and larger with each passing second. The man in the dinghy flailed away at the water with the oars. His panic was impeding his ability to go about rowing in anything resembling an efficient manner. In the end, though, it wouldn't have mattered, because the pirate ship was simply too big and powerful, and the dinghy had not a chance. Mary Slash herself was at the wheel and was taking great delight in sending her mighty vessel barreling toward their target. Even the shade of her late brother had taken interest and was watching from the prow of the ship.

Here's a bit of irony.

It was Yorkers's turn to serve as second watch, meaning that if the crew's attention was focused on one place, Yorkers was to patrol the deck and keep an eye out in all other directions so that no one could sneak up on them. Since Mary Slash wasn't in charge of handing out deck assignments, however, she didn't know this. She'd just picked him at random to drive home her point (no pun intended). With Yorkers very likely bleeding to death below deck, no one else had stepped in to take up the slack. All attention was being paid to the man in the dinghy, and thus the crew of the pirate ship was unaware that it was under attack until the booms of a fusillade alerted them. By then, of course, it was a little late. If someone is setting upon you, you want to know about it before you find yourself under fire.

It was a stray gust of wind that saved them from immediate demolition. Just as the far distant thundering sounds of cannon reached them, an unexpected crosswind hit the sails. Before Mary Slash could make the adjustment, the ship was sent careening to port. Consequently, several cannonballs flew past, missing the mark and splashing harmlessly into the water beyond. What could have been a killing, or at least very destructive, stroke was reduced to a series of warning shots across the bow.

Still, whatever its initial intent, the result of the attack could not be argued with. And that result was to get the attention of the ship's denizens.

Mary Slash spun on her booted heel, and her eyes widened in shock as she saw a massive man-of-war bearing down upon them, its guns at the ready. To make matters worse, a fearsome storm was rolling in right behind it, propelling it toward the pirate ship with all speed.

Simon the Dancer, from the crow's nest, said, "Vessel off the starboard bow!"

"Oh, really!" shouted back Captain Slash, sarcasm drenching her voice. She refocused her telescope, wondering who in the world would be daft enough to challenge the most formidable pirate vessel afloat. She got her answer quickly enough when she peered at the oncoming ship and saw none other than The Boy perched in the rigging, gesturing straight at them with his sword. And running about on the deck, obeying his orders with remarkable precision, was a small army of painted Indians, with bows, arrows, and spears at the ready to supplement the array of guns bristling on the forecastle.

Mary Slash let out a scream of indignation and fury. *The Boy! The cursed Boy!*" Then she saw something else through her spyglass, namely Paul stalking the deck cloaked in the mantle of the white tiger. It took her only the barest of seconds to work out for herself how they'd been fooled, and her ire was almost so much that her body couldn't contain it.

Instantly forgotten was the small dinghy they'd been pursuing, and the head of state sailed away into irrelevance so far as our story is concerned, except to say that the crisis was averted and he was voted out in the very next election by an electorate that thought him too passive and insufficiently confrontational, to say nothing of having a newfound strange aversion to the yearly yacht races.

The crew of the *Skull n' Bones* scrambled about, with Mary Slash shouting all those nautical things that captains always shout when preparing for battle. The pirates sprang into action, raising and lowering sails in rapid succession while rolling out the guns. This time Mary Slash was going to make no mistakes.

The man-of-war bore down upon them, and through her spyglass she was able to make out the ship's name, etched on the side in proud, gilded letters: *Toy Boat Toy Boat Toy Boat*. Her eyebrows knit in confusion. The name made no sense to her, and she supposed it was an attempt at humor. She didn't find it remotely funny—as I'm sure you didn't either—but The Boy did, and that is all that matters.

Meanwhile, aboard the man-of-war, The Boy was bounding about, the incarnation of excitement. He waved his sword around with such gusto that he nearly sliced through one of the sails. Irregular and Porthos, pressed into service as gunnery mates, were preparing another round of shots for the cannons. Paul was at the helm, which he would have thought would be a far more difficult job than it was. But the *Toy Boat* was a gloriously responsive ship, reacting to his slightest touch. It was as if all he had to do was think about where he wanted the ship to go and it would move in that direction . . . which wasn't far off from the reality of it. Gwenny was standing in the prow, shouting updates to The Boy and Paul.

"We're closing the gap!" she said. "But I think they're . . . yes! They're coming about! Bringing their forward guns to bear!"

"Let them!" said The Boy, confident in his abilities and invulnerability.

Paul didn't sway from his course, but he called worriedly to Gwenny, "Is this ship impervious to cannon fire?"

There were three distant booms, and Gwenny said, "I think we're about to find out."

Sure enough, three cannonballs were flying through the air, coming straight toward the man-of-war in a graceful arc. It was a formidable piece of shooting, and it appeared to Paul that they were going to be struck directly. His first instinct was to cut the ship hard away from the oncoming projectiles.

"Stay the course!" said The Boy as he rocketed through the air toward the missiles. He met them halfway and bounded from one to the next to the next, bouncing off them in rapid succession like a child leaping across rocky islets across a river. In each case, The Boy brought his feet down and sent the cannonballs splashing harmlessly into the water. The waves were kicking up furiously, thanks to the storm that was rolling in directly behind the man-of-war, pushing it even faster.

Paul glanced over his shoulder and saw that the Indians were still engaged in their rain dance, with Princess Picca in the middle, shaking a spear and imploring the storm gods to keep doing what they were doing. Paul wondered briefly if it was the same storm deities who had sent that gigantic wave crashing down upon the Indians and nigh flooding out the entire island. He wondered how the Piccas could have suffered at the hands of those whom they were now imploring for help. But then he considered all the "acts of God" that fell upon people who then went right on praising that same God in the highest, and decided that it was probably a wiser course to practice forgiveness and humility when it came to beings who could wipe you out with a shrug of their shoulders.

Closer and closer they drew, and Paul was now able to see the pirates scrambling about on the deck of their ship. A second barrage of cannon fire fared exactly the same as the first, thanks to The Boy's deft footwork and reactions. Then the long guns of the *Toy Boat* cut loose, sending their own assault flying at the

Skull n' Bones. It was a carefully placed launch, aimed at taking out the sails, because they didn't want to risk sinking the vessel. After all, Fiddlefix was still aboard somewhere.

And then something moved through the air in front of the pirate ship. Paul recognized it instantly, and The Boy's breath caught in his throat as the shadow of Captain Hack advanced to defend his vessel. As opposed to leaping aboard the cannonballs, Hack simply moved from one cannonball to the next as soon as they came within range of the ship. His speed was far greater than The Boy's, since he was capable of moving at the speed of light (or dark, as the case may be). Nor was he vulnerable to the impact of the balls themselves. Instead, he smacked them aside with the blade of his hatchet.

Then the shadow pointed at The Boy in an unmistakable gesture that, even though offered in silence, spoke volumes: It said, *Come and get me, if you dare.*

The Boy pointed back in return. "I'm for you, Hack! We finished it once! And we'll keep finishing it until there's no returning, even for you!"

It was rapidly becoming clear what sort of climax events were coming to. This was not a battle that would be settled through force of cannon fire no matter how much weaponry the ships might have been respectively packing. This was going to be face-to-face, hand-to-hand.

Lightning cracked in the sky behind the *Toy Boat,* and the fearsome gusts of wind propelled it forward even more viciously. Rain began to pelt down, and Paul struggled manfully to keep the ship on its course. The Boy was perched atop, still pointing defiantly at the shade of his archenemy, who pointed back in return. The Indians were howling fury all the louder. Gwenny could make out the faces of the Bully Boys and pirates, twisted in rage and barely recognizable as anything human.

And a fearful thought crossed her mind unbidden: *This is going to end badly. We're not all going to make it.* But there was no one for her to share her concerns with; and even if there had been, it wouldn't have made much difference.

Suddenly the *Skull n' Bones* was coming right at them.

The abrupt change in the ship's course had been deft and swift. The man-of-war was indisputably the more powerful of the two; but the pirate ship was faster, more maneuverable, and under the helm touch of Mary Slash was simply the better piloted as compared to the novice hands of Paul Dear. All the crew of the *Toy Boat* knew was that the *Skull n' Bones* was coming right toward them, dead set on a collision course.

"Hard to starboard!" said The Boy from on high, but the wind carried his words away. Not hearing any countermanding orders, Paul kept the man-of-war straight on toward the pirate ship.

Gwenny ran to him and shouted in his ear, "What are you doing? We're going to ram them! Turn off!"

"They'll turn first," Paul said grimly, his voice a tiger growl. "They're pirates. They're cowards."

Clinging to the rigging above, The Boy waited for Paul to cut hard to starboard. But there was no movement save dead forward, and The Boy looked down to see that Paul hadn't altered his direction in the slightest. "Hard starboard!" The Boy called once more, and still their course didn't change. He started to leap down toward Paul, but his foot snagged in the rigging, and The Boy dangled upside down, trying to pull his foot free from the rain-soaked ropes.

The storm had now spread beyond the man-of-war. The skies were solid black; and bizarrely the winds were coming from two different directions, one pushing the man-of-war, the other the pirate vessel. It was as if two different groups of storm gods had chosen sides and were curious to see who would triumph.

At the helm of the pirate ship, Mary Slash held firm to her course. She was convinced that the man-of-war would try to get out of the way; and when it did, then the *Skull n' Bones* would ram her amidships. With any luck, it would be enough to break apart the man-of-war and send both halves to the bottom of the sea. She was even more convinced of the viability of her plan when she saw that the youthful Paul was at the helm. "Come on, then," she snarled. "It's one thing to have your fun at our expense when you're hiding in the high weeds! Let's see what you're made of when confronted with impending destruction!"

They hurtled toward each other, two determined juggernauts, neither one backing off. Gwenny was shouting to Paul that perhaps he should reconsider what he was doing, but Paul's jaw was set in determination, convinced that he wasn't going to turn away in the face of bullying behavior. Captain Hack, meantime, was gesturing wildly to his sister to turn from her course, but she naturally couldn't understand what he was saying; and, besides, she would be blasted to perdition if she allowed herself to back down in the face of an attack by a slip of a boy, of all things.

Closer and closer still, and both Paul and Captain Slash came to a mutual realization at about the same time: namely that neither was going to turn away. At the last second, both of them decided to cut hard; but there was a split-second hesitation as to which way to go. In that fraction of a second, the final gusts of wind from either side shoved them forward faster than either anticipated.

As a result, with much accompanying alarmed shouts from both crews, the two vessels crashed head-on. There was a thunderous splintering and crunching of wood as the ships collided.

Gwenny was thrown backward, tumbling behind Paul; and Paul barely managed to hold on to the wheel. The Indians and the other boys were sent staggering as well. As for The Boy, he was jolted free from the rigging and, before he could gather his wits to fly, wound up tumbling down the rigging and hitting the rain-slicked deck.

Over on the pirate vessel, Mary Slash slammed up against the steering wheel and almost managed to put out one of her own eyes with her sword blade. The pirates rolled about the deck like pinballs, crashing up against one another. The only one who wasn't thrown about was the shadow of Captain Hack, who simply floated there, shaking his head.

Neither ship was damaged so calamitously that they were in danger of sinking, for what had really engaged were the bowsprits of both vessels. The large spars, projecting from the prow, collided not head-on but just to the side of each other. As a result, they ran the length of each other, like two swords coming together and sliding down their respective blades. The figureheads of the two vessels then crashed into each other, the fearsome skull of the pirates smashing directly into the rather attractive mermaid that decorated the bow of the man-of-war. They both shattered under the impact. Meanwhile, the forward sails that had been anchored to the bowsprits broke apart, sending piles of canvas collapsing to the respective decks.

Rain poured down all the harder, and for a moment the two mighty vessels bobbed in the water like corks. The only sound to be heard was the creaking of wood as the two vessels remained there, enmeshed and entangled.

And then The Boy was on his feet, and he pointed his sword at the pirates and said, "Teachers of betrayal and mistrust, have at thee!"

And then Mary Slash pointed her sword at him in response

and shouted back, "Students of the naive and credulous, prepare for thy final lesson!"

The Indians massed behind The Boy, while the fearsome pirates came running at the behest of Captain Slash, and, charging across the engaged bowsprits, the two forces of good and evil crashed headlong into their final battle.

Chapter 18

Death at Sea

As Yorkers lay below deck, he was barely aware of the crashing together of opposing forces above him. Instead, his attention was entirely inward as he contemplated the length and breadth of his life and came to the conclusion that he had wasted it.

This was a crushing realization for him, because here's the truth of it: When young men misbehave, they do so in the belief that eventually they'll have the opportunity to correct their behavior. Youth is the time for wrongheaded actions. As long as they straighten out by the time they become adults, they will wind up good husbands, good fathers, and good men...a goal held by far more nasty young men than you could imagine.

The advantage of residing in the Anyplace is that the time for misbehavior can be extended indefinitely, at least in theory.

Where the theory falls down is that people can die violently in the Anyplace as readily as elsewhere.

Yorkers was beginning to understand that such was the case

with him. A wasted life, a wasted death, and nothing else to come was all that awaited him.

He lay there, clutching at his chest and sobbing piteously. Slowly he became aware that there was some sort of major battle going on overhead. But it had decreasing relevance to him.

He heard the distinctive shouting of The Boy, which was surprising since he had supposedly been eaten by a tiger, and Captain Slash shouting back at him, and the clashing of swords. There were war whoops from Indians, which was even more surprising to Yorkers, since Captain Slash had been convinced that they'd been wiped out and he'd had no reason to doubt her. There was the pounding of feet overhead—people running back and forth—and Yorkers tried to bring himself to standing so that he could be a part of it. Except he realized at that moment that, even were he capable of joining the battle, he couldn't be entirely sure which side he would fight on. After all, the captain to whom he'd sworn fealty had stabbed him, possibly to death—that remained to be seen. On the other hand, The Boy was not noted for his compassionate and forgiving nature; he was just as likely to run Yorkers through as look at him.

Finding a bulkhead to lean against, Yorkers forced himself to stand, even though his legs were shaking violently. He licked his lips, which were suddenly bone-dry, and then he heard the light footfall of someone coming down the companionway. Yorkers had his short sword tucked in his sash, and he pulled it free and held it with both hands, even though they were both covered with his own blood.

A lithe figure landed directly in front of him. They both gasped upon seeing each other.

"Gwenny," he managed to say.

For it was indeed Gwenny. Her hair was slicked down, her clothes plastered by the rain to her body. She was holding a broken belaying pin in her hand, for she had shattered it on the head of the fearsome pirate Agha Bey. She'd hit the pirate from the side while he had been facing off against Paul. Paul had voiced a brief protest, his pride not allowing him to admit that he was relieved at her intervention.

Having taken it upon herself to try and find the missing Fiddlefix, Gwenny had come below deck and was quite surprised to discover Yorkers facing her. Her surprise was quickly replaced by alarm when she saw the spreading red stain upon his shirt. "Yorkers! You—you need help!"

Yorkers shook his head, keeping his sword up so that Gwenny couldn't proceed. "Nothing can help me," he whispered, surprised at the hoarseness of his voice.

Gwenny's mind raced, trying to figure out a way past him, and suddenly she said out of nowhere, "Fiddlefix can help you."

He looked at her suspiciously. "She—she can?"

"Of course. She can cure that wound with pixie magic. Didn't you know that?"

Yorkers shook his head. "Are you sure?"

"Yes, absolutely sure. Don't you remember all the times she cured us of various wounds and ills? Certainly you must!"

He didn't recall a single incident, but he was loath to admit it. "I—I guess I remember . . . something like that. . . ."

"Take me to her! If you do, and we free her, she can cure you. Fix up that wound in your chest in no time."

For a long moment his determination wavered, and then Yorkers saw all hope of future redemption sliding away from him, and he said, "Come with me."

Gwenny followed him as he took her directly to the cabin of Captain Mary Slash. It was ornately decorated; and, left to her own devices, Gwenny might never have located what she was looking for. But Yorkers, leaning against the captain's reading desk, pointed with his sword toward a cabinet and said, "In there. Second drawer down."

She pulled open the drawer and removed a tightly locked box. "Fiddle?" she called softly. "Fiddlefix? Are you . . . ?"

She didn't need to finish the question as a spirited chatter issued from within the box. Gwenny sagged in relief. "Thank heavens we found you!" She turned toward Yorkers and started to say, "The key! We need the key to open—"

Yet again she did not finish what she was saying, but in this case it was out of surprise. Yorkers had collapsed to the floor, lying motionless. She took a step toward him and then stopped, for standing in the doorway, looking as fearsome as ever, was Agha Bey. He had his saber in his hand, and his face was twisted in a terrible scowl. There was blood on the side of his face, but otherwise he seemed none the worse for wear.

"Put that down," growled Agha Bey.

Gwenny stood her ground. "Get out of my way," she said defiantly, hoping that spunk and bravery would win the day.

Her hope was short-lived. It lasted for exactly as long as was required for Agha Bey to advance upon her, the edge of his sword gleaming and looking thirsty for a new victim. Gwenny didn't flinch but instead held the broken belaying pin up in as threatening a manner as she could muster.

Agha Bey let out a coarse, confident laugh and drew back his sword in clear preparation to retrieve the box by chopping it right out of Gwenny's hands. Suddenly he gasped and looked down in surprise at the sword point that was protruding from his chest. Agha Bey looked over his shoulder and saw Yorkers directly behind him, desperately holding his sword as if it was the only thing keeping him on his feet. As it turned out, that was exactly the case: When Agha Bey, with a final curse in his native tongue that neither Yorkers nor Gwenny could understand, collapsed to the deck, he took Yorkers with him. They lay there in a tangle of arms and legs; and now we must tragically say farewell to Yorkers, for the truth was that Fiddlefix had no such power as Gwenny ascribed to her, and Yorkers's fate was already sealed. But at least he achieved some degree of redemption in his final actions and thus was satisfied with the way things turned out.

Gwenny, spared from having to admit to Yorkers that she had been lying, and knowing it would be a sin that she would carry upon her soul forever, stepped over their unmoving bodies and clambered back up the companionway. She emerged upon the deck and saw chaos everywhere.

The Boy was battling furiously and with greater energy than ever against the shade of Captain Hack but was regrettably having no more luck against his unreal opponent than he'd had earlier. Paul, meantime, was battling Mary Slash; and, although he was proving a deft opponent, he was still clearly not in her league as she effortlessly turned aside every one of his thrusts.

Scattered throughout the rest of the pirate ship were the Indians in savage battle with the pirates. Lightning danced overhead, as if the gods of storm were applauding their entertainment.

"Let me out!" Fiddlefix cried from within. "Let me out! I can save the day!" Gwenny didn't know what she was saying since she didn't speak the language of pixies, but Fiddle's urgency was impossible to misinterpret. She looked desperately around for something that she could use to break open the lock upon the box. Finally she spotted a knife a short distance away. Tossing aside the useless, shattered belaying pin, she moved quickly toward the knife, holding the box firmly in one hand.

Not firmly enough, as it turned out.

A sudden lurch of the ship, and Gwenny was off balance. With her free hand she grabbed at something, anything that would enable her to maintain her footing, and at that instant a crack of lightning in the dark skies caused her to stand out and catch Mary Slash's eye. The pirate queen realized what Gwenny was holding and intuited the danger that an unleashed Fiddle presented. Stepping back from Paul, she lashed out with one foot and connected, kicking the box out of Gwenny's grasp.

"Fiddlefix! No!" shrieked Gwenny, but it was too late. The box spiraled away from her and over the side of the ship.

The Boy was too far away to do anything about it, but Paul did not hesitate. It was Fiddlefix who had brought him to the Anyplace, who had helped him in his endeavors, even if her reasons were entirely selfish. And it was Fiddlefix who was now in trouble as the box that imprisoned her tumbled into the sea.

Shoving his blade into his belt, Paul vaulted after the box. Mary Slash tried to bisect him as he passed, but he somersaulted in the air before passing out of her range. He saw the box just as it hit the water and vanished. Keeping his arms and legs in perfect diving position, Paul hit the water cleanly and descended after the box.

Mary Slash turned and saw Gwenny standing there, looking not only distraught but helpless. Gwenny was as plucky a heroine as they came, but she really wasn't all that much for fighting; and, besides, she wasn't holding anything that could match the terrifying blade nestled on the end of Captain Slash's arm.

"Now you die," Mary Slash said, and she came straight at Gwenny.

And something suddenly blocked her way.

Captain Slash took a step back as a vicious spearhead nearly split her face in two. She steadied herself on the pitching deck and saw that Princess Picca was facing her. The princess was holding a spear crosswise, and on her face was an expression of supreme confidence.

"Pick on someone own size," said the princess.

With an angry shout, Captain Slash came at her with her blade. The spear whirled like a propeller in Princess Picca's hands, batting away the sword and returning with a thrust that nicked off a small swatch of fabric from Slash's coat. Slash jumped back, regarding the princess with far more caution as the two of them lobbied for a superior position.

Beneath the water, Paul Dear swam as hard and fast as he could. He saw the box falling through the water, falling, and there was the softest of glows from within. The box slowed ever so slightly, and he realized that Fiddlefix was trying to prevent it from sinking through sheer force of will. He made a desperate grab for it, but then it fell once more. He felt the air starting to burn in his lungs, and knew he was running out of time. He realized he was rapidly approaching a decision point, that he was weighing his own life against the possibility of saving Fiddle's. He was keenly aware that there had to be an airhole in the box, and if that was the case, the box was doubtless filling up with water. It meant that Fiddle was going to drown unless he snagged the box within seconds.

And then, below him, he saw something looking up at him. It was an eye.

It was a huge eye, as big as Paul himself if not bigger. Then something appeared next to it, and he realized it was a second eye, having lazily opened.

In the darkness and murk of the waters, he saw the shadows of gargantuan tentacles moving about.

The box tumbled down, down, and struck directly between the two round eyes. They blinked in surprise as the box ricocheted and landed in one of the tentacles.

Paul's heart sank. His breath was screaming to evacuate his

lungs, and those tentacles looked large enough to crush a city bus. He had no idea what he was facing—kraken, squid, octopus, or something else entirely—but there were two things he knew without question:

He could talk to animals.

He was out of time.

Staking everything on one roll of the dice, Paul opened his mouth and burbled out, "Help us . . . please . . ."

Then he closed his mouth as quickly as he could, but seawater was already working its way into his lungs. He started to sink, clutching at his chest, despair overwhelming him. *I've failed,* he thought miserably.

Suddenly he felt something pushing him upward. He realized immediately that it was one of the creature's tentacles. The box was flipped into his grasp in an almost offhand manner, and he clutched it to his chest. Quickly he slapped his hands over the airhole to try to prevent even more water from flooding into the box, if it wasn't already too late.

And then the surface of the water was there. With one final push the tentacles shoved him upward, and he was hurled up and out of the water. He still had enough ability to fly left to him that he rocketed up onto the deck, landing while coughing water violently out of his lungs.

He saw that the pirates were putting up a mighty battle, but they couldn't begin to match the savagery of the Indians. Princess Picca was still trading blows with Captain Slash, while The Boy was making absolutely no progress against Captain Hack.

Paul overturned the box, allowing the water to pour out. Fiddlefix wasn't saying anything. A grim dread began to grow in him that he had been too late to save her. Rain continued to pour down, as if the skies themselves were crying for her.

"Paul! Look out!"

Gwenny's cry alerted him to the danger. The shadow of Captain Hack was coming right toward him, having turned its attention away from The Boy. Paul knew right then that Hack wanted to make sure Fiddlefix did not break free of her confinement. Running their previous encounter through his mind, he suddenly realized that Fiddle had never gotten near the shadow of Hack at all. Instead Mary Slash had intercepted her with a well-thrown weapon.

The Boy, seeing that Hack had broken off the battle with him, mistook it as a sign that he had Hack on the run. This resulted not in his pursuing Hack, as would have been the wise move, but instead in his doing a small dance of triumph that accomplished nothing other than showing that The Boy could dance quite adroitly. By the time he realized that Hack was running toward something rather than away from him, it was too late to intercept the shade's course.

Hack swung the hatchet and Paul darted under it. The shadow pivoted with such speed that Paul never even saw the turn. Captain Hack's silhouette pursued him, swinging furiously in an attempt to crack open Paul's skull like a cantaloupe.

It was at that instant that Paul's racing mind came up with a move that would serve as both defense and offense, provided he could pull it off.

The pirate shadow was coming at him—left, right, left, right—swinging the shadowy ax blade in a regular, rhythmic manner. Paul timed it perfectly, and brought the metal box up just as the ax was sweeping past.

Captain Hack's blade crashed against the lock on the box, shattering it.

Paul threw open the box and tossed it to the ground as if it were suddenly scalding hot. The lid fell open and, in a small wave of water, Fiddlefix was spilled out onto the deck.

Trying to grab its opportunity, the shadow of Hack swung its hatchet directly at Fiddlefix. Paul knew he was helpless to stop it, because the shadow was still fully capable of touching whatever it wished, but anyone who endeavored to initiate contact wound up with large handfuls of nothingness.

But Fiddlefix recovered with amazing alacrity, and she darted up and out of Hack's way as his ax hit nothing. Freed of her imprisonment, ripe for vengeance against those who had discommoded her, Fiddlefix started to glow with the force of a miniature sun. The intensity of her illumination was directly proportional to the ferocity of her temperament, and at that moment Fiddlefix was feeling temperamental enough to blind a herd of bison.

"Get him, Fiddle!" said Paul, pumping the air. Realizing what was happening, The Boy followed suit. Even Captain Slash and Princess Picca briefly halted their battle, standing frozen several feet away from each other with their weapons at the ready, to see what was transpiring.

The blinding glow of Fiddlefix approached Captain Hack, driving the shadow backward. It tried to ward her off with its hatchet, but the more brightly she glowed, the more daunted did the shadow become.

It all made perfect sense to Paul. Darkness was helpless in the face of light.

"Get it, Fiddle!" Paul said. "Break it into shards! Blind it into nothingness! Destroy it for all time!"

All of that Fiddle seemed more than happy to do. Her light escalated in brilliance, as if she were a spotlight that someone was increasing the wattage of. No longer appearing remotely as certain or confident as it had been, the shadow fell back, back.

It didn't even have the strength to strike at Fiddle. She was scolding him furiously in her native tongue as she drew closer. She darted forward, grazing the shadow, and it grabbed its arm where she had come into contact with it.

And then Paul saw The Boy, hovering overhead, watching Fiddlefix systematically demolishing their mutual opponent.

He looked resigned to the shadow's destruction.

He looked . . . old. Or older.

That was when Paul realized the horrific flaw in the proceedings. If Fiddlefix succeeded in destroying the fearsome shade, as it now appeared she was going to be able to do through the sheer nature of her glow, then there was every chance she would destroy the shadow of The Boy as well. If she did that, The Boy was finished.

Without thinking, Paul darted forward, interposing himself between Fiddlefix and the shadow of Hack. "No, Fiddle!" he said, bringing her up short. "We need to—"

What Paul needed to do was never uttered, for Captain Hack chose that moment to bury his shadowy hatchet deep in Paul's back.

The Boy cried out his name, but it was too late. Paul had allowed his guard to lapse for not more than a second, but that was all the time that a miscreant such as Captain Hack needed to do his dirty work.

Paul turned to face Hack, which was the absolute worst thing he could have done, for Hack sliced forward with the hatchet once more, cutting deep into Paul's chest. It was a miracle that he missed Paul's heart, but for all that it added to Paul's survival, he might as well have cut that mighty muscle in twain. Paul staggered, blood trickling from between his lips, and Gwenny called to him, as did The Boy. He didn't hear them. All he heard was the voice of his own conscience, berating him and telling him that he had completely botched everything. That not only was his mother going to be bereft of a daughter, but now she wasn't going to have a son either.

Probably for the best. I bet she won't even miss me, thought Paul as he stumbled over his own feet and pitched forward. He struck the shadowy figure of Captain Hack headfirst and vanished into nothingness.

Gwenny's high-pitched scream of alarm served to halt much of the remaining fighting aboard the ship. Everyone sensed that something fundamental had changed . . . that the challenges presented them were about to be brought to a new level far beyond the simple brutality of knife against ax and sword against spear. The Boy floated several feet away from the shadow of his late enemy and snapped angrily, "Let him go!"

There was no sign of Paul. None of him had reemerged on the other side. It was as if he had fallen through a hole in the air itself.

"Let him go, I said!" The Boy said, and threw himself directly at the shade of Captain Hack. Cold overwhelmed him for a split instant and then he reemerged on the other side, trembling. He spun to face the shadow of Hack again, knowing that any attempt to assault it would simply have the same result . . . a result he didn't pretend to understand.

Captain Slash stepped near him, grinning lopsidedly. "You understand nothing, Boy. Don't you see? Only the dead or dying may enter the twilight realm from which my brother's shadow emanates, dwelling in a half existence between life and death. You are neither dead nor dying. So you have no hope of retrieving the lad. Not that you could have anyway; he is beyond all help or salvation."

"No," The Boy said fiercely. "Nothing happens in the Anyplace save that I want it to."

"Then you must want the other lad dead," suggested Captain Slash. "Not that I blame you. So brave and adventurous, selfless is he. He makes you look bad in comparison; certainly you must see that."

"You lie!"

"About which part?" she said innocently.

"About all of it!"

"Boy, don't listen to her!" Gwenny said.

"Yes, Boy, by all means, don't!" said Captain Slash. "I've no doubt you're afraid of what you'll hear."

Both Gwenny and Princess Picca started to speak, but he made a preemptive gesture, silencing them. "I'm afraid of nothing," The Boy told her, wanting it to be true, knowing it wasn't, but not caring.

"Well, then . . . after him you go."

And Mary Slash stabbed forward with her sword. The Boy made no move other than to throw wide his arms and welcome the thrust as it bit deeply into him. He heard Gwenny cry out, and Princess Picca made a noise like an outraged hawk; and Fiddlefix shouted his name, his true name; and then he fell forward into the welcoming darkness of Captain Hack and heard nothing more.

Chapter 19

Anyplace and Noplace

Paul was dangling from a very high place when he saw The Boy in the distance.

The Boy was looking around in bewilderment, probably thinking that nothing had changed since he was still standing on the deck of a pirate ship.

It took him a moment to realize the first thing that was different: It was much colder.

Much, much colder.

The ocean was frozen. Ice stretched out in all directions, and there were several large icebergs dotting the area. A steady wind was blowing, causing the sails to flap, but the ship was incapable of moving anywhere. It was completely locked into the ice.

The Boy looked up. The sky was as a second home to him, so it was natural for him to do so.

The blue of the Anyplace sky was gone. Nor was there any sign of the storm that had been hammering the ships. Instead, there was gray, nothing but gray. So much gray as to be unnatural.

Then The Boy thought to look at his own hands. They were gray as well, along with his clothes. It was as if all sense of color had been sucked out of the environment.

"Boy!" Paul shouted, his distant voice finally managing to capture The Boy's attention. The Boy turned in the general direction he thought it was coming from.

It was from one of the icebergs. Paul was hanging off one of the projecting cliffs, very high up. But he wasn't hanging from his fingers or any such thing. Instead he was being dangled, his arms and legs flopping about helplessly. And The Boy's heart threatened to stop when he saw who was holding him. As I'm sure you've surmised by now . . . it was Captain Hack.

But he was no longer a mere shadow of himself. Instead there was the villain, big as life—or unlife, or whatever it was that passed for existence in this land of black and gray. His greatcoat flapped in the wind, and he was holding Paul with his good hand while keeping his hatchet poised near the lad's throat.

"I see you down there, Boy!" he called, the wind carrying his evil voice all the way to The Boy's ears. "Come to me! I've been waiting ever so long for you, Boy. Come and entertain the hatchet!"

The Boy hesitated there on the deck of the immobilized sailing vessel. He was still feeling disoriented, unsure where he was or how he had come to be there.

The Boy took several quick steps, bounded to the rail of the ship, and leaped skyward.

All the more depressing, then, when he discovered himself utterly bereft of flight. His arms pinwheeled in alarm, as he tumbled and struck the ice-covered water below. The ice was so thick that he didn't even come close to cracking through it. He did, however, manage to bang himself up rather impressively. But he held up his scraped elbows and examined his knees and saw there was no bleeding.

Paul's spirit plummeted when he saw that. He knew that he was lacking the power of flight, but he had hoped that The Boy, more accomplished in the art of flying, would still have the knack. He was crushed to find otherwise.

Meanwhile, The Boy, just out of curiosity, put his hand to his chest.

There was no heartbeat.

He didn't panic about this latest development or let it bother him overmuch. Nor did he raise any of the sort of deep, philosophical questions that you or I might have conjured. Instead he simply accepted it as a reality of his new environment. Then he set off for the iceberg on foot, the thin layer of snow crunching beneath his feet.

"No hurry, Boy!" said Captain Hack, seemingly overjoyed to be able to communicate once more beyond futile gestures. "We have all the time in the world here!"

The Boy had no clue where "here" was, but that didn't deter him from striding across the ice. He didn't run, for the ice and snow were slippery and he was uncertain of his footing. His inelegant attempt to fly already stung him sufficiently, and he had no desire to provide further amusement for the onlooking pirate captain. Were he capable of flying, he would have been soaring around Captain Hack, hurling taunts and reveling in his superiority. Absent that, he didn't feel much like engaging in banter. So he set his jaw and made his slow, measured way along the frozen sea.

The pirate captain, however, didn't feel the least disinclined to palaver. "Do you sense the cold beginning to set in, Boy?" said Hack. "Oh, you don't feel it at first. At first you have to get used to your surroundings. But it should be working its way into you by now. The cold in your muscles, your joints. If your blood were flowing, it would be slowing down about now. Figured it out yet, Boy? Know where you are?"

The Boy didn't know, nor did he care. What he knew was that, annoyingly enough, the pirate's words were starting to affect him. Whereas before he had felt nothing of this inhospitable place, now a bone-crushing chill was seeping through him. By the time he reached the base of the frozen mountain upon which Hack was perched with the helpless Paul, the icy wind was suffusing his being and he couldn't remember a time when he'd ever been warm.

Paul, meanwhile, had changed his tune. Seeing The Boy's fallen state, he had begun warning him to keep his distance, urging him not to risk himself on Paul's behalf. Captain Hack had responded by shaking him violently and snarling, "This has almost nothing to do with you, lad. There is unfinished business between The Boy and me, and you are simply a means to an end...an end that would have been forthcoming whether you were here or not."

The Boy climbed and continued to climb. The wind became fiercer the higher he ascended. The entire time he made his way up, he was convinced that he was not alone. Every so often he would stop and glance over his shoulder, but there was nothing there. Just the stark whiteness of the icy mountain. Light flurries of snow were swirling around him like so many tiny white insects. He brushed them away, looked again, saw nothing again. This place was playing vicious tricks upon his very consciousness.

"Just a little farther, Boy," came the taunting voice. "What's the matter? Slower going when you can't just flap your arms and fly?"

The Boy wanted to have some sort of clever, biting response, but nothing came to mind. And suddenly he rounded a corner and there was Captain Hack, holding Paul over the drop.

"Put him down," said The Boy very quietly, very firmly.

"You don't issue dictates to me, Boy. Not here. Not in this place. I have waited too long for—"

Displaying absolutely no patience for the back-and-forth that Captain Hack so famously enjoyed, like a cat slapping around a small rodent, The Boy interrupted him and said in that same quiet, firm voice, "Put him down gently, now, and deal with me, or I'm leaving."

"I don't believe you."

The Boy shrugged, turned, and started to make his way back down the icy mountain. Realizing The Boy was completely serious, Captain Hack quickly dropped Paul at his feet, clear of the drop. Paul fell roughly onto his rump and tried to stand. But The Boy turned back and said coolly, "Stay down, Paul. This is between Hack and me."

"It always has been," said Captain Hack with a sneer. "And how fitting that it should come down to the two of us here, of all places."

"But where is here of all places?" Paul said. His head was swimming; he had no idea what was happening. He only knew that the wind was cutting into him like a thing alive and that if he didn't have the tiger skin wrapped around him, he would be freezing to death . . . assuming death was even an option for him.

"Why don't you tell him?" Hack said to The Boy, gesturing with a nod of his head toward Paul.

"Tell him what? What do I know of this, whatever this is?"

"Oh, you know. In your heart, you've always known. Come on now. Think." Rather than villainous, Captain Hack sounded almost avuncular, as if he were pulling for The Boy to pass some particularly challenging test. "Just as you share all with the Any-place, so too is this part of you. It's simply a part that you've never wanted to admit to. It's the part you don't like to think about. Let it seep into you now so you can answer Paul's question . . . for him and for you."

There was something in Hack's words that prompted The Boy to do as he said. The opening up of his mind to the Any-place was something he had learned to do almost instinctively. This place . . . well, it was something else again, but that didn't mean he was incapable of connecting with it in the same way. He did not close his eyes because he did not want to remove his gaze from Hack for even a moment, although the pirate did not especially look as if he were about to make a move against The Boy. But he turned his vision inward, letting his mind wander across the vastness of the black and gray wasteland that lay all around them.

His inner eye, the center of his imagination, showed him a realm of terrible foreboding. His mind soared above it, as he himself would have if he'd had the power of flight. It looked much like the Anyplace, but the gray and black hues perme-ated every aspect of it.

And there were inhabitants, yes. But they were nothing like the joyful, spirited, adventurous denizens of the Anyplace. No, these inhabitants were not living in their surroundings. They simply existed there.

And they burned. They burned with frustration or sadness or hatred. They burned for goals unaccomplished, for words left unsaid, for emotional turmoil unresolved. They seethed be-cause they were unable to communicate with those who really mattered. They went neither forward nor back. They just . . . were . . . and were not.

"Boy?" Paul said softly. He didn't move from the place Captain Hack had dropped him. "Boy?" Then, angrily, he turned on Hack and said, "What did you do to him!"

Credit Paul with courage. He still had his sword, and he pulled it out now to face the pirate as The Boy simply stood nearby, rocking slightly on his heels but otherwise looking as if he had completely lost touch with his surroundings (when, ironically, just the opposite was true). Captain Hack noticed the defiant gesture and simply chuckled softly. "You have determination, lad . . . but not much wisdom." Hack had his cutlass out, and the hatchet that adorned his wrist was at the ready.

Paul charged him, hoping that youth and determination would win the day. Such was not the case. Their swords clashed for mere seconds, and then Hack knocked the sword out of Paul's hand. Hack brought his sword around, looking prepared to sever Paul's head, and suddenly The Boy's blade intercepted his swing. Hack grinned. "So you've rejoined us, I see. And what, pray tell, have you managed to discern in your ponderings?"

The Boy stepped back, keeping his blade leveled. "This," he said, his voice carefully controlled, "is the Noplace. If the Anyplace is the place between dreaming and wakefulness, the Noplace is the place between dreaming and the end of life."

"Just so," Hack said proudly. Again, he could have been no more pleased than if The Boy had been his own son, answering difficult questions for a grueling exam. "People in comas reside here, helpless to reply as their loving relatives sit at their bedsides and chatter to them endlessly about this, that, and the other thing. And this is also the residence of those who have passed, or are about to, but have scores to settle. Vengeance left unaccomplished. That which people call 'ghosts' exist here, with pale reflections of themselves occasionally seeping over into the world of man." He gestured toward the expanse of it. "Is it not magnificent, Boy? All your life you've taken refuge in the Anyplace so that you would never grow older. And now you've taken up residence in the Noplace, where you will elude death... but on my terms this time. My terms." And suddenly he said, "Mine!" and came straight at The Boy.

The Boy darted back, deftly keeping his blade up. He did not have the power of flight, but he still intercepted Hack's charge with accuracy and certainty. Their swords clanged together, running up each other's blades, bringing Hack and The Boy together with their sword guards locked, each pushing against the other.

"We end this now," said The Boy.

"You don't understand. It never ends."

With that declaration, Hack shoved The Boy backward down the icy path that he had climbed to get there. The Boy tumbled foot over face, and when he managed to skid to a halt, he saw Captain Hack coming right after him, laughing loudly, and his cutlass shaking with urgency.

The Boy rolled out of the way, falling off the edge of the icy mountain. Fortunately it wasn't far to the bottom at that point, and he landed nimbly on his feet. He was amazed to see Captain Hack leap into the air, somersault, and land squarely in front of him.

"Let me explain to you what the rest of your existence will be like," Hack said generously.

He attacked then with eagerness and ferocity, and The Boy found himself retreating.

"Imagine a future where, since you are not truly alive, you cannot truly die," said Hack as he thrust forward. The Boy parried desperately. Hack continued to come at him, his sword blinding. "Nor will we ever truly tire. We will spend the remainder of our twilight existence, if not eternity itself, battling fiercely without letup or respite." He lashed out with one

booted foot, catching The Boy squarely in the chest and knocking him back. The Boy, feeling leaden, fell, and then scrambled
to his feet. Hack advanced, the point of his sword shaking not
from fear but anticipation.

"This will be your punishment, Boy, and I could never have
conceived of a better one if left to my own devices fore'er." Captain Hack chortled as he spoke. The Boy had already managed
to stab his opponent several times, but none of them mattered.
The cuts healed instantly; death would not take him. "Until the
end of reality and unreality itself, we shall battle! No quarter will
be asked or given, nor will it matter. Do you not see the glorious
irony of it? You, who hid in the Anyplace so you would never
have to move forward in your development, have now gotten
your wish! You shall never move forward, nor back, nor side to
side, nor any which way. You will always be no more and no less
than you are right now: the eternal opponent of Captain Hack!"

They battled around the perimeter of the iceberg, Hack
more relaxed and amused by The Boy's defenses than he'd ever
been. The Boy shouted back defiantly, "You're insane if you
think I'm going to spend the rest of eternity just existing to be
your fencing partner!"

"I don't see that you have much choice, Boy," Hack said.

"I could put up my sword. I could stop."

"Quitting isn't in you, Boy," Hack said, and that was true
enough. Then he added, "Besides, here's what you haven't considered: If you do not fight, I will have off your legs. Your arms.
Your head. And you won't die, because in this realm you cannot. Instead, you'll simply lie there, resting in pieces, while I
stand and laugh at you. Then I will do the same to your little
friend, and laugh at him. And when I am bored with that, I'll re-
assemble you and we'll begin the entire process over again. Face
it, Boy. You are trapped. Trapped!"

Back and forth across the ice they battled, The Boy now putting on an aggressive display of bravado. But it seemed as if Hack was playing with him. That he didn't care much what The Boy did, for the ultimate laugh would be from Hack directly at The Boy.

"How does it feel, Boy?" Hack said, his cutlass deftly slicing a pattern in the air. "How does it feel to know that I was in your mind like no other? How does it feel knowing that you're going to be staring into my face for ever and ever, unable to escape me or the knowledge that, once and for all, my triumph is com- plete? And you know what else? You never defeated me in the first place! Not ever! It was the beast that was my demise, and you've no fearsome creatures to help you now! Here, there is just you and your wits, and that is not enough. Not remotely enough by half!"

Slowly The Boy's spirit began to shrink. He was starting to realize that Hack was correct. The odd thing was that Hack was embracing the notion of eternal battle, which should have pleased The Boy as well, since there was nothing he liked bet- ter than a good scrap. But he wasn't pleased. The concept of never moving forward, of seizing upon one aspect of his life and never moving beyond that—in those terms, it seemed one of the most pointless endeavors in creation. But was that not, at its core, the philosophy of The Boy himself?

The Boy looked into the face of his enemy and saw the waste of his own life there, and he did not like it in the least.

Paul had clambered down from the iceberg, but he was help- less to intervene, and Captain Hack was laughing loudly and tri- umphantly; for as you know he is a most educated villain and could appreciate irony in a way that most other pirates never could.

That was when Paul felt something, something ... pervading

the area. They were not alone. Something was there; something was watching them.

The Boy obviously felt it, too. He closed his eyes, reached out, tried to get a sense of what was near them, inviting it to reveal itself to him. Hack did not hesitate and thrust forward with his sword, howling in triumph before remembering that he might as well have stabbed a cloud for all the good it did. The problem was that his sword was now lodged in The Boy's chest, and he was having trouble removing it because The Boy was gripping it firmly. Angry, Hack brought his fearsome hatchet up to try to bury it squarely in The Boy's face, but at that moment The Boy kicked away into Hack's chest, knocking him back. The Boy pulled the pirate's cutlass from his chest and for a moment stood there with a sword in either hand, looking as fierce and primitive as he ever had.

He was about to attack yet again, but suddenly Paul was in the way, and he was facing Captain Hack.

"Stand aside, Paul," said The Boy. "He's mine."

"No. He's ours," said Paul, intuiting what he needed to do. Yanking off the tiger skin that he'd been wearing as a cloak, he threw it as hard as he could toward Hack. The throw wasn't an especially good one and the wind began to carry the skin, to send it skimming across the ground.

And then something seemed to ripple through the air, as if the air itself had come to life. It seemed like a mirage, or perhaps a fast-moving patch of fog. Paul realized it was not random currents of air or casual happenstance. Whatever it was, it was moving with distinct purpose and was heading straight toward the tiger skin that was flying on the fierce breeze that had just kicked up.

Suddenly the tiger skin conformed around it. As opposed to being carried by the wind, the skin began to move of its own accord, charging forward with feline grace. Because there was no skeleton to support it, the skin stretched as if it were elasticized. The jaws, no longer confined by a skull, stretched wide and even wider. Although there were no teeth within, it didn't matter, for the mouth was of sufficient width that it could easily swallow whole anything it desired.

At that moment, it clearly desired Captain Hack.

Captain Hack, who had already been devoured once in his life, shrieked in uncomprehending terror. For a heartbeat he brought up his hatchet to try and ward off that which was descending toward him, and then his lack of true nerve betrayed him. He turned and tried to outrun it, but alongside him, keeping easy pace, was The Boy. Paul was on the other side, likewise keeping pace.

"How do you think it feels for him, Tigerheart? For that great bloody salmon," The Boy said, probably taking a bit more pleasure in someone else's misfortune than one would consider appropriate—but boys will be boys. He was speaking almost conversationally to Paul, as if they were discussing Hack's fate in the abstract. "How do you think he feels, Tigerheart, to have a beast at his heels once more, knowing he will now pay the price for his crimes?"

And Paul said, "And I wonder, Boy, how he feels knowing that even here—in the Noplace, where death has no meaning— it will have a unique meaning for him?"

"Get away! Get away!" Hack's voice went up several octaves, and somehow he heard his own voice and the lack of manliness in it.

Hack was ashamed.

He stopped in his tracks, and even though the phantom tiger was barreling toward him, he didn't deign to look its way. Instead he said with decided heat, "You, Boy, ruined my life, and you, Tigerheart, have ruined my death. I certainly hope you are both satisfied."

At which point the creature that had been pursuing them— the thing that was a tiger neither alive nor dead—vaulted the remaining distance and descended upon Captain Hack. Paul looked away, flinching. The Boy never averted his eyes but instead grinned, his sharp little front teeth making him look like a triumphant wolf.

Thus was the last of Captain Hack swept from the No-place, destined now for the final place from which there is no return.

When Paul finally steeled himself to look, Captain Hack was gone. The phantom creature that had devoured him, however, was walking slowly toward Paul, one paw padding in front of the other. Paul braced himself, not at all sure what to expect. Would he be next? And what did "next" represent?

The creature rubbed its mighty remains of a head against Paul's leg. "Snow tiger?" Paul whispered.

"Of course," said the snow tiger. Its mouth was not moving, yet Paul could hear its voice clearly in his head.

"But—but why are you here? *How* are you here?"

"Because of you, Paul."

"Me? I—I don't understand."

"Because of your grief over slaying me. Your sorrow was so overwhelming that it held me to this place. I tried to ease your mind as much as I could through my very hide that adorned you quite well. And I was with you in the jungle when you were tracking The Boy, helping you, giving you all of myself that I had to give."

"Forgive me," whispered Paul.

"There is naught to forgive. Just as I did what I must as a beast, you did what you had to as a hunter. But if it will help...then I forgive you. Does that attend to your sense of guilt? Can we, in the end, be friends once more?"

For answer, Paul reached down and placed his arms around the beast's mighty neck. Although it was mostly just fur hanging in the air, Paul was still amazed at the solidity of it; and the warmth of the tiger's presence swept over him. He saw nothing, yet something warm and rough slid across his face. His tiger was licking his face.

"I still taste guilt," said the tiger. "Why?"

"They..." Paul felt ashamed even to say it. "They call me Tigerheart. The Picca. The Boy just now. I can't seem to stop them from doing it."

"Why would you want to?"

"It's disrespectful to you."

"Nonsense. There is nothing the Picca value more than the heart of a warrior and no warrior they valued higher—or feared more—than me. To call you Tigerheart is to say that you are like me. It is a compliment that reflects as much on me as you, and I can think of no more deserving owner of the name. Wear it as proudly as you would my coat, Tigerheart."

"I will never forget you."

"Of course not. Who could?"

Paul heard something then, a deep sighing from the innermost recesses of his tiger that blended with the howling of the wind. Then the fur sagged, bereft of the spirit that had supported it. It took with it the spiritual remains of Captain Hack and the first love that only the heart of a young boy can give to the first individual, aside from his parents, who ever gave his life real meaning.

"Farewell...my best friend," Paul said, and although he couldn't hear a reply in the wind, he was certain there was one just the same.

He sat there for a time, uncertain how long, and then he realized The Boy's legs were directly in front of him. Happily, the rest of The Boy was situated above them.

"Now what?" Paul said, not unreasonably.

"Don't you want me to ask if you're all right?"

"Do you care?"

It was a fair question. The Boy considered it and then shrugged, which was about as much answer as Paul had expected.

"So...now what?" Paul said again.

"I don't know."

"You don't know?" Paul was dumbfounded.

"We could explore, I suppose." Even The Boy wasn't completely taken with the notion, but it did appeal slightly to his adventurous heart. "I admit, it seems rather bleak here, but—"

"There can be no 'but' here!" Paul said. "We have to return to the land of the living! This—this half-life is no place for us!" Then he looked down at the vicious wound he'd sustained from Captain Hack, the one that had propelled him into the twilight realm of the Noplace, and the full weight of their dilemma settled upon him. "We—we have no choice, do we?" he said, touching the wound. "We can't return. Even if we did manage to somehow...I would then die from..." His voice trailed off and he stared at The Boy as if seeing him for the first time. "How came you here? If this is a land of the dead or near dead..."

The Boy, with a curious display of pride, pulled aside his tunic to reveal the deep thrust he'd taken from Mary Slash. Paul gaped, standing and walking over toward The Boy, staring at it in wonderment. "You did that for—for me?"

"Of course not. I did it for me," The Boy said curtly. "The villains were trying to write the end of the piece, and I wouldn't have any of it. Things turn out the way I want them to. That's simply how it works."

"Well, then . . . you couldn't possibly want things to turn out that we're left here to freeze or be miserable? What sort of ending is that?"

"Not an especially good one," The Boy said. "Bleak and depressing enough to have been conceived by an adult."

"All right, so . . ." Paul's mind raced, and then he recalled something from very long ago. "There was a time when you were in trouble—no, when Fiddlefix was in trouble—and you asked for all the dreaming minds of children to help you, to restore her . . . to make things work out, to—"

"We're not in the Anyplace," said The Boy, impatient that he should have to point that out. "We're in the Noplace. And that's—" Then he stopped as an idea leaped fully formed to him. His enthusiasm began to grow as he spoke. "But there are still people here. Many people. Not children, for the most part, but dreamers nonetheless, most of them dreaming of a time when they *were* children and their whole lives were ahead of them, instead of dwelling in darkness as they do now, waiting for their end to come at last. I can give them a chance to make one final difference. Perhaps they couldn't partake of the adventure, but at least they can help see it to its proper conclusion."

Paul started to ask how, but he never got the chance. The Boy began to turn in a slow circle, as if addressing everyone and no one all at the same time.

"You can hear me," he said. "I know you can . . . all of you. You are adults, and I freely admit that in the past I have had little use for you. But I need you now for you to set things right, so the villains do not triumph. Just as you need us to survive so that there remains a spirit of youth, joy, and laughter for you to cling to, as you would savor a long-forgotten taste upon your tongue.

"If you have hands to clap, clap them now. If you have lips to speak, move them now. Believe, as I do, that matters can—should—must come out aright. I need you to have faith with every fiber of your being—with your minds that others believe cannot think, with the faintest whisper of a mouth that others believe cannot speak—believe that we should be delivered, hale and whole, from this place."

And Paul, hearkening back to his own experience with clapping his belief, realized what The Boy was doing. He joined in, speaking to that which he could not see, but with no less emphasis. "You cannot follow us, but you can send us on to be your proxies. Our triumph will be your triumph, and in the depths of your despair will be a single glimmering ray of light for you to bask in and take with you to your ultimate destination, whenever and wherever that may be.

"Believe in us. Believe in a happy ending. Believe... believe..."

Their words echoed throughout the entirety of the Noplace and resonated into the rest of mankind.

It was an extremely cruel time.

We cannot fault Paul and The Boy, really. They were simply trying to salvage their situation, to give themselves a way out. They could not know the harsh result. They cared merely about the ends, and gave no thought to the means through which it was acquired.

Throughout the world, for a very brief time, people lying in comas, or with multiple tubes invading their bodies—people who were incredibly aged, sitting in a haze of uncertainty as to whether they were alive or dead, their own memories suspect and their own children strangers to them—for a very brief time, those peoples' families were surprised and stunned to hear them speak or whisper with a clarity and certainty of purpose that they had all assumed to be long gone.

"I believe," whispered the elderly and infirm.

"I believe," whispered people lying in hospitals.

"I believe," whispered coma patients who had been declared to have lost the ability to string words together.

Individually, not a one of them would have been able to embark on anything approaching a heroic quest or a world-saving mission. But together, collectively, they joined their will and determination and recollection of what it was like to be young and carefree and triumphant, rather than laid low by the curse of relentless age and cruel nature.

Their nurses jumped and their family members started, and throughout the world hope swelled that a miracle had been handed them from on high. A million tiny miracles presented in one brief, glorious instant, like a star exploding in the mind of humanity.

And then it faded.

The aged slipped back into their twilight worlds, the comatose back into their comas. They left behind them a vast array of momentarily stoked hopes that would convince their families and caretakers that there was a possibility—however slight—that their loved ones would return to them. It would sustain them for a terribly cruel period of time until, one by one, they were doomed to disappointment.

'Twas a fleeting moment . . . but, as the Bard once said, "'tis enough, 'twill serve."

A door that neither The Boy nor Paul knew was closed opened wide, and they were pulled through. A happy resolution had been determined, not by me, certainly. I am but the recorder of events; and honestly, I had no idea how matters would turn out until just now, and to speak truly, I am of mixed feelings on it. I do not believe that heroic quests should end in failure if it can be helped, but I despise the notion that innocent bystanders are made to suffer without even comprehending why things transpired the way they did. But no one asked for my opinion, which is probably just as well, since it was a vacillating one at that and not of much use to any. Best, then, that I simply relate what happened next rather than dwell upon yet another example of life's cruelties.

Chapter 20

The Strange Fate of Mary Slash

Anyone who has ever had a dream—which is, in fact, anyone—can tell you that the speed with which time passes in one place is not remotely relevant to the speed with which it passes elsewhere. Many has been the time, I'm sure, when you've fallen asleep at the witching hour and had enough dreams to fill an entire night's sleep—only to awaken and discover that mere minutes have passed.

So, too, was it with the transition from the Anyplace to the Noplace and back again. Mary Slash had just sent The Boy tumbling into the shadow of her brother with a vicious thrust of her sword, and she was now holding the bloody implement over her head and laughing her triumph.

It is difficult to say whether she would have lived long to celebrate it. Upon seeing what had transpired, Princess Picca let out a savage howl, leveling her spear and preparing to charge right at the pirate queen. For her part, Captain Slash was brimming with confidence over her latest victory, and confidence can go a long way in a battle to the death. All other fighting had ceased aboard the pirate ship, with all eyes now upon the princess and the pirate. There was a sense that the winner of this impending and no-doubt fearsome battle would determine who was the victor in the war that had consumed the two vessels.

But before any move could be made, there was a loud sound like a sudden rushing of air, as if a small tornado had leaped into existence right there on the deck of the ship. All of them watched in astonishment as the shade of Captain Hack trembled, flinched, and suddenly seemed to be pulled right into itself, like a shirt being turned inside out. Then, from out of the space that had been occupied by the piratical shadow, two forms leaped, although really they were as much propelled as they were jumping on their own.

The Boy and Paul landed on their feet, and Gwenny, who was looking on, waited for them to collapse and die. Instead, they stood tall and straight, looking first at themselves and then at each other.

Then The Boy looked down.

His shadow was secure at his heels, as if it had always been there and was slightly puzzled over the notion that it should be anywhere else. Of the outline of Captain Hack there was not the slightest trace.

"That's as it should be," said The Boy, and "I should say so," agreed Paul, and then the two of them grinned in that insouciant way that only triumphant boys can. Gwenny let out a squeal of delight, and Princess Picca a war whoop of triumph; and Fiddlefix turned lightning-fast circles, chiming out in her pixie language so rapidly that not even Paul or The Boy could comprehend what she was saying, but the general thought was that it was approval. The clouds parted, the rain ceased, and the sun shone down.

At which point, Mary Slash went berserk.

"Foul boy!" she said. Her body was trembling and her face was purpling; and the sword upon her wrist was vibrating with such force that it was making high-pitched, irritating sounds. *"Vile boy! Contemptible boy! Where is my brother? What have you done with him?"*

"He is not 'done with' so much as simply done," said The Boy. "He is gone, woman. Face it."

"I don't believe you!" said Mary Slash. Her anger was towering and seemed to have a force all its own, as if it were coming from somewhere else and she was merely the channel for its ferocity. *"He cannot be gone! You cannot have triumphed! It's impossible!"*

"And yet here we are," Paul told her, feeling a touch smug about the ordeal. "Your beastly brother now resides in the belly of the beast, in this world and the next."

She attacked Paul in a blind fury. She was so angry that she couldn't see him, her world having been reduced to a sheer blanket of red. *"You lie, wretched thing! I hate you! I despise you!"* Her sword went wide of him, and he easily sidestepped it. She stumbled forward, banged against a mast, turned, and charged once more yelling, *"You can't have won! You can't! You're just a couple of pathetic boys!"*

"Wrong," said Paul defiantly. "He is The Boy—"

"And he," said The Boy, "is Tigerheart."

Again Mary Slash missed in her thrust, as reliable in her aim as any drunkard. Her sword bit down into the prow and she yanked it free, sending splinters of wood flying.

"And to think I was once afraid of you," Paul said, his tiger's heart pounding proudly in his chest.

Captain Slash tried to go for him once more, but this time her wrath was so all-consuming that she wasn't able to stay upon her feet. She took two steps and stumbled forward, landing heavily, and she started pounding her fist impotently on the deck. For good measure, she started kicking her feet as well; and for a moment Paul thought she was going to explode, so irate was she. *"I don't believe it! I refuse! It's not true! I hate you! I despise you! You cannot have won! I won! Me! Mary Slash, the most dreaded pirate captain in the seven seas!"*

As you might imagine, this wasn't going over particularly well with the rest of the pirates. Pirates stake a good measure of their pride and self-esteem to their commander, and Mary Slash's meltdown was taking their confidence and loyalty— what there was of it, considering they were pirates—along with it. Even worse, the Indians and The Boy's followers were doing the unthinkable: They were pointing and laughing at Mary Slash's tantrum. Let me say that again: pointing and laughing. Small wonder, then, that the pirates and the Bully Boys exchanged silent looks and began to sidle away, all unobserved by the amused onlookers. By the time Mary Slash's strange fate overtook her, her crew was long gone, having taken the closest small boats and longboats and gotten away as quickly as they could.

Mary Slash, meantime, was still venting loudly. One could almost feel a measure of pity for her. After all, she had thought that she had triumph within her grasp, and now she had nothing, while that damnable Boy looked on in amusement. She flipped over onto her back, continuing to pound the deck with her hand and booted feet, like an irate tortoise. All thoughts of her mother's fate were gone, so furious was she.

"Oh, come now, Captain," The Boy said, "act your age!"

It is impossible to say whether she heard him or not, but she very well might have, considering the results. She howled for her crew to cut down these smirking invaders where they stood, but her crew was already well under way. *"I want my brother! I*

want my crew! I WANT MY TRIUMPH! I WANT MY DAY OF VIC-
TORY! I WANT MY SHIP! MINE! MINE! ALL MINE! GIVE IT TO
ME GIVE IT TO ME I WANT IT I WANT IT I WANT IT—"

Gwenny was the first to notice what all the others were laughing too hard to realize: As she purpled in rage, as her cheeks seemed to balloon, as her eyes scrunched up, Mary Slash's voice was getting higher pitched. The words were running one into the other into near incomprehensibility.

And then Princess Picca's eyes narrowed, and she saw something else, and she pointed and said, "Is pirate captain . . . shrinking?"

Paul tried to wipe the tears of laughter from his eyes, and then he saw what Picca was talking about, and so then did The Boy. They stopped laughing, consumed by the wonderment of it all.

Mary Slash didn't realize they had stopped laughing. She was far too involved with herself, and it was not just that she was shrinking. She was growing backward very rapidly. Within seconds she was a teen, then a young girl, and the tantrum continued. Her hair grew shorter, her face rounder, her arms and legs chubbier. She was no longer speaking anything approximating words, but instead had been reduced to one long, ululating cry.

She disappeared within her clothes; and in very short order, there was only a moving lump beneath her shirt. It was thrashing, still crying, but it was more of a reed-thin wail; and then even that tapered off and there was nothing.

They all exchanged looks, and then slowly Paul moved forward toward the pile of clothing. He pushed the garments aside and then realized that the crying had not ceased entirely. There was still a faint snuffling, like the sound of an infant that had exhausted itself but was trying to work up its energy once more.

He pulled the clothing back, and, lying there, with a

scrunched-up face and discontent expression, was a round-faced, pucker-lipped infant girl. The sword was lying nearby, having fallen off her wrist since the cuff was now far too large, although the stump still remained from where she had severed her hand. She had a small tuft of hair atop her head. She looked as if she was about to start crying again.

"Hunh," said The Boy. "I guess she really did decide to act her age."

"Swaddle her," Gwenny said quickly. "Infants like to be swaddled."

Paul quickly ripped up the pirate shirt, fashioned a diaper out of it for her, and then drew her pirate coat around her like a swaddling blanket. If the infant had been intending to cry once more, she changed her mind. Instead she nestled her head against Paul's chest, her eyes rolled up in her head, and she drifted to sleep as if she had just had the longest day ever.

"Never seen anything like this," Princess Picca said.

"Oh, I have," Gwenny said confidently. "It's called a 'second childhood.' It happens all the time to adults. Granted, not usually this dramatically or reflective of the true nature of the attitude, but things do tend to turn out rather literally around here."

"So—so what do we do with her?" said Porthos, looking a bit disconcerted over the entire business.

"It's obvious," said Irregular, and he pointed at Paul. "He said he wanted a new baby sister to replace the other. Here she is."

"What? Her? This?" Paul looked with uncertainty into her sleeping face. "You want me to bring a pirate home for my mother to raise?"

"She's not a pirate now," Gwenny pointed out reasonably. "She's a blank slate. You can write whatever destiny you wish upon her."

"But what if you're wrong, and she does grow up into a pirate?"

"Then she'll doubtless be the most successful member of your family," said Irregular, "becoming a captain of industry and making more money than any of you know what to do with."

"Oh," said Paul, giving it some thought. "Well . . . that would be okay, then."

It was at that point that they realized the pirates were gone. For a moment Paul was concerned that The Boy was going to want to go right after them, but instead The Boy simply shrugged and said, "It wouldn't be fun. They need time to regroup, choose a new leader, and become a threat again. Far more sporting to wait so I can kill them later." So The Boy and his shipmates set to separating the vast vessels. This took them a bit of time, but they managed it. Even though both ships were somewhat damaged, neither was holed below the waterline, and so they were able to sail them both back to the Anyplace while The Boy bounded from one to the other and kept declaring himself to be commodore.

The Indians, knowing that Paul would soon be on his way, held a farewell celebration in his honor. The Boy, as was typical for him, joined aggressively in the festivities, dancing about almost exclusively with Princess Picca. This left not only Gwenny disgruntled but also Fiddlefix, who alighted on Gwenny's shoulder and complained at length and in very colorful language—of which Gwenny only understood every third word, but it was enough—about the Indian way. It was the first time that the two females, albeit of different species, found themselves in agreement on something.

Paul did not participate in this celebration all that much, but not—as was the case the previous time—because of grief. Instead he spent the entire time off to the side, cradling baby Mary in his arms and watching her with wonderment. After a time she awoke, and the Indians were able to provide her with a drinking skin filled with milk, which she delicately sucked from. Paul held it carefully, making sure not to let her drink too much at once, and stopping every so often to wipe dribbling liquid from her chin. The infant finally stared him straight in the eyes, and there was such unadulterated love and peace in that look that Paul felt the last vestiges of his concern melting away.

"Was she worth it?"

He looked up to see that The Boy was regarding the infant with faint suspicion. "You gave up your tiger for her, and everything he represents. You'll never be what you were before. Was she worth it?"

"If she makes my mother smile, she's worth all that and more."

"And if she doesn't?"

There was a challenge in his voice that Paul couldn't help but notice. "What do you mean, what if she doesn't?"

The Boy squatted near him. "Your mother is a mother, no different from any of the breed. She probably has not even noticed you have left; and if she has, then she will probably not care when you come back . . . and wonder what the point of the infant is to boot."

"You're wrong."

"If I am right," said The Boy mischievously, "then come back here to the Anyplace with me. We could have grand adventures together."

Paul thought of all the things his mother had said to him, and the way she really seemed to greet him with nothing but anger. There was just enough truth, or so he thought, in the words he was hearing to make him think that maybe, just maybe, The Boy had a point. But then he rallied his confidence and said, "And if I am right, you have to stay with us. Let my family adopt you. Leave behind childish games and make your mark as a man."

The Boy spit in the palm of his hand, said "Agreed," and held it out for Paul to do likewise. Paul spit into his own palm, joined hands with The Boy, and shook firmly, as Mary dozed peacefully in the arms of her new big brother.

Chapter 21

Why the Window Was Barred

We now return, at long last, to Paul's home, where things were not at all as Paul had left them.

The cleaning woman had found Colleen Dear the morning after Paul's abrupt departure, lying upon Paul's bed as if she were one dead. She was staring straight up at nothing, and her arms were crisscrossed on her breasts. The poor cleaning woman tried to get her to stir, tried to get some sort of response from her. The missing boy was quickly noted, and the police summoned. But there were no clues, except a slightly dented pot. The police in turn summoned Paul's father, Patrick. It is tragic to report that in such cases, departed fathers are often the first suspects when their children go missing. But Patrick's conscience was clear, naturally. He answered every question the police asked, his small apartment was searched in vain for some sign of the lad. So although the police still looked at him a bit suspiciously, he was to all intents and purposes eliminated as a potential suspect.

With his son missing and his wife unable to attend to herself, Patrick opted to stay with the insensate Colleen. She was of no use in providing hints as to where Paul might have gone. But that did not stop Patrick from speaking to her constantly, as if she could hear him. He talked of their time together, and their shared life, and of how much he still loved her and wished that they could remain together. And most of all, he kept reassuring her that somehow, in some way, Paul would return to them.

There was one point when Patrick thought that he was getting through to her. Late one night, as he sat in a rocking chair next to her bed, he thought he heard her whisper something. He leaned forward. "What was that, darling? What did you say?"

"I believe," she whispered, and then fell silent once more. All Patrick's attempts to coax more words from her ended in failure, so his brief surge of hope was terribly dashed.

The only other sign he got from Colleen was when he tried to relocate her to their bedroom. Her body went from limp to resistant, from supple to rock hard, and he quickly understood that on some fundamental level, she absolutely refused to move from Paul's room. So he had made no further effort to challenge it. Night after night she lay upon Paul's narrow bed while Patrick resigned himself to sleeping as well as he could in the rocking chair he had pulled into the room.

And then one night, Patrick was downstairs making tea when he heard what sounded like burglars coming in through the second-story window, the one that led into Paul's room... the room in which Colleen had taken up residence. Grabbing the closest weapon he could find, which was a butter knife, Patrick sprinted up the stairs, two at a time. He darted into Paul's room and froze in the doorway.

Colleen was on her feet, her eyes wide and focused, staring at the open window. Standing on the sill was Paul, cradling a small, blanketed bundle in his arms.

No one moved, not so much as an inch. Patrick had to pinch himself to make certain that he hadn't fallen asleep in his rocking chair and was dreaming this. Once he had ascertained that he was awake, he was then afraid to make the slightest move, lest he shatter the fragile tableau and send Paul back off to wherever he'd fled to and now just returned from.

Paul looked nervously from one parent to the other, and then extended the bundle toward them. "I brought her for you, mother. For us."

Colleen took one slow step toward him, then another, looking as if her legs were trembling, but then gaining strength with every move closer to her son.

"I believed," she whispered, and suddenly she was across the room and clutching her son to her. She sobbed his name over and over, and she scolded him fiercely for terrifying her while at the same time apologizing profusely for everything she had ever done or might have done or might ever do that could make Paul think, even for a moment, that a mother was something you ran from rather than ran toward. Paul tried to speak but was not able to, overwhelmed by that knot-in-your-stomach feeling one usually gets when one's mother is crying for whatever reason. Moments later Patrick had joined them, lifting his son down off the windowsill, the three of them embracing and promising that they would never, ever, ever be apart.

The baby, who was becoming well and truly smothered from all the hugging, let out a yelp of protest. Colleen stepped back and took the infant in her arms, looking at her in wide-eyed wonderment. "Paul . . . where did this child come from? And— good heavens, look! The poor thing is missing a hand!"

"I'm sorry about that," Paul said. "I wanted her to be perfect, but this was the best one I could find there."

"There? There where?"

He took a deep breath, let it out, and said, "The Anyplace. That's where I went. The Anyplace, brought there by a pixie to find a new baby sister to replace Bonnie," and steeled himself for his mother's immediate repudiation of the very notion of such a thing.

Colleen stared at the child, who in some ways reminded her very much of what she herself looked like when she was a baby. Then she turned to Patrick, who simply shrugged. Finally, to Paul's utter astonishment, she said firmly, "Of course you did. Where else would she have come from, and would you have gone, save the Anyplace?" She paused, and then added, "Paul, understand: No one could ever replace Bonnie in my heart, nor you. Nevertheless, this is a beautiful little girl, hand or no, and she clearly does need a mother."

"And she's not the only one," Paul said, barely able to keep the triumph out of his voice. "Boy!" he said, turning toward the window. "I know you're out there! We had a wager, Boy, and you have lost! Come in and meet your new mother and father!"

There was a long pause, and then to Patrick's utter shock, a young lad stepped through, dressed in garments that seemed plucked from impossibly green trees. He recognized him instantly.

"You," he whispered.

The Boy drew himself up and, although he did not drop his suspicious attitude, nevertheless bowed grandly as he had seen other gentlemen do. "I have to be going," he said abruptly.

This shocked and angered Paul, as he said, "Wait! You can't! We had a bargain!"

"Did we?" The Boy said carelessly. "Can't say as I recall it."

"You lie!"

"Never."

"What do you mean, never! You are half brother to the trickster god Coyote, first cousin to Puck, grandnephew of Loki. You lie all the time!"

"Half brother of . . ." Paul's father, who had looked stunned, seemed to be recovering. He almost laughed at Paul's recitation of The Boy's proclaimed lineage. "Is *that* what you've told him, Boy?"

Not perceiving his father's amusement, Paul said with a wounded tone, "Yes, he did. So maybe I should have known"— he turned back to The Boy—"that you were lying when you said you'd allow my mother and father to adopt you! That you'd—"

"What? Trust them?" The Boy said. "Have you learned nothing from adults? From me? From my warnings of what you can expect? Maybe not today, but sooner or later."

"I know, I know what you said! How you flew away from home, and when you returned, your parents had shut the window against you. That they'd forgotten about you. But my parents are different"—and he gestured toward them. "Can't you see? They can love you, tend to you. My mother can be your mother, my father your—"

"No." It was Patrick who had spoken, and there was unutterable sadness in his voice. "No, Paul. I can never be his father."

Paul looked at his dad in shock. The Boy smirked and said, "See? Now do you understand?"

"No, he doesn't," said Patrick. "And neither do you."

"What do you mean?" The Boy looked with renewed suspicion at Patrick. "Why do you look at me that way?"

"Because I know that you're wrong. I know that your mother didn't shut the window to keep you out."

"And how do you know that?" said The Boy.

To which Patrick replied with infinite tenderness, "She didn't shut the window to keep you out, Boy. She shut the window to keep me *in*, because I was so desperate to follow you. Even as an infant, I tried on three separate occasions to escape out the window after you. So she kept it shut until I grew up. Don't you see, Boy? I'm your baby brother."

The Boy gripped the edge of the window frame. "You—you lie," he said, suddenly feeling short of breath. Paul was looking from The Boy to his father in amazement, seeing now resemblances that he wondered why he'd never noticed before.

"This," Patrick continued, and he put a hand on Paul's shoulder, "is your nephew. I can never be your father, but I can be your brother and we can be your family, for now and forever."

The Boy refused to believe. It was too confusing for him to deal with. He backed away, loudly declaring, "No! You're lying! I know what I know, and I don't need to know any more than that!"

"You're sounding more like an adult already," Paul commented.

"Come back! Please!" Patrick said, and he reached for his big brother, but his grasp came up short. The Boy bounded back, off the ledge and hung in the air, and he said, "I'm always going to remain exactly the way I am! Always and always, and you can never change that no matter what lies you tell me and excuses you make! Never! Never ever!"

The Boy spun in the air then and arched himself skyward. Patrick went to the window, and as loudly as he could, said, "You will always be welcome here, and the window will always remain unlocked for you, my brother! Always!"

He kept repeating that, long after The Boy was out of sight. Patrick sagged against the windowsill then, and Paul thought that tears were welling in his eyes. But he quickly wiped them away.

"Father," Paul whispered, "did I—did I handle things in a grown-up enough way?"

His father laughed, although it sounded like a choked and saddened laugh, and he said, "You know what, Paul? Even when you're all grown-up ... as long as you have parents, you're never really grown up, because you've got parents who will always think of you as their little boy. That's what my—what The Boy—doesn't understand. He could have everything ... be a grown-up and child all at the same time. But maybe he'll realize that someday."

And as Mary cooed in the arms of her new mother, a small bird chirped brightly out on a tree branch and then flapped away.

Paul's family never moved out of the house. Patrick bequeathed the house to Paul and his adopted sister, and even though they each went out and started families, inevitably the families returned to live there. There Paul and Mary remained until the end of their days, leaving it to their children in turn. (Although it should be noted that Paul continued to have adventures all the way into adulthood, because once adventure knows your name—especially when your name is Tigerheart— it tends to call on you whenever it sees fit. Perhaps we will tell you of those further adventures someday. It depends upon whether you behave yourself or not. It's up to you.)

Their upstairs window was never ever barred, because they always hoped that one day a young boy who refuses to grow up will return home. At that point, he would be tended to and loved and helped to grow up, so that he would no longer be unique and special, but merely another adult. And so it will always be for as long as adults are naive and hopeful and childish.

Acknowledgments

Although he was mentioned in the dedication, we cannot emphasize enough the debt owed to the works of James Barrie . . . not only for *Peter and Wendy* but also for *Peter Pan in Kensington Gardens*. It begs the question why we did not just call The Boy "Peter Pan," particularly since Peter and company have fallen into public domain, thus removing any legal barriers. The reason is simple: The story is really Paul Dear's story. His quest, his ambitions, and his character development are what drive the book. And Peter Pan, quite the arrogant and saucy fellow that he is, wouldn't deign to be associated with any story in which he is not the prime mover and shaker. So as this story developed, Peter bowed out and The Boy bowed in. We are sure that you will see the resemblances in the end, although we suspect that Peter and The Boy would look at each other sideways and crossways and see no likenesses whatsoever. Ultimately, we suppose that if literary pastiche is good enough for August Derleth and Philip José Farmer, it's good enough for us.

Nevertheless, as a result of our indebtedness to the source material, a percentage of royalties for this book will be donated to the Ormond Street Children's Hospital, to which Barrie left the original copyright lo those many years ago.

We wish to thank the individuals who got this book into print: our agent, Matt Bialer; our editor, Betsy Mitchell, who never lost faith in the title (in several senses of the word); and her assistant, Kaitlin Heller, who offered a number of very useful suggestions to improve the manuscript. And of course my wife, Kathleen, who remains my first and best source of commentary and critique.

And lastly, again we acknowledge Ariel David, who read the manuscript and dubbed Paul "Tigerheart" before the book ever called him that. He remains flattered by the name and will strive mightily to live up to it.

About the Author

PETER DAVID's novels include the fantasies *Sir Apropos of Nothing*, *Wode to Wuin*, and *Knight Life*, and the quirky werewolf story *Howling Mad*. He is famous for writing some of the most popular of the original *Star Trek: The Next Generation* novels, as well as the official novel of the movie *Spider-Man*. In the world of comic books he has written just about every famous comic book superhero, including The Hulk, Captain Marvel, Spider-Man, and the futuristic Spider-Man 2099, and he is currently scripting the graphic adaptation of Stephen King's acclaimed Dark Tower series. In his spare time, David writes movie screenplays, children's books, and TV scripts.